The Strength Of A Woman

LOUISE ALLISON

For Mark

ONE

Rose had looked in the mirror this morning. What she saw, she had found hard to understand. Her hair and features had appeared blurred. It appeared that parts of her face were subtly repositioning themselves, in a sneaky bid to start relaxing towards middle age, as she was reluctantly sucked towards forty.

Often, she had imagined looking at herself in the mirror one day and seeing a quick, obvious decline in her looks. She had visualised the surprise would be like the swift, sudden way a child grows up in front of you. She knew no one's face stayed sharp and new their whole life. Using one's brain was far more important than looks, and there was certainly nothing blunt about her mind. The changes she noticed bothered her because, deep down, she read them as a symptom of what struggled inside her.

Make-up might help. Perhaps she would try a fringe. She was not really bothered about her looks. The rest was more complicated. She reminded herself that she had been up for large parts of the night with her two-year-old daughter, Evie, for weeks. No one remained sharp while sleep-deprived. However, the way Rose felt could not be simply brushed away as sheer, physical tiredness. Anyone who has a child signs up for sleep changes. The worst nights would pass. She knew all of this. It made sense. She managed well. Friends constantly told her how she made motherhood look easy while remaining well groomed. She welcomed these compliments but nothing quelled her new feelings of being invisible and unfulfilled. She had imagined herself fresh, frivolous and fulfilled at forty. Instead, she felt something close to raw bewilderment. That did not make sense.

In her mind, no one dressed up to walk a dog unless they were looking for attention. Even so, she dared not think what she looked like now in the woods. It did not matter, as she was unlikely to bump into anyone. She wore old jeans and a shapeless jumper retrieved from the charity bag under the stairs. The wellingtons were borrowed from her mother. There was a bite out of the top of the left one, a stolen snack for Bobble, her mother's Labrador. Rose's hair was held loosely in a messy bun on top of her head.

She smiled to herself as she silently peered past a tree at the group of deer ahead of her in the clearing. She believed spotting deer was lucky. She paused as she relished the sense of calm they brought her. Carefully, she edged closer towards the oak, stepping around the slippery, protruding roots so as not to become unbalanced. She got as close as possible and counted eight. They stood strong and regal as if trying to overhear a bit of news in a coffee shop. Their mischievous-looking mouths always amused her. She imagined them spreading the story like cartoon characters.

She pulled her scarf up higher around her neck, and raised her shoulders to her ears, in an attempt to protect herself from the cold. She noticed the spicy smell of the woods. A different language was spoken here. Peaceful sounds were made. Some meagre, rustling leaves still hung from the trees despite it being late autumn. The trees creaked and cracked. There were no interruptions from people. A welcome escape, anonymity, momentary freedom from responsibility.

As her left temple hit the oak's hard, rough trunk, she yelped. Lost in her thoughts, she had forgotten where she was and that she was supposed to be walking Bobble. Unable to contain his excitement, he had jumped up at her, knocking her into the tree. Having almost knocked her out, he danced around with his prize. A dead rabbit hung from his mouth. The deer had vanished.
"You're a bad boy. I've told you not to jump up at me like that. Sit down. Now. Come on, calm down." Feeling angry at being disturbed and hurt, she rubbed the bruise on her head. She snapped his lead back on and carried on walking. Looking sheepish, he trotted alongside her. The rabbit remained in his mouth. Rose checked the time on her phone. No reception so no messages but it was time to head back.

She strolled along the hard, muddy track, flanked by tree trunks and bushes. Soon, as winter bedded in, these tracks would turn into bogs and strong legs would be compulsory. The cold made her ears hurt. Next time a

3

hat would be a good idea, or earmuffs. She always liked an excuse to go shopping. She wondered about earmuffs being a difficult look to pull off. The ones she had tried before were too tight or too small to go over her head. Some covered her ears but not quite the lobe, an odd look on anyone. Her friend, Kate, said they were for little girls, not full-grown women. However, Rose would keep looking. She did not take such comments seriously. In fact, she had wanted to tell her London friend how different things are in the countryside. People appeared less bothered by appearance. She had thought better of it. After all, this was about more than a pair of earmuffs. It had been the first time she had wondered if she was drifting away from some of her childless, hedonistic, working friends. Her priorities had changed. She was still very particular about her clothes. That was never going to change but it felt good to wade around the woods in any old thing. She smiled as she imagined the look on Kate's face while telling her that. Humour would not come into it. Funny though, Rose did feel a pang of envy, thinking about Kate and her life.

Rose drew nearer to the edge of the woods and prepared to leave the cocoon of peace. Her thoughts returned to her family. She felt she had missed out so much with her first two children, Anna and Thomas. She had returned to full-time work after a few months off with each. With Evie, she had been determined to put her career away for longer. She had wanted to experience full-time motherhood. It had been amazing; for a while. She had imagined lots of laughter, no stress, baking bread, cheesy cheerfulness all day, every day, like in the magazines. She had not considered how relentless and isolating it could be. There were no days off and few adult conversations about anything other than children. She felt that, although she was visible to her husband

and children, she was invisible to society. The silence when new acquaintances asked what she did, many lost for words, was infuriating.

Her present state of exhaustion, she knew, did not promote positive thoughts. She would get Evie to sleep properly again. She would keep trying. During the night, Evie had tried to sleep on top of Rob's head then Rose's head, Evie's ever-expanding nappy becoming more and more like a boxing glove. At one point, Rose had woken up to her eyes being prised open,

"Morning time! Time to get up! Breffit time!"

"It is? Really?" The room was in total darkness. The illuminated figures said 3.47am.

"For God's sake, Evie, it's the middle of the night. Stop it and go to sleep. Now! Please! Mummy's very tired." Evie had sighed and tried to settle again on Rob's head,

"Oh my God, this is driving me mad. I'm knackered. I need my sleep. I've got work tomorrow. Sorry, Rose, but I can't sleep here. Evie, just sleep. You're going in your room tomorrow all night because I'm getting a lid for your cot." He had grabbed his pillow and gone downstairs to sleep on the sofa.

"Is Daddy cross?"

"No, Evie. He's tired. We're all tired. Go to sleep." Rose gently pushed her away into his empty space, "Think about animals sleeping, Evie, and copy them. Good night."

"The animals want to play, Mummy."

"They can't in the dark. They'll hurt themselves. Everyone sleeps when it's dark."

Rob woke up on the sofa miserable, complaining of being cold and stiff, but he quickly cheered up,

"I think I'll move into my hut! I get warmth, stimulation and adult conversation and not the slightest hint of wee in my face. Bye!" He sauntered off with a mug of coffee. Rose knew that Jan, his secretary, was in today. He was always cheerful around her. Rose felt jealous. The sleep deprivation made her feel hung-over. Certainly, she was not. She could not remember the last time she had touched a drink. The fuzziness returned. She envied Rob who still had the focus and satisfaction of a stimulating career away from her and the children. What she missed most from her old life was how her career had made her feel more equal to Rob. She had depended on him only for his love and support.

On leaving London, he had set up as an architect on his own. He worked on his own projects and completed those for his old employers on a contract basis. He had never mentioned it but she knew that he could have settled for anywhere in the countryside, after they left London. He had been kind enough to move really near to her mother, Cathy. She also knew he had taken a risk going alone. He had forgone the luxury of the benefits associated with being a salaried member of staff. He was brave. He appeared happy, even on little sleep. She was not.

In theory, she could rest during the day as far as he was concerned. In a way, he was right. The cooking, cleaning, washing, tidying, ironing, household administration and helping with homework could, theoretically, mostly, wait. The backlog this created was just too overwhelming, not to mention the response from everyone affected, especially when they all ran out of clean pants.

Her friends often reminded her that to get two children to school age only to get pregnant again was enough to shake up anyone's world. They were right. She had always felt the door was open to more children after her first two were born. Evie was a much-wanted child, an important part of their family. However, if the truth be known, she had really been the result of rather casual planning and possibly triggered by a bottle of red wine too many. Lately, Rose found herself literally at the mercy of her family. Sometimes she wondered if she was cut out for motherhood at all.

She was almost out of the woods, wondering whether she would have been wiser to take up her mother's offer for an hour of rest instead of walking Bobble. Even so, she was glad she had cleared her head, despite the bump on it. She felt too keyed up to sleep during the day anyway. Too often, it had the undesired effect of making her crave even more sleep. The signal had returned to her mobile. It buzzed a message in her pocket,

"Hi Rose, thought you said you were coming straight back after school run? Where are the tea bags? Rob. X"

"Gone for a walk - back at lunch time. New tea bags in the cupboard at back under the kettle."

"Looked there - can't see any"

I'm not replying to that. I'll have to pretend the reception has gone, if he says anything later. If he can't find them, tough, he can walk to the village shop or get Jan to totter along, in her heels. I'm not his mother. The sooner the builders get going on that office, with its own kitchen and toilet, the better, otherwise I might throttle him.

On moving, he had erected a temporary, wooden office in the garden. It would be transformed into a summer house once all the changes had been made to their property. He referred to it as 'the hut'. He liked it. It was comfortable and cosy with enough room for two. However, it had no plumbing so he and Jan, his helper, often came into the house, a challenge in the wind and rain. Rose found this intrusive as she believed home and work should be kept separate. He was in the process of getting the plans approved to improve their house, and erect a separate building with garages and a large office above. She knew she needed to be patient.

Gaining planning permission was typically slow. The council kept asking for the office plans to be modified. Two departments were involved, commercial and residential. Sometimes, it seemed that they were at opposite ends of the country not in the same building. However, the biggest problem was one of their neighbours, Ed, a redundant pilot, possibly with time on his hands. His property bordered the bottom of their garden. He questioned, and tried to object to, everything they wanted with the council. His partner, Nicky, never seemed to have anything to do with any of it. The reason for all these objections eluded Rob because they could barely even see each other's properties. Nothing would be visible to Ed once finished. The office, to which he objected most, would be tucked away to the side of the house, screened by metres of foliage. The council had an obligation to acknowledge all queries, which took time. Rob decided not to take it personally.

It was exciting. Once the new office was complete, he would take on another architect, and gradually expand his practice. He had been lucky to find Jan after putting an advert in the local paper. She had made it clear from the start that her priority was her twelve-year-old son. She was a single mother so a degree of working-flexibility was necessary. Although initially nervous that she might take too much time off, being new to employing someone himself, he had, nevertheless, agreed to this. She had proved invaluable to him, so efficient, a welcome addition to his business. He only saw joy in Jan. What had impressed him straight away was the fact she seemed genuinely unbothered about having to enter her boss's home for a cup of tea or to use the toilet. Rose was not so keen. She worried that Jan might be a busybody. Jan had lived in the area all her life. If Rose ever wanted to know about someone or something, she only had to ask her. Rose warned her husband to be careful what he told Jan. Also, Jan appeared to flirt with Rob which was annoying. She had a flirtatious nature so it was likely to mean nothing. It was easy to be critical. Still, Rose kept an eye on her.

Feeling hungry, she was glad to turn onto the wider track, with hoof prints, which led directly onto the road where her mother lived. A few more minutes and she would be back with Evie.

She heard a loud crunch in the bushes. It sounded like something big was stamping on fallen branches, cracking them like a bear might. She looked into the bushes and saw a large, dark animal with a smaller one next to it. In a flash, she remembered a holiday she once took in Sardinia. She was told to stay away from the wild boar if they had just had babies. Now, she was back there. That day, the sound of them grunting had been enough to make her run. Now she was running again. Bobble, alongside her, bounding along with excitement, the dead rabbit still in place. She looked back while still running. She collided with another tree hard enough to make her fall backwards into a pile of damp, fusty leaves. A cow with a calf stood in the distance placidly chewing.

"Are you OK?" came a voice. She could not quite make out a face in the strong light but took the offered hand, "Let me help you up."
"Thank you, I'm fine, just slipped."
"Are you sure? You let out quite a scream. I couldn't ignore that! Were you running from someone or something in particular?" He looked amused as he stared past her at the cow, her calf almost leaning on her. *Oh God, how embarrassing.* She brushed some mud off her jeans, amazed that the lead was still around her wrist. The dog was sitting patiently beside her, guarding the rabbit at his feet.
"Um, no, well err, not really; just a cow and a... um... a calf. They were chasing me."
He looked bemused. She felt really stupid, "Except they weren't following me or chasing me really. They spooked me, that's all. Look, this is embarrassing. I'm very tired, my toddler kept me awake most of the night, probably not thinking straight. I am sorry if I worried you."
"Not at all, just glad you're OK although I think that bump on your head looks sore, like it might need some ice." He looked concerned. He had probably only just noticed it. She hoped he felt guilty for appearing to find it all so amusing. She fumbled in her pocket for a tissue, and started to feel even more embarrassed. What was wrong with her? She felt like a teenager again, talking to the boy she secretly had a crush on.
"No problem! I'm Will by the way."
"Rose," she offered her hand but realised it was muddy and there was blood on her finger so quickly withdrew

the offer. He glanced at the other hand and spotted her wedding ring.

TWO

Rose led a slower Bobble up her mother's steep drive towards the Victorian, semi-detached house. This had been Rose's childhood home. A black, wrought iron gate led into the back garden. She unclipped the lead, "Right, Bobble, run around the garden and shake off some of that mud before you go inside while I rinse these wellies under the tap." He dropped the rabbit at her feet and obediently did a quick circuit of the garden, pausing to check and sniff under a couple of bushes along the way. After messily slurping up the entire contents of his water bowl, by the back door, and vigorously shaking, he sat patiently, his enormous tongue hanging out, watching the door, waiting to be let in.

She found visiting her mother's garden like escaping into an awesome place of freshness and tranquillity. The view across the neighbouring farm was breathtaking. A paved path ran around the garden's perimeter and beds with mainly evergreen shrubs ran alongside the path. The bottom third of the garden was paved with sandstone, a suntrap in the summer and a great place to entertain. A couple of silver birch trees marked the boundary. When she was a child, the garden had contained just haphazard grass. Now, that grass resembled a soft carpet. It was so perfect that it could be fake.

"Not that difficult to keep the weeds out with a little bit of effort." David, her mother's friend, would state in response to any comments, "Of course, drainage is important too." He would drone on at length if unchecked, always invading your space, moving in too close, keeping intense, blue-eyed contact. Cathy appeared unbothered by David's obsession with grass perfection, often commenting on how lovely it was to walk around the garden bare foot in the summer, knowing there were no thistles hiding in the grass to stab you. In fact, David's general eccentricity never seemed to bother her mother at all. They had an unusual relationship. David spent an enormous amount of time at Cathy's house, but continued to live by himself, as did she.

"Rose! ... Rose!" It was Cathy calling from the back door. Bobble had dashed inside. "I thought I heard you. Don't worry about the boots. Come in and have a coffee." Rose walked towards the house. The two over-sized, terracotta pots she had given her mother years ago as a birthday present stood proudly either side of the back door. Each contained fresh, moist soil, one with a dancing windmill propped up in it, the shiny, multi-coloured sort you get at the seaside. Come spring, one pot would produce tulips, the other daffodils. Her mother would tie a fine wire around the tulips to keep them from wilting under their own weight. They would always be red, a reminder of the first flowers Rose's late father, Johnny, had given her mother.

Evie sat comfortably on her grandmother's hip and thrust a blue-tipped finger at Rose,
"Fingle painting, Mummy!" she exclaimed. Evie wore a thick, waterproof smock with a smiling, pink elephant on the front. She had a blue spot of paint on the end of her nose, as did Cathy.
"So you have, Evie, lucky you!" She tickled Evie gently under her ribs and Evie squirmed as she started to examine her decorated, index finger as if it was the first time she had seen it.
"Gramma fingle paint too!" She exclaimed breathlessly. "And ...and ...and... I show you, come on Mummy!" Evie freed herself and wriggled down Cathy's leg. Her enthusiasm was mesmerising. How Rose loved her. Evie proudly pointed up at a makeshift clothes line with six pictures pegged to it, all similar, blue, finger paintings.
"They're great. Did you do them all, Sweetie?"
"Yep and Gramma but not Dava as he at goff today. That's what gramma said." Evie spoke as if Grandma was not in the room.

Rose turned to her mother and pecked her on the cheek,
"Thanks for painting with her, Mum."
"Evie's lovely company. We've had fun. She's an artist in the making. She's made some beautiful pictures. You should have seen the thought she put into them all. Each finger was carefully placed on the paper. There was no aimless flicking of paint. I like the dog picture best. The dog's not Bobble. It's a dog from the TV, Evie said, a small one that runs a lot and has teeny, tiny ears. She's hilarious, and her speech is amazing." Evie was not listening. She was busy climbing on and off a kitchen chair.

"Well, if she is artistic, she gets that from you, Mum, and maybe Rob's side, definitely not from me. I really don't have the patience to get the paint out for her at home. It's just so messy."

"Patience comes with time, love, and you don't have a lot of that. It's a grandparent's job. I enjoy it and things like this are fun when you're not thinking about the next school run and everything else you have to do." She smiled, "If Evie's not sleeping, well, it's hard to recharge. It will get easier, you know, it really will. Look at Anna and Thomas now. You hardly know you've got them!"

"Don't worry about me, Mum. Let's have the coffee. I need to sit down."

Her mother half turned towards the kettle then did a double take at Rose and stared right at her face, her eyes narrowing,

"Goodness, Rose, your face! What happened?" Cathy moved in for a closer look. Rose laughed,

"Bobble knocked me into a tree at the beginning of the walk. He found a rabbit and was excited. I didn't see him coming as I was watching some deer and day dreaming, so I lost my balance when he jumped up."

"Oh, I'm sorry about Bobble."

"Really, Mum, it's not a big deal. After that, you're not going to believe it but, Bobble was being perfectly well behaved and I got spooked by a cow, wasn't looking where I was going and hit my head again." Cathy looked amused. "Oh, Mum, it's not funny. You're just like the man who came to my rescue and helped me up."

"Rose, you're blushing. Handsome, was he?" Nothing ever got past her mother.

Evie picked up her covered cup from the floor and took a hearty gulp from it before dropping it carelessly back onto the floor. Rose reminded her,

"Evie, pick the cup up and put it in the sink like you do at home, please." Evie did as she was told and reached up above her head before cautiously dropping the cup into the sink, shutting her eyes tightly as if she was expecting something to fall down onto her, at the same time. Cathy picked Evie up and hugged her.

"Thank you, Evie. I think we'll put the paint away while you watch TV if Mummy's all right with that." Rose smiled and nodded. Cathy started to take Evie out of the room, "Make the coffee, please, Rose, and I'll wash the paint off Evie's fingers and change her nappy. I've got a great 'Peppa Pig' DVD." Rose filled the kettle and plonked it on top of the Aga. She was about to sit down again but realised how damp her jeans were.

"Mum!" she called from round the door, "May I borrow a blanket to put round me while my jeans dry?"

Rose retrieved her bag from the car. As David was out, she wrestled her jeans off in the kitchen so she could put them straight over the Aga rail to dry. Her cold, mottled legs looked lifeless.

In the cloakroom mirror, the rest of her looked lifeless too. Perhaps, she had expected too much from the walk. The bruises were not very obvious but both her eyes had white, dried tears at the edges, like dribble. She removed a tiny twig from her hair and a live insect, thankfully not a nit as it had noticeable wings. A hairbrush, baby wipe and some pink lipstick made her feel better, as did the dry knickers at the bottom of her bag, even if they were covered in biscuit crumbs. She knew Thomas's missing biscuit would turn up at some point.

She poked her nose round the sitting room door. Evie had fallen asleep as hoped. Peppa Pig waddled across the screen followed shortly by Daddy Pig oozing and waving from his car. Rose left the television on. Evie was a light sleeper. Any change in her surroundings could wake her. Rose went back into the warm kitchen. Her mother was sitting at the table with two mugs of coffee and a plate of biscuits in front of her. Rose felt like a little girl all over again. A soothing drink, cosy blanket and her solid, strong, stoical mother's full attention.

"How's David? Evie said he's at golf," enquired Rose.
"Very well, thank you, a lesson today not a game. I think that's what he said so he'll be back soon. You might see him."
I hope not. Rose did not feel in the mood for talking to David today even if he was a good friend of Cathy's. David and Johnny had worked as partners in a solicitors' practice. Both families had socialised together yet Rose felt she had never really hit it off with David's children, Cressie and Giles. They were much the same age as her.

Rose's father had died suddenly of a heart attack the day after her twenty-fifth birthday. He was only fifty-five and had complained of stomach ache on and off for a brief time leading up to it. The pain had been dismissed as indigestion by his family and friends so he had not bothered the doctor. Rose and her mother had been racked with guilt. They recounted, numerous times afterwards, how they had rolled their eyes at each other when he reached for the indigestion remedies once again, and at his birthday meal the week before that fateful day. The uncomfortable question burned Rose's heart. Had they taken proper notice, could his death have been avoided?

David was a rock in the months that followed, writing letters, making telephone calls and giving helpful advice. He remained consistently stable and supportive as they stepped through the insurmountable fog of grief and guilt, even though he himself was mourning the loss of a good friend and colleague.

David encouraged Cathy to return to teaching as a way of hauling herself back up. She took his advice, and gradually threw herself back into teaching adults, running two evening classes in the village hall, one called 'sewing machine basics' for beginners and another more advanced class. Cathy became interested in gardening for the first time too and it was not long before David was helping almost daily, fitting it in around his work then doing more once he retired. Later on, Cathy started a business making curtains and blinds. She still ran this on a small scale.

About eight months after Johnny's death, David suffered his own personal loss. His wife disappeared overnight without any real explanation, just leaving a note to say she was fine but had had enough and would not be returning. David was devastated, especially by the sudden surprise of it all. It was Cathy's turn to bolster him. Their friendship was sealed.

"Rose, you look miles away. How are things with you?" Rose sighed. For a moment, she thought she might burst into tears,

"Things are fine, Mum. We're all well. Rob's work and the house plans are all moving ahead. I suppose, I'm a bit bored really but then I'm too tired to do much about it. I keep thinking about starting the business I told you about but I don't know if I'd cope with more to do. I'm stuck." She paused as her mother took a sip of her coffee and nonchalantly bit into a corner of shortbread. Rose continued, "Never happy are we? Probably not the best time to talk about this considering I've been up most of the night. I'm feeling negative and sorry for myself."

"Rose, don't take this the wrong way, and I know you're not having the best day, but is being at home full-time enough for you? I know you love being a Mum and Rob likes having you all around but are you really happy with…?"

"Oh, Mum..." Rose was about to interrupt when the kitchen door swung open.

"Ah, here's David," exclaimed Cathy, "We didn't even hear you open the front door."

"I came in very quietly because I saw your car, Rose, and guessed Evie might be asleep. Lovely to see you, you look well." Sensing something in the air, David asked,

"I'm not interrupting anything am I? Sorry, if I am." Cathy got up and kissed David on the cheek,

"Of course not, would you like a coffee?"

"Yes, please."

"Are you well, David?" Rose felt she should ask.

"Yes, very well thank you. My golf lesson was rescheduled for tomorrow so I'm back earlier than expected. I won't have my coffee with you. If you don't mind, I was going to check the lawn but it's raining now, so I might have a look at your computer, Cathy, check that virus is definitely gone." He was looking at the lawn out of the window.

Rose swallowed her urge to laugh out loud at the mention of the grass, fearing she might lose control. Her mother shot her a glance. Rose managed to ask,

"How are Cressie and Giles?" David launched into a speech. Cressie, an orthopaedic surgeon, was up for promotion, and Giles, a solicitor, was soon to be promoted to partner. As always, David did not mention their relationships or any other interests, just work-related achievements.

David never mentioned that Cressie and Giles had little to do with him. David had once told Cathy that they preferred to avoid trying to be close to him to steer clear of the risk of being let down again, as their mother's desertion had disturbed them so much. He entirely blamed any problems they had, as a family, on their mother's departure.   David even wondered if they blamed him in some way for her leaving.   However, Cathy had suggested to Rose that this may have nothing to do with the past, but could be down to David himself. Often, he was too controlling towards his children. David made it clear that he did not approve of Cressie's boyfriend, a nurse. David had expected Cressie to settle down with a fellow surgeon and had told her exactly that.   David was equally disappointed in Giles's choice of partner. Giles had ruined his marriage to a 'top girl', David's words, a fellow solicitor, by having many affairs, before settling for 'some girl, a mere typist', David's words, again.

Having droned on, David finally paused for breath.
"So, they're happy?" Rose asked tentatively.
"Who knows? Who knows!" exclaimed David, with a forced laugh.
 "Would you like a biscuit, David?" Cathy lifted the plate towards him.
"No, thank you. I'll stick with my celery!" David patted his stomach. He rinsed the celery and, as he did, the water managed to pour down onto his trousers creating a wet patch. "Oh, damn. Look what I've done, damn, damn." David grabbed some kitchen roll and started dabbing at his trousers. Cathy acted like nothing

had happened but Rose felt uncontrollable laughter rise within her again. In an attempt to quell it, she took a large, ill-advised gulp of coffee which left her spluttering.

Handing Rose a tissue, David, mumbling something, strode out of the kitchen. Rose, working hard to stifle her laughter, had to stand up to catch her breath. She was trying not to laugh loudly as she did not want David to hear her. She need not have worried about upsetting her mother, by laughing at David, because Rose noticed her mother's shoulders were heaving with stifled, silent laughter. Cathy managed to say,
"Try to find a place for him in your heart, Rose. He's so kind to me. We'd be lonely without each other."
"I know, Mum. I do like him. He's just so very serious all the time." Rose stopped laughing, "You're not are you, Mum? I hope you're not..." She was going to say lonely but before she could finish David appeared in the doorway with Evie in his arms. Evie's eyes were wet with tears and her hair unkempt. David carried her like an awkwardly shaped, fragile object. He seemed unsure how to hold her, before clumsily lowering her onto the chair next to Rose,
"She was calling for Mummy." Evie looked up at Rose who stroked her hair. Rose thanked David,
"I'll be going in a moment. I'll see you again soon, I'm sure."
"Yes, of course. Say hello to Rob for me...and your other children!" As David walked away she noticed he was wearing a white, frilly apron around his waist, the sort that would not look out of place teamed with a French maid, fancy dress outfit. Obviously, David felt it covered the wet patch nicely.

Rose struggled back into her dry-enough jeans. How she hated the unpredictability of jeans. They felt much tighter around her thighs. They had either shrunk or she had instantly put on weight from the biscuits.

THREE

Rose arrived home. Through the kitchen window, she could see Rob and Jan enjoying a tea break together. A stranger, looking in, might think they were a couple. Hugging their mugs, they were chatting and laughing, leaning against the kitchen surface, seemingly oblivious to the arrival of Rose and Evie.

Evie ran over to Rob,
"Daddy!" Rob quickly managed to put his mug on the surface, in order to catch her, as she jumped into his arms. She put her head on his shoulder as if she had not seen him for weeks. He felt her head,
"Hi little Evie Boo, hi Rose!" He moved closer to kiss Rose briefly on the lips. "Feel her Rose, she's warm. I think she's got a temperature. Have you not noticed?"
"Really? Oh, poor Evie. No, I hadn't noticed. I'll check her with the strip in a minute." Feeling criticised, Rose turned away from Rob to greet Jan,
"Hi Jan! How are you?"
"Very well, thank you," Jan smiled then took a sip from her mug. Rose could not resist saying,

"Looks like you found the tea bags." Jan cut in, still smiling,

"Yes, I found them, your husband can't see for looking!"

"In the cupboard there?" Rose pointed.

"Yep, right there staring at him they were!" Jan let out a loud, easy laugh.

"All right, ladies, sorry, I didn't look properly. Did you have a nice walk, Rose?"

"Apart from a few bruises, yes, thanks, I did."

"Bruises?" Rob and Jan said in unison looking straight at her. Rose felt embarrassed at such attention and wished she had not mentioned it.

"Yes, long story, nothing serious, it was good to get some air." Rose looked at an expectant Jan and felt the need to elaborate, "I walked my mum's dog while she watched Evie. I needed some space, you know, to try to clear my head, a break from Miss Night Monster who kept me up yet again last night. Anyway, I knocked my head off a couple of trees. I won't bore you with the details. You'd think I'd been drinking." Jan looked sympathetic,

"Actually, Rob was telling me earlier that Evie won't go to bed or stay there. That must be awful. Hard to believe really, she's so seriously cute. Nothing like her Dad." She winked at Rob. Rose wanted to tell her to go back to work. Jan was unconscious of this, "Have you tried homeopathy to help her sleep? It's very good and all natural, definitely safe for kids?"

"Jan, I've tried everything I can to no avail. It's just so exhausting!" Rose did not want any sympathy, especially from Jan, for fear she might burst into tears of exhaustion. It was none of Jan's business anyway. Rose added quickly, "I'm sure she'll sleep soon. No point making a big deal about it." Still, Jan continued,

"Mind you, I never used any remedies on Fred. I was always lucky with him. He was a good sleeper. In fact, he still is, except now he's older, I have a problem in that he never wants to get out of bed." Jan turned to Evie, "You need to sleep at night, Evie, otherwise Mummy and Daddy will be too exhausted to look after you." Evie acted like she had not heard a word. Jan looked at the clock, "I must get back. See you in a minute, Rob. Nice to see you, Rose." Jan teetered off in very high heels, leaving Rose wondering how she negotiated the path through the garden to the hut without ending up on her bottom.

"I won't be long, Jan." Rob called after her before turning to Rose, "I really must get on. You look tired. You really should try to get some rest. Everything here can wait." Rob darted out of the kitchen. Rose felt a pang of envy that he was able to escape so easily, especially to Jan, who Rose was finding increasingly irritating. Jan had done nothing wrong except be herself. It did not make sense.

Evie was not hungry and spread her food all over the table, which was unusual for her. Her temperature was slightly raised. Rose put it down to teething and tiredness. She was not surprised when Evie chose to lie on the sitting room floor and play with her teddy and a brick, silently and slowly arranging and rearranging them.

Rose whizzed round the house making beds and tidying up. She thought about the question her mother had asked her that morning. Rose knew the answer was no, staying at home was not enough. Her mother had noticed this, almost before Rose herself. What was she going to do about it? She would have to put it right. Whenever someone well meaning commented that she was lucky to be able to have the choice to stay at home with her children over going out to work, she felt awkward, not lucky. Things were starting to make sense. The awakening of new beginnings could no longer be ignored.

What nagged at the back of Rose's mind was that she was gradually becoming more disconnected from a world that had once given her so much satisfaction. She missed it, and needed to retrieve some of it. The stimulation of working was different from anything she experienced with her family. As she picked up another dirty sock, she muttered to herself,
"Perhaps I should just go ahead and do my own business. I could make it work. I would still be a good-enough mother." Her old enthusiasm was returning as she started to acknowledge what she might need.

As Rose managed to reach the sweet wrapper under Thomas's bed, she became more excited by her plans,
I could get a shop; make sure it's local so there would be no commuting to worry about. If the children needed me at any time, it would be easy to be there for them. This was not a new idea, running her own shop in town selling fabrics and gifts while also offering coffee, as well as sewing and craft classes at the back.

She imagined teapot collections and bunting scattered around her shop and a relaxed buzz. Rose had visualised all this for years. Her idea had started as escapism a long time ago after a bad day at work. It was exciting to think she could make it happen.

Rose took a container full of Duplo Lego upstairs with her so Evie would have something to occupy her on the bathroom floor while Rose took a shower before the school run. No sooner had she finished and wrapped a towel round herself than Evie started crying and pointing to her mouth. Rose thought Evie had bitten herself chewing on the Duplo. Rose bent down for a closer look before a fountain of vomit projected from Evie, all over the floor and Rose's feet. Evie screamed with shock.

'Oh darling, it's OK. It's OK." Rose quickly carried Evie over to the toilet and stroked her hair. Evie howled before vomiting again. It was almost unbelievable that so much rotten liquid could pour out of such a small body. Rose gagged as she stripped Evie who looked pitiful, her flesh covered in goosebumps. Rose sprayed Evie down in the shower, dressed her in warm clothes and left her lying on the bed with a bucket next to her. Rose prayed Evie would not be sick again. Rose dressed herself and dragged a comb through her hair as fast as she could, working out how late she would be for Anna and Thomas.

Rose dumped her used towel on the sick all over the floor hoping it would stop it spreading and make clearing it up easier, when she got back. She grabbed Evie and the bucket.

Evie cried for almost the entire ten minutes drive to the school, a weak, fed-up cry. She clutched her favourite, pink beaker in one hand and Marge, her floppy bear, in the other. Rose prayed she would not have to pull over if Evie vomited again as she was already late enough. Rose collected Anna and Thomas from the office where the teacher was so nice to her that Rose, again, nearly burst into tears.
"We thought you had forgotten us," said Anna.
"Yeah, you're always late." chimed Thomas.

"I'm sorry but Evie was sick and I'm not always late. In fact, I've only been late twice this term and on neither occasion was it my fault."

"Alex's mum is never late and she always brings a cake for him. She makes them. I wish she was my mum." Thomas said to his feet. Rose knew they were right. She always seemed to be running against the clock. She never seemed to be able to arrive on time for anything. *Wouldn't it be wonderful to be so perfect, like Alex's mum?*

As Rose pulled into the drive, Evie let out a wail before vomiting again. There was much less of it this time but enough to seep into the car seat. Anna appeared to be holding her breath, grabbed the keys off Rose and bolted out of the car into the house while Thomas sat there with his school jumper pulled up around his mouth so only his eyes and tufts of hair poked out.

"Thomas, stop being silly and just get out of the car. In fact, hurry up and get me some kitchen roll. I said, hurry."

As Rose extracted a dripping Evie from her car seat while trying not to breathe the smell, Jan breezed past still so steady in those heels as if she were wearing trainers. She mumbled something to the effect that she would help but she had to go home and get changed, something about a karate competition and her son. Rose wanted to say that she did not blame her but just smiled as Jan looked disparagingly at Rose's old tracksuit bottoms.

Rose surprised herself at how quickly she cleaned it all up. The children were so good. Thomas was mesmerised by an episode of some fighting monsters on the television and Anna sat on the sofa stroking Evie's hair until she fell asleep, giving her occasional sips of water from her beaker, not allowing any gulps, on Rose's instruction.

Rose dumped the carrier bag containing the car and bathroom clean up in the bin outside thinking how clearly different an average day was from her old working days. Until Evie was born and the move to the countryside, apart from a relatively brief period working for a friend, Rose had been a buyer for a well-known department store and had been involved in the sourcing and price negotiation of merchandise. Her bosses loved her because she had an eager eye for what would sell and always drove the suppliers prices down. Rose delivered every time and became affectionately known as Ruthless Rose behind her back as she steamed ahead in her career. She enjoyed trips to China as part of her job where she would be treated like royalty. Rose would always remember the time she sourced a best selling tee-shirt for the ladies department for such a low price that each one managed to retail at twenty times the buying price she had negotiated with the factory owner. The marketing and advertising department convinced the customers that this was the new-season-wardrobe staple. It was available in three key colours, black, white and neutral. Satisfied fully by work, marriage and children had not yet crossed Rose's mind.

Rose's father had expected her to follow him into law. However, Rose had made up her mind, while still at school, that her future was in retail and managed, at only fifteen years old, to secure a Saturday job in a small boutique in the local town, without discussing it with her parents. She smiled to herself now as she remembered the argument with her father about this,

"But why, Rose? I give you enough pocket money. I don't understand why you want to do this, and without even discussing it with me first! Why would you do such a thing? I pay for everything so you can study, Rose, without having to worry about anything else."

"I know, Dad, I appreciate that. Really, I do, but I want to do this. It's not just about money. It's about learning new skills and getting work experience."

"Well, if it's work experience you want then the firm can give you that at any time. You only have to ask." Her exasperated father had yelled, "And retail, Rose for goodness sake, what about the fact you'd make a damn-good solicitor and you wouldn't be constantly dealing with disgruntled customers? We can give you work experience or the other firm in town if this is about not wanting to work with me. It would look so much better on your CV."

"Dad, I want to make my own way. I'm sure I want to be on the management side of retail anyway so I wouldn't have much to do at all directly with the customers. It really excites me. It's fun and interesting."

"But so is law," he exclaimed.

Despite his concerns, Rose's father did back down and was supportive of her decision but she knew he was disappointed. She wished, as she had many times before, that she had had siblings to take some of the spotlight off her.

Rose loved her Saturday job. After graduating with a degree in business management and marketing, she joined a supermarket chain as a graduate trainee. Shortly after finishing this training, she managed to secure a role in buying. Luckily for Rose, someone left. She took their place. However, she preferred clothes to food and household items. She could not believe her luck when she was headhunted for the role of buyer at a well-known department store for less pay but, she knew, better prospects longer term.

Her father remained largely unimpressed and could not understand why anyone would take a new job for less money. He did manage to say that he was proud of her and admired her determination. This meant so much to her. She finally had his blessing, something, she believed, every girl wanted from their father, whatever their age.

Rose turned on the oven and left it to heat up for dinner. Rob appeared behind her and made her jump,
"God, it stinks in here, Rose, almost like sick. I'll check the fridge. Maybe something's gone off." Rob looked inside the fridge. Finding nothing, he looked flummoxed, "Right, I'm just calling round to Ed and Nicky's with the latest plans. I want to make sure they're happy. I really want the building to start, in earnest, next spring, as one winter in the hut will be enough. It's very noisy when it rains; wish me luck. Ed's an awkward bugger. I'm sure he'll find something he's unhappy with." After glancing at her tracksuit bottoms, he skipped off out the front door before Rose had a chance to say anything.

With the children still hypnotised by the television, before Rose started to prepare any food, she poured herself a large glass of chilled, white wine into the biggest wine glass she could find. She smiled as she took the first, cooling sip.

FOUR

At thirty, Rose had been exactly where she wanted to be in her career. She had not shared any of the insecurities, regrets or feelings of lost youth that a lot of her friends felt this milestone birthday signified. Still single, Rose had been in no hurry to meet Mr Right. She had barely entertained the notion of having her own children even though she knew she might want them eventually. They belonged very far into the future. Her substantial salary had enabled her to buy her own flat in London near the King's Road and near where she worked. Despite having a mortgage, she never felt tied down by the responsibility of it because she had made sure she had bought in an area where she could let or sell overnight if she wanted a change.

She had kept the same circle of close friends, most of them from university. She spent a lot of her free time with them. They enjoyed cinema, pub and theatre trips. She loved shopping and treated herself to regular manicures and visits to a prestigious hair salon in Covent Garden. She felt fulfilled and happy. Even her father had managed to swallow his pride and tell her how well she had done for herself, even if he had spoiled it a bit by adding that it would never be too late to study law, or indeed anything else if she so wished. She had managed to see humour in this with the help of her friend and colleague, Sarah. She had pointed out that it was really a compliment that Rose's father thought her so capable because her own father was the opposite. He had never expected her to pass an exam let alone hold down any kind of job for long. She claimed she did not care what he thought but Rose could tell she did.

It was at the wedding of an old school friend that Rose met Rob. She fell so in love that it literally knocked her off course. Never, since wanting to work in retail, had she been so sure of what she wanted. Almost immediately, she imagined a life married to Rob, with children playing a prominent part. She felt this so strongly she could barely control any of it.

As everyone had taken their places at the wedding breakfast, she had spotted Rob at a table adjacent to hers. Throughout the meal, she had felt unsettled and unable to concentrate fully on the conversation. She had willed herself to stop gawping at him. She had seemed unable to stop herself. She had been aware of flushing every time she looked over at him. How could someone she did not know have this effect on her, and from a distance? She had not even spoken to him for goodness sake. She had been aware of someone looking at her. She had turned towards Rob again. This time their eyes had met. She had looked away almost immediately but, before she could stop herself, had sneaked another look. Rob had smiled. She had smiled back and dared herself not to look again. *Must be very strong champagne if it can do this after a few mouthfuls*, she had thought, trying to rationalise her madness.

Once the meal and speeches were over, Rose, knowing she had to drive later, had bought herself a sparkling water at the bar. She had a presentation to finalise in the morning for a business trip to China the following day so needed to stay sharp. She did not plan to stay late but wanted to speak to as many people as she could, many she had not seen for ages. She was replacing her purse in her bag when she heard a male voice asking politely for two beers just behind her.

This voice had actually made her quiver inside with delight. It sounded husky and smooth, with a hint of the North. She did not want to look round for fear of looking obvious but she could not stop herself. When she saw who the voice belonged to she almost laughed out loud as she remembered what Sarah had said about men and voices. The nicer the voice the more gross the bloke. *Well, not on this occasion, Sarah.* It was the man from the adjacent table. Rose found herself dumbstruck as they came face to face. She remembered how she had smiled at him before attempting to move away. Buying two drinks probably meant that he was with someone special already even though she had not noticed whether he had been. She wished she had been more observant.
"Hi, I'm Rob. Bride or groom?" he beamed.
"Um, bride, definitely bride... yes, I went to school with her, with Tilly." Collecting herself, Rose managed to offer her hand. "I'm Rose." He looked amused as he shook her hand,
"I went to school with Ben, the groom, in case you didn't know. Anyway, good fun all of this don't you think?" She was staring up at Rob and had not really

heard what he had said. Aware that she had been staring right at him, she asked,
"Haven't we met before?" As it slipped off her tongue, she cringed at her own rubbish chat-up line. She smiled to herself now as she remembered how Sarah had roared with laughter when she had later relayed this conversation.

Rob had looked even more amused before saying, kindly,
"I'm absolutely sure I would always remember someone as beautiful as you." She had felt weak with excitement despite his corny line but, before she could say anything, had been literally carried away by an extremely excited friend she had not seen in ages. This friend had quickly apologised to Rob before grabbing Rose's arm. She was yanked towards another group of fervent people. She did not see Rob for the rest of the evening until she left, a little earlier than everyone else, to drive back to London. As she had pressed the key fob, her car lights had sprung on. Rob had literally jumped out of the bushes.
"Um, me again," he beamed, "I don't normally do this kind of thing but is there any chance I could have your phone number? Err... " He ran his hands through his hair. "It would be nice to meet for coffee or a drink or something... well... you know what I mean. It's just I would have liked to get to know you a bit better here tonight but... well, you know... well, could I have it... please? The number, your number...?"

Lost for words again, she managed to fumble in her bag for a business card and handed it to Rob. It never occurred to her to give him her home telephone number,

"I'll be in China for most of next week on business but you can always leave a message with my secretary. And, yes, it would be nice to meet up. I'd like that."
"And, this is my business card but I was thinking more of a social get together than a business one." He joked and handed it to her. She looked at it but was so excited that she did not take it in. It could have said get lost for all she knew.

She had been aware of sounding business like but her mother had always taught her never to seem too keen with men, even if you wanted to grab them and run, and this message was now ingrained in her psyche,
"A social meeting sounds nice." She replied, "I live in London, though. Where are you based?"
"Well, as luck would have it, London too. I'll be in touch." She smiled. Rob looked awkward as if he did not want to leave. Rose felt rooted to the spot too but both were saved from saying any more when a stunning woman stumbled towards them, whining,
"Oh, my darling, there you are!" She planted a huge, smudgy kiss on his cheek. "Take me home pleeeeease, I'm so knackered and pissed." Rose raised her eyebrows at Rob, turned around, got in her car and drove off.

Once on the motorway, Rose felt furious. She said out loud to herself,
"Two beers! Lovely to meet you, my arse!" She continued to punish herself thinking *but, of course, how could I be so stupid? Someone as good-looking and suave as him would already have a girlfriend and would play the field. Forget him, he's probably got a different woman every day of the week and is riddled with 'stds'.* At this, she had tried to firmly push him out of her mind, had dismissed any chance of moving forward with him as a fantasy, a hope that did not exist. She reminded

herself that she was independent, very much able to look after herself. However, he would not leave her thoughts. For the first time, she was smitten, by a man.

The business trip to China went perfectly. She closed the deal in her usual no nonsense way. Everyone was happy. What had marred the trip for her was an unprecedented, creeping sense of dissatisfaction stirring inside her. She had woken in the middle of the night hot and breathless after a nasty dream about the loneliness she had often felt as an only child, the exclusion when she saw other children playing or arguing with their siblings. Although she had frequently had friends over for tea or sleepovers, and her parents had been very encouraging and accommodating of this, it had not been the same.

It seemed that Rob had stirred up feelings in her she thought had long blown away. Something in her, despite her suspicions that he was a relationship player, yearned to get to know him. However, sharing a man with other women had never appealed to her. Even so, for the first time, she was not sure she wanted to be alone any more and certainly not for the rest of her life.

On her return from China, she had entered the office satisfied with her new deals. She was looking forward to the meeting scheduled with her colleagues to discuss it all.
"Hi Rose, how are you? Hear you've been to China again. How did it go?" It was Bob, one of the security guards.
"Hi Bob! It went very well, thank you. And, how are things with you?"
"Oh, not too bad, not too bad...." She smiled at Bob and was about to walk through one of the turnstiles when he

continued, "I'm OK but my son injured his back bungee jumping at the weekend and my daughter gave birth to son number five a few days before, massive, he is. She only had another for a girl, of course, so she'll probably need counselling to get over it!" He laughed, "She'll be having a sixth, you heard it here first, I can guarantee that! Never gives up, my daughter!" Before Rose had a chance to say anything, wondering why the sex of a baby would be so important to someone, Matt continued, "Anyway, you still single?" She flinched at this unexpected question, which she found over familiar coming from someone she barely knew.

"Well, yes I am." Even though she knew she did not have to explain herself she had added that she did not really have time for a relationship. Matt had looked delighted as he said,

"Well you might just have to make time, love, as there's a massive bunch of flowers upstairs for you and they're not from a client we don't think...got a secret admirer have we? You kept that quiet!" Before she could say anything, the telephone rang on his desk. He picked up the receiver, gave her a knowing nod and buzzed her through the turnstile.

Bet they are from a client. She climbed the stairs to her office. The Chinese boss she had met on her trip had been pretty smooth. They were probably from him. An enormous bunch of pink peonies wrapped in pretty, expensive-looking, pink, tissue paper were waiting on her desk. The accompanying card was sealed in a gold envelope.

"Fancy a drink in town after work next Thursday, 8pm The Old Steine? Rob xx PS The other woman is my sister!!"

That moment would always remain clear in her mind. It was one of the happiest and most significant of her life. She remembered finding it hard to concentrate on the simplest task at work for the rest of that day, wanting so badly to be with Rob. She had fallen totally in love with someone she barely knew.

"Mum... Mum!" shouted much louder the second time. Rose jumped as she returned from her daydream. It was Thomas. He was almost growling her name while tugging frantically at his school tie. It had developed into a tight, tiny knot, nothing like the chunkier one she had sent him to school with. "Get my tie off now," he exclaimed while doing a jig to demonstrate his frustration. Removing his school tie had become impossible. Usually quiet and content, Thomas could spend hours creating Lego villages and battles. Clearly, this was one that he was losing, one that would be enough to enrage even the calmest of little people. With the tie safely removed, Thomas seemed embarrassed at having made such a fuss before rubbing his neck and running back upstairs to his room.

"Thomas, Anna and Evie, I've got a surprise for you!" Anna appeared at the door almost instantly followed by the other two. Even though it had not been forty-eight hours since Evie's last vomit, Rose felt she was better. Where had she caught it anyway? Rose decided that, as it was Friday, and she was tired, and Rob was going to the pub with his golfing mates, she would take the children out for dinner. The local pizza restaurant had a good children's menu. It would give her a break.
"Can we have chocolate ice cream with a flake pleeease?" said the chorus of three.

"If you eat your main courses, yes, you can."
"Yes!" Thomas and Anna both jumped on the spot and Evie let out a screech of delight. A frenzy of toilet trips and grabbing of coats and shoes followed as Rose ran upstairs to check her hair and put on some make-up.

Seeing the children's eager, excited faces made her smile. *This is why we become parents, for these happy moments.* She felt proud. She was looking forward to taking them out on her own, showing them off and having them completely to herself.

The pizza trip was fun. The children behaved well. Anna and Thomas spent time engrossed in the pictures they coloured, provided by the young waitress. Evie emulated them, clumsily holding the pencils in her chubby, dimpled hands. The children ate all their food. They chatted about school telling Rose about the naughty things some of the children did like pumping all the liquid soap out of the dispenser in the toilets. She wondered if they made some of it up.

The children went to bed when they were told, much to Rose's relief and surprise. She kissed each child goodnight. Thomas seemed pensive.
"What are you thinking about, Thomas?"
"Alex is going to be a teacher like Mr. Allen when he grows up."
"Would you like to be a teacher?"
"No," Thomas sighed, "I don't know what I want to be. I have no ideas. I like Lego but that's for children. I'm not going to get married, though. Girls are horrible."
"Well, you've got me and you've got plenty of time to decide what you want to be. You might change your mind about girls one day. Anyway, you can always live

with me forever. You could do my gardening." Thomas looked stunned before adding,
"I know what I'm going to do! I'm going to live underwater and marry someone like Jan."

FIVE

The children remained in bed all evening, a first, in a while, for Evie. With no Rob, Rose enjoyed a rare evening on her own. She painted her fingernails and read a sizeable chunk of her novel. Her nails had the unusual chance to dry properly. It tickled her that there would be no sheet imprints on them in the morning.

She fell asleep reading. She slept so peacefully that in the morning she woke in a panic wondering if Evie was actually all right and if Rob had indeed come home. His pillows were dented and his dressing gown had gone from the hook on the back of their bedroom door suggesting he had. Becoming fully awake, she heard him moving around in the kitchen below. She grabbed her dressing gown and went downstairs. Evie was sitting in her highchair eating *Coco Pops*, her eyes and milk-soaked lips glistening at Rob, clearly glad to have Daddy all to herself.

"Hi Rob. I can't believe I slept so well and for so long. It's disorientating, no trouble from Evie. The other two,

42

are they not up yet?" Rose pecked him on the lips trying not to inhale the stale beer and curry.

"Nope, just the three of us. I'm afraid I've got a bit of a hangover after last night but it's my own fault so I don't expect any sympathy." He smiled meekly. "You didn't even stir when I came to bed. Your book was resting on your neck. Nice nails by the way."

"Oh, thank you, you noticed!" She admired her perfectly polished fingernails. "I didn't hear a thing last night. I actually feel quite refreshed, not to rub it in about the hangover or anything." She laughed and sipped the tea Rob had made her. She sat down at the table with Evie while Rob continued to stir the porridge he was making. "Was it a good night? How is everyone?"

"Yes, it was, thanks. Tasty curry, flowing beer; you know, the usual, drunken antics of men, on a tight leash, given a bit of freedom." Rob winked, "No news for you, though. We talked cars and golf all night. Aren't you going to ask me how it went with our lovely neighbour, Ed, yesterday?"

She wanted to reply that she had purposely not asked. She assumed it would not have gone well, bearing in mind how awkward Ed could be. She did not want any stress to cut into her current, relaxed state of mind. She was tired of the petty scenarios erupting from the bottom of the garden. She wanted to dismiss Ed as crazy and tell Rob to accept this and move on. However, she did not dare. Rob needed to vent his frustrations, even if he was making a habit of going round in circles.

"Oh yes, I forgot you went round there. Did it go OK?" Rose lied. Rob smiled and raised his eyebrows. After a sip from his mug, he began,

"Well, Ed is being unreasonable about the plans again, no surprise there. He's still harping on about a window overlooking his property. He owns the bushes and the tree which will completely obscure the offending window of the future. It's metres away from the boundary.

"Also, he's saying that he might have to put in a new objection to the council about the roof windows, for the proposed loft conversion, because they might overlook him too, even though they aren't even going to be pointing in the direction of his property. We're not going to be craning out of them, like giraffes, hoping to catch a glimpse of him. God, he's so annoying. Honestly, he's doing all this to wind me up because he doesn't want us to live. Later, he started going on about building noise and possible compensation because ... wait for it ... it's hard enough on a good day here, apparently, with our kids screaming and shouting in the garden. I wouldn't mind but the kids hardly play outside as it's nearly always raining so the garden's a bog, and they aren't screamers because I wouldn't stand for it."

"It went well then." Rose said meekly more to her cup of tea than Rob.

"Oh, come on, Rose, doesn't he get under your skin too?"

"Yes, but we know he's weird and makes things up. I've chosen not to let him bother me. We've pretty much got everything we want, permission-wise, and he knows that. There is enough distance between our properties for us not to have to bump into each other very often, if at all. He's just flexing his muscles for reasons that probably have nothing to do with us. A lot of it is in his head. I would imagine we're not the only people he rubs up the wrong way. I bet Nicky won't hang around for much longer, you'll see. Just don't go round there any more. You won't change him and being open and honest with him obviously doesn't help. You can never level with people like him." Rose took another sip of tea before continuing, "Actually, um, talking of Nicky, did she have anything to say? Does she agree with Ed?" Rose could not imagine Nicky making a big deal about something like a window she could not even see.

"She didn't say much. In fact, at one point, she actually left the room. Can you believe that?" Rob smiled and shook his head, "Something about letting the cat in or out, I can't remember. I reckon she knows what an awkward bugger he is and couldn't bear to listen to him any longer."

"Well, perhaps you should take a leaf out of her book and not let him bother you either. Like I said, you won't change him, Rob. Try not to react as much. You've gone about everything the right way and you get on well with Mr. Smithson from the council. He likes you. It'll all be OK. They must be used to dealing with people like Ed so I'm sure it wont slow anything down for long. Once you've got the project manager in place, I would leave it all to him, and let Ed bend his ear, not yours. Come on, it's exciting. We'll have the home of our dreams soon."

"I know, Rose, you're right. Sorry for ranting. I must stop." Rose had stopped offering to help where the plans were concerned. Rob had made it clear that he did not want any help. It was his venture. She just listened when he needed her to. Increasingly, she felt her job had become one of pacifying the children and him. This needed to change. She needed another focus. Otherwise, what would she do when the children left home? She shuddered at the thought of her life only revolving around Rob.

Her thoughts shifted to Jan. She wondered if Rob ever shared his worries with her. Perhaps she would be shocked if she knew he was not always the easy-going, cheerful chap he appeared to be when Rose saw them together. She doubted Jan would put up with any nonsense. There were always other jobs.

Rose decided to have a look at business premises in the estate agents' window later that day. Looking was harmless, and did not have to lead to a commitment to anything, so why not? She went past it almost every day on her way to the supermarket or the school. She needed to stop off for milk and bread, at some point, anyway.

She timed the afternoon school run well. She parked easily just as the children were coming out meaning she did not have to make polite conversation with anyone, which suited her today. After piling the children into the car, Rose managed to stop in the street right outside the supermarket enabling her to leave the children in the car while she nipped in. On coming out, she remembered to have a quick look in the estate agents' window. Anna and Thomas seemed very settled in the back of the car. Anna was reading her book. Thomas was mesmerised by a lorry on the other side of the road delivering massive pallets of stock, the tailgate going slowly up and down. Evie was fast asleep. Without saying anything, so as not to break this quiet spell of calm, Rose carefully shut the car boot. She darted along to the estate agency, two doors down.

Acutely aware she had left her children unattended, she quickly scanned the window. A property caught her eye, a pretty cottage that had been a coffee shop until recently. It was situated a short distance from the high street, up on the hill, in a courtyard, surrounded by other businesses. It would be ideal for what she had planned.

She went in and asked for a copy of the details from a lady who caught her eye. Despite explaining that she had very little time, having left her children in the car, the agent seemed in no hurry. She found a copy of the details, in a filing cabinet. She dangled the paper in front of Rose,

"This is a very cute property. It won't hang around." The agent looked hopeful, "so, if you are keen...?" The agent clearly wanted to know how serious Rose was, "then, you'll need to move fast. The property is up for rent or to buy. The owners died, old couple, and the family don't want it." Realising what she had said she backtracked, "Of course they want the going rate for it and don't especially need the money, so won't give it away. They'll wait for the right deal. Do you have finance set up to cover this? We have an excellent financial adviser we can put you in touch with."

"I'll let you know. My children..." Rose grabbed the details from the agent's hand and ran out the door calling thank you as she went.

She hopped back in the car and looked at the children. Evie was still asleep but she noticed tears in Thomas's eyes,

"What happened?" Anna was looking very sheepish and could not meet Rose's eyes.

"Anna hit my arm because she said I breathed bad breath on her."

"Oh for goodness sake, Anna, why? Poor Thomas, just leave each other alone."

"Anyway, where were you?" asked a tearful Thomas, "You took ages."

"I wasn't that long, sorry. We're going home now." She sighed as she turned on the engine and pulled away to go home.

Rose stopped the car on the drive. Anna and Thomas raced straight into the house leaving the car door open and a trail of bags, coats and shoes behind them. They grabbed a biscuit each and plonked themselves on the bean bags, in front of the television. Rose left Evie asleep in her car seat with the window ajar. Rose needed five minutes rest. She opened the sitting room window slightly, too, so she could hear Evie once she woke up.

Rose slumped onto the sofa, pulled a soft, warm blanket over herself and fell into a deep sleep. She was dreaming about trees, of running through the woods, of Bobble and of entering an unfamiliar house where she went upstairs to find a lump, resembling a body, under the covers, in her bed. Even though she knew it was the man she had met in the woods, she was going to pull back the covers, to check.

"Rose, Rose... Rose, I've made you a cup of tea." She opened her eyes, abruptly leaving her dream, and wiped sticky saliva from her chin with the back of her hand. She noticed a dark, damp stain, on the satin cushion, where she had dribbled. Gingerly, she turned the cushion over, hoping Rob had not noticed.

He was holding a smiling Evie, fresh in her pyjamas, ready for bed. Rose was struck by how similar to each other they looked. They had the same wide smile and large, hazel eyes. Daddy's girl. Rose swung her legs off the sofa, onto the floor, and moved the blanket to one side. The tea tasted perfect.
"How come Evie's in her pyjamas?"
"Well, it's her bedtime soon! She's had a bath. They've all had dinner, fish fingers, smiles and peas, with ice cream to follow. Thomas and Anna are getting changed for bed now. I said they could watch television for a bit

longer, if they were quick and hung up their uniforms ready for tomorrow."

"Wow, thanks, Rob. How long have I been asleep for? What time is it?"

"It's six-thirty so ...I don't know. When did you get back?"

"Usual time, around four o'clock. I only meant to rest for a little while. I thought Evie would have woken me. You should have."

'It's fine, Rose, you needed to sleep. I finished early today anyway. The children have been really good. I suppose, it's a novelty for them to have Daddy doing dinner and bed. It was funny because I came in to find you. Evie was calling at you from her car seat, her legs and arms flailing around, like a stuck tortoise, but you were dead to the world, so I released her. She could see you through the window. You didn't even stir. Anna and Thomas were playing upstairs."

He stopped and stared at her cheek.

"What on earth happened to your face?"

"I thought I told you. I knocked it in the woods, the other day. The bruising must have come out. Actually, it's not sore."

"I do remember now, yes. It wasn't that noticeable before. Drink your tea. I'm going to put Evie to bed. We're going to read 'The Tiger that came to tea'." He handed Rose the local Indian takeaway menu. "Pick something on that. I don't feel like cooking and you look like you definitely need a night off. I'll go and pick it up once Evie's settled."

"Thanks, Rob."

As he carried Evie upstairs, he was concerned at how tired Rose looked. He worried about her. She seemed worn down. He wondered if it might be more than just physical fatigue from Evie's antics. Perhaps Rose had done the child thing for too long and needed another outlet, like work, to give her a separate sense of purpose, while someone else took over the children for a while. She had mentioned going back to work, come to think of it, but he wondered how she would manage. Still, she would work it out. He had always admired her resilience and ability to make whatever life had in store for her work to her advantage. She would soon rise up again.

Rose was looking forward to her takeaway and to catching up with Rob. After a quick shower, she slipped into her favourite black wrap-dress, comfortable and smart, drew lipstick over her lips and went downstairs to warm some plates in the oven, and lay the table. After much blind rummaging in the high kitchen cupboard, she could not be bothered to get the step as she knew they were in there somewhere, she located the matches and lit a candle in the centre of the table, just as Rob arrived back with the food, the fresh smell of outdoors on his clothes.

He poured them each a glass of red wine,
"Just to let you know, I left the property details I found in the car, which I assume are yours, by the bed. So, come on, Rose, do tell, what are you up to?" He smiled. She felt bashful. She had not planned to say anything, not just yet anyway, not because she was being particularly secretive but because she was getting used to her idea herself. Grabbing details was easy. Doing something with them required determination. Even so, holding those details had given her a certain feeling of excitement, which she had not felt in a long time.

She told him all about it,

"I've done my homework. There's certainly a market for something like this around here. The business would work well. No one else is doing it. I wasn't going to say anything because it's been a dream of mine for a while. Something's pushing me to do it. I grabbed the property details on a sort of whim. It's only a fifteen-minute walk from the town centre. Sorry, I'm galloping on a bit aren't I?"

"Not at all. It sounds like you've already given it a lot of thought. You seem really alive when you talk about it. I've got no problem with it, Rose. I don't wish to sound sickly but sometimes dreams have to be allowed to come true, you have to trust in them. Look at me, working from home, building up my own practice and us in this house, something we always dreamed of when we were in London... More rice?"

"Yes, please," Rose looked down, "I know, Rob, but Evie still needs me a lot and I don't want her at a nursery all day. I'd hardly see her, and then there's Anna and Thomas to consider. I missed out on a fair bit with them. I don't want to abandon them all over again."

"I know but no one is asking you to abandon them, Rose. You must never think you have. You are entitled to a life too. Isn't a happy mum a good mum?" He smiled, "you'd be local anyway. As they get older, they could come and see you after school, even help out for pocket money, and perhaps you could aim to delegate in the long run, as you become more established, you know, employ a manager, and please yourself a bit more, full-time one week, part-time the next. You don't have to be a slave to the family. I realised tonight that the children are capable of doing a lot more for themselves than we allow. Eventually they'll leave home and then what?"

"I know. I've been thinking about that too. Don't wish all our lives away, though." Rose exclaimed, "Anyway, enough about me, how was your day?"

"Very good! I got a lot of those jobs, the ones everybody puts off, finished. You know the ones, collecting information for the accountants, filing, answering queries, checking post... It was quite therapeutic. Of course, I couldn't have done it without Jan. She's amazing, so efficient and light hearted. It must be so hard for her being a single mother, no one else to turn to for support. She's got no boyfriend or anything. Hardly goes out. Hard to believe really. Says she spends her evenings reading and watching soaps! Must be lonely for her. She's very pretty, don't you think? Don't take this the wrong way but I'm surprised she hasn't been snapped up!"

Rose felt a stab of jealously at her husband referring to Jan as being pretty, even if he was stating a fact. She had no intention of letting Rob know this, though,
"She is pretty. She doesn't need you worrying about her, though. She has her mother there for her, to help with her son. She's fine." She got up from the table to bring the wine over and poured them both another glass.

With the meal finished, Rob cleared the table and took the rubbish out while Rose slipped the plates and cutlery into the dishwasher. She thought about Jan and why the mere mention of her was enough to unsettle her. Was her sixth sense trying to tell her something or was it just her insecurities pestering her, regrettably and currently, an all too familiar feeling? After all, Rob was married to her and she was the mother of his children. Jan was just his helper.

"Fancy a cup of tea and an early night, missus?" Rob pecked Rose on her cheek and brought her out of her thoughts, "You look miles away! What are you thinking about?"
"Just the children, hope they're still asleep," she lied, "And, yes, an early night, why not? See, I wasn't really miles away," she grinned.
"I'm sure they are asleep. I'll make the tea and check everything's locked up down here if you want to check them."

The children were beautifully settled. Rose slipped into bed. She was acutely aware of how tired she felt. It had been a long day and the wine, along with the rich food, had made her feel soporific. She willed herself to stay awake. Soon, Rob climbed in next to her,
"The coast is clear. We're in luck." He put a reassuring arm around her waist and pulled her towards him. She felt a familiar, quivering feeling, like butterflies in her stomach, as he kissed her. Nothing else mattered in the world as they became all consumed with each another.
"I love you so much, Rose." He whispered close to her ear.
"I love you too." There was a bang against their bedroom door before it was flung open. They jumped apart and managed to pull the duvet up to their chins, hoping they had been quick enough.

"Mummy," Evie cried while swinging off the doorframe, "Can I sleep in your bed?" Rob had managed to pull his trousers on under the duvet and stomped off to the bathroom moaning under his breath. Rose fumbled under the covers as she tried to put some clothes on without Evie noticing she was naked. Rose mumbled that Mummy was hot but had now cooled down, just in case.

"Oh, Evie, for goodness sake, why can't you just sleep in your own bed? It's sleep time until it's day again. You know that."

"I don't like it. It's too dark. I'm scared."

"Please, Evie."

"No, I want to sleep with you."   Rose could not be bothered to argue because she knew, from experience, that Evie would just keep reappearing all night until she got what she wanted and Rose did not have the will to argue.

A seething Rob stomped out of the bathroom, took one look at Evie who had confidently taken up residence in the middle of his side of the bed and announced he was off to sleep in Evie's bed.

"Except, I might put her back in soon if she's restless," said Rose gently, carefully negotiating the imaginary egg shells. He flounced over to the bed, gently eased one of the two pillows from under Evie's head and stuffed it under his arm.

"I'll sleep on the sofa downstairs then," he leered at Rose as he continued, "but you and I both know that it's highly unlikely Evie will be back in her own bed by the morning." He stomped out of the bedroom leaving the door ajar and the landing light shining directly into Rose's eyes.

She waited until she heard him settle downstairs on the sofa, and the click of the light going off, before she crept over to turn the landing light off and close the bedroom door. Evie's eyes were like saucers, she was taking it all in, and, yet, she seemed unaffected by the tension she had created, as she asked,

"Mummy, can I have some water?"

"No, Evie... Night, Evie,". Rose felt dejected about Rob and drained by the familiar night disturbances from Evie but, as Rose reached over to turn off her bedside light, she eyed the property details next to it. She smiled as she drifted off to sleep thinking about her future business.

SIX

Jan was making coffee in the kitchen when Rose and Evie returned from the morning school run. Jan was attractive. At thirty-eight, she could pass for thirty. There was not a blemish on her skin, not even a sun mark. She was petite, five-feet-two and an hourglass shape. She had a tiny, defined waist, long eyelashes and massive, chocolate-brown eyes. Her lips were full. Her wavy hair was blonde and shoulder-length. Rose reckoned Jan could not know the meaning of a bad-hair-day. Rose wondered if Jan had had Botox or some other kind of cosmetic help because she always looked so flawless.

She dressed to suit her shape, normally in a dark coloured, tight, short skirt and high-heels, with a jacket drawn in at the waist. The skirts, often reserved for much younger women, suited her. She appeared classy, never overdone. She was bubbly, chatty and sometimes flirty with a girly, almost doll-like voice. Despite Rose's concerns, and as far as she could tell, Jan was loyal to Rob.

She claimed to have no interest in finding another partner. Her divorce, three years before, had drained her. Rose knew she should accept this, move on. However, it niggled her that Jan dressed up to work with Rob. It was not like she did any client-facing work. He saw her dressed up more often than he saw Rose at her best. That bothered Rose. Frankly, Jan could turn up in jeans and it would not matter. After all, Rob, her boss, often dressed down. After thinking all this, Rose felt a pang of guilt at being, frankly, bitchy about Jan. Rose well knew, from her own experience, that part of being professional was to look the part. She was being unfair. She, herself, was fed up with having nothing regular to dress up for except the odd night out with Rob. That was hardly Jan's fault, though. Rose dismissed her negative feelings towards Jan and decided to concentrate on her own inadequacies. Rob was happy with Jan and that should be the end of it. Even so, Rose wondered if Jan was maybe subconsciously trying to attract a new partner. She must have realised that Fred, now thirteen years old, would eventually leave home. What would she do for company then?

Rose set Evie down on the kitchen floor to play.
"Hi Rose! Fancy seeing you here!" Jan giggled, "Rob's been filling me in on your latest nightly escapades!" There was a momentary, awkward silence as Rose felt bashful, wondering what Rob had said. "Oh gosh, not like that! I meant with Evie. It sounds like a nightmare but, as we mothers well know, it's a phase and phases pass quickly. Hopefully, soon, you'll look less tired and feel less bedraggled." Jan turned to Evie, "You are a very naughty little sausage still waking up your mum and dad at night." Evie squealed with delight at the attention.

Rose bristled,
bedraggled, tired, God you are as annoying as hell. She
smiled through gritted teeth, replying breezily,
"Actually, I'm used to it. I've decided to accept it. I
don't feel that tired at all."
"That's not what you were saying this morning." Rob
laughed as he appeared in the doorway. Rose wanted to
hit him. Jan seemed unaware of any atmosphere,
"I've just made coffee for Rob and myself. Would you
like one?"
"Yes, please." Rose felt she really could do with some
coffee. It might wake her up a bit. As Rob picked up
his mug to return to the hut, he commented cheerfully,
"See you in a moment, Jan." He was gone. As Jan
grabbed a mug for Rose, showing she was very familiar
with the kitchen layout, she continued,
"Having said Fred used to sleep well, I do remember for
about a month, little rascal, him getting me up at five
thirty every morning. It was way too early but I just
used to send him to bed at nine every night and that
solved it. I'd then go off to bed myself. Mind you, I
didn't have a gorgeous hub like yours to maintain and I
had to get up early for work so that was not too much of
a sacrifice." She winked, "At least you don't need to
rush off to work every morning! Here's your coffee. I'll
let you do your own milk." And with that she was gone,
like a pantomime fairy in a puff of smoke.

As Rose added milk to her coffee, she thought to herself,
*How does Rob put up with her? She'd drive me mad,
with that constant champagne fizz, if I had to work with
her.* After sipping her coffee, Rose mumbled to herself,
thinking no one was listening, "For the record, some
women, like me, actually want to work even if we don't
need to, bloody cheek."

"Work!" Evie announced as she scuttled towards Rose, bringing her back from her thoughts.

"You are sweet, Evie." Rose scooped her up and kissed her as she cuddled her. Evie wriggled free and slid down back onto her feet. "Come on, Evie, let's tidy up a bit before the day runs away with us and we need to collect Anna and Thomas." Evie seemed to like this idea. She picked up a doll by the ankle and threw it roughly over her shoulder into the toy basket. "Good shot, Evie."

Rose continued to tidy up, loading the dishwasher and washing machine before checking the fridge for any signs of something she could serve the children for their tea. Evie happily toddled around, periodically pausing to look at stray toys before throwing most of them over her shoulder.

After making all the beds upstairs, Rose realised that she had not heard from or seen anything of Evie for a while. Rose found her fast asleep on the sitting room floor. Even though Rose had decided earlier to keep Evie awake all day, in the hope that it might make her sleep better at night, she looked so settled that Rose left her. Rose welcomed the peace. She draped a blanket over Evie's chubby, baby-like body. Rose used the time to call the estate agency about the coffee shop. She booked a viewing for Friday morning. Her mother agreed to look after Evie saying how David would be there this time. They would do a jigsaw together. She had bought a new 'Peppa Pig' one in the sale. Rose decided not to discuss anything with Rob at this stage, preferring to view the property alone. She would make up her own mind and not be swayed by anything other than her own instinct.

It was nearly time to leave for the children, when she caught a glimpse of Jan, from the upstairs bedroom window, tottering away, along the drive. Rob crept up behind Rose and made her jump as he threw his arms round her. Noticing Jan too, he commented to Rose,

"She's a funny little thing, isn't she? So lovely, though. I couldn't manage without her. She's a fantastic organiser. In fact I was thinking only this morning how lucky I am to have her and I think I'll promote her once I expand and take on another architect. It'll be nice once I get there. I'll feel like I've accomplished something big, pretty much on my own."

Rose said nothing. All she could focus on was Jan's perfect bottom, clad in her tight mini skirt, as she tottered out of sight. Rob appeared blind to any negative feelings Rose had towards her. This was probably just as well as Jan had not done anything bad to Rose. "Before I forget to tell you, I've got a meeting with Mr. Chapman, a project manager, tomorrow morning, if you'd like to come? I'm sure your mum would have Evie. It would be nice for you to meet him with me because I'm pretty sure he's the man for the job. He has a great list of projects behind him. I really won't be able to oversee all this building work on my own, you're busy and anyway, I need to start growing my practice. Someone like him will be invaluable, to liaise with the planners and any of the neighbours, should the need arise. I don't want to have to go back to my old colleagues with my tail between my legs!" Rob laughed. "Rob, I can't do tomorrow morning. Sorry but I have promised my friends that I'll go to the singing class with them. I cried off last time. I can't do that again at such short notice. I want to get to know them better. It's good for Evie too."

"That's fine, don't worry!" Rob smiled, "You can meet him another time. It's early days anyway and I like the sound of him, having spoken to him on the phone a couple of times. His experience is impressive, from what I've found out, so I'm pretty sure he's the one we'll go with."

"You're a good judge of character so I'm sure if you like him, I will too. Thanks for understanding. I know this house means so much to you so next time give me a bit more notice and I'll make sure I can be there."

"Another good thing is he thinks everything should be approved very soon after a few, minor tweaks. And, he doesn't think Ed should be a problem, even if he continues complaining, as he has nothing substantial to complain about, as we all well know. Mr Chapman, I can't remember his first name as I stupidly forgot to write it down, well, he thinks Ed is just flexing his muscles, which is quite common when a neighbour smells change. No one likes change. It's unsettling, especially on your doorstep. It never brings out the best in people. Mr. Chapman reckons a year from start to finish so, just think, we'll have our dream home by then. No more living with draughts and no more log cabin for me." Rob punched the air as he spoke.

"Sounds like he'll provide the help we need. Rob, I'd love to chat more but I must go. I don't want to be late for Anna and Thomas. I need to wake Evie and change her nappy before I go."

"Oh, I assumed Evie was at your Mum's or something." Rob laughed.

"No, she's here, asleep, where she literally dropped, on the floor. Have a look if you like. She looks so funny. I probably shouldn't have let her sleep but I'm really beyond knowing what to do about her behaviour in the evening and at night." Rose said glibly.

"I know, as Jan says, it will pass. Just think, soon the house will be the way we want it and Evie will sleep.

She has to. That's what keeps me going, change itself."
Rob joked.

"I look forward to choosing cushions and vases and
other fun bits and bobs." she laughed, "I can't wait to
turn this place into the home we've always dreamed of.
I do wish Evie would settle down though. It's started to
get me down, to be honest." A cheerful Rose had
returned to looking sullen. Rob wished she would cheer
up a bit. After all, she was the one who chose to stay at
home with the children all the time and it wasn't like
Evie was always going to wake at night, surely. Rose
should be counting her blessings not moaning.
However, he had to acknowledge how tired she actually
looked. She was always busy, a bit too rushed and,
possibly, not particularly happy. That might be the
problem. He wanted his old wife back, the happy,
energetic, spontaneous one. He wished she would visit
him in the hut during the day if Evie slept rather than
catching up on chores. She never seemed to have a lot of
time for him and yet they saw more of each other than
ever. And, there were the property details she had got.
How did she plan to fit that in? He had noted she did not
want to give much away. Here she was, clearly
planning a business, and yet she was too busy to pay him
much attention. Still, he wanted her to be happy. If
working were what she needed, then he would accept it.
Perhaps this is how life will be from now on. A feeling
of having never bought into this started to rise up inside
him. He needed a break. *I need to get away for a night,
stop mulling everything over. Perhaps the clear, country
air is getting to me. Yes, a lads night out, in London,
with Andrew and the gang is called for; let go a bit, have
a few drinks, blow away the cobwebs. Probably all I
need to put everything in perspective.*
He pecked Rose on the lips,

"Enjoy the school run," he said jovially as he turned on his heel to return to work. He would organise that night out right away.

SEVEN

Rose approached the school pushing Evie in the buggy. She caught sight of Mel, one of the more zealous members of the school community. *I really don't need this today. I'm not in the mood for you, Mel.* Rose immediately caught the eye of her friend, Sam, someone she trusted. She pushed Evie towards Sam but after a quick hello, Sam breezed past,

"Hi Rose, Evie, sorry, I can't stop. I need to catch Miss Greene. Talk later, maybe coffee soon, yes?" Sam rushed off to find the teacher. She managed to stick her tongue out behind Mel's back as she saw her moving towards Rose.

Mel's loud, monotonous voice hit Rose. Mel spoke in a set tone. She never got louder or softer. She drowned out any other sounds. This trapped people into listening to her. Most were too polite to walk away. She liked to stand way too close, a proper space-invader. The more Rose backed away, the more Mel closed in. Rose imagined Mel would eventually pin her up against the wall.

Mel had four boys at the school. She had an amazing head of wild, dark-grey hair that, in the wind, looked like a dense, hay-ball that had blown onto her head. She was obese and wore her version of a uniform each day. It consisted of an ample, loose piece of thick, man-made material with neck and arms holes in it. She had a black one and a dark-grey version. Over it, she favoured a well-worn, waterfall, black cardigan. Bright-red lipstick added colour but had a tendency to leak into the creases around her lips, drawing attention to her moist, top lip. Even on the wettest, coldest days she wore flip-flops that had had every last breath of air flattened out of them. However, her toenails were always manicured and polished which left Rose wondering how she reached them or if someone else did them for her.

Mel irritated most people and many at the school gate completely ignored her but when it came to fundraising, it had to be acknowledged that, she was very effective at it. She was able to persuade people to part with their money, possibly just to make her go away. Fundraising was a necessary, yet often thankless, task. Rose felt the least she could do was be civil towards her. Rose just wished Mel did not assume everyone agreed with everything she said. She needed to give people a chance to raise their opinions occasionally. Her habit of talking at people, never pausing for them to say a single thing, was terribly irritating,
"The fund for the new playground equipment is growing nicely. It would be lovely if some people would dig a bit deeper into their pockets and give a little more but then some people think a nice, new car is far more important than the children's development. I suppose as long as they're all right and their kids are OK, the rest aren't their problem!" She announced this while glaring in the direction of Sue, another mum, who had just

bought a brand-new car. Rose felt uncomfortable and hoped if Sue had heard Mel, Sue did not assume Rose agreed with Mel. As far as Rose was concerned, it really was not anyone's business how other people spent their money. No one ever knew the full details of anyone's life anyway. How did Mel know that Sue did not give money, or time, to a charity outside of school? A swift change of subject was required.

"Mmm..." muttered Rose, "sounds like you're doing a good job! Hope the fundraising is not taking up all your time. How are you, yourself, Mel?"

"I'm very well, thank you! I am cooking lasagne tonight, my favourite. I've already made a tiramisu for pudding. I've bought ice cream for the kids as the booze might make them hyper! Actually, was it you I saw dashing into the estate agency?"

"Um...no, I mean..." Rose laughed trying to sound natural, annoyed that her movements might be tracked. For once, Mel had stopped talking, and was staring right at her, awaiting a response.

"Er, I was just picking up some details for Rob, you know, him being an architect. Why?" She enquired.

"Oh, just wondered if you might be moving or if you'd kicked Robbie out!" She chuckled. Her face wobbled, "Only joking!" Barely pausing for breath, Mel continued,

"And how's lovely Robbie? Great, I'm sure. You look a bit tired, though." Rose could not work out if she was being honest or a little bit off. Rose had told her numerous times it was Rob, never Robbie. "Actually," Mel continued, "I bumped into dear Robbie earlier at the post office. He's so kind to have put the school down, as a charity, for his old firm to organise a collection for, as part of their charity ventures. To think that people who don't even know this school will donate money and yet some of those that directly benefit from it don't give a penny. Selfish, that's what these people are!" Mel was off again. As she droned on, Rose felt deflated at the conversation having gone full circle.

Her thoughts drifted, as she half-listened to Mel, willing the children to be released from their classrooms so they could save her. Her thoughts rested upon the house. She had booked an expensive cleaning firm to come in, a rare extravagance for her. She supposed she would need a permanent cleaner if she went ahead with her business. Perhaps she could advertise for one in the local shop window. She suspected finding a good one would be difficult, in this area. People she knew seemed reluctant to share contacts like that. Most fobbed her off, saying they would ask their cleaners if they needed more work, and never got back to her. She felt that there was no excuse for withholding contacts, even if there was a shortage of good ones and a risk they could be poached. It was an untrusting, frosty way to behave towards others. Surely, the cleaners deserved a chance to speak for themselves?

Mel's lecture must have moved on without Rose noticing,
"Lewis has got nits again." Rose stiffened at the mere mention of the word. She was now alert and listening. Shortly after moving to the area, she had joined other mothers, from the school, on a night out, in a bid to make new friends and a good impression. After a few drinks, she had imparted too much information to Mel. Rose had found nits in Thomas's hair. She had assumed Mel's discretion on the matter but had misjudged her. Mel happily broadcast this to all the mothers, round the table. Some said the usual things like nits only go for clean heads but Rose could tell most were unimpressed, some claiming their children had never had them.

Mel's loud laughter shook Rose from her uncomfortable thoughts, "His head was jumping again this morning but then you know all about that don't you?" She winked. Rose tried not to visibly squirm. "I've got to go now and get the chemical stuff and treat him tonight as well as the other three. I can't be combing through all four heads for ever. I'd rather sit down with my gin and tonic. I was hoping he'd been climbing that tree in the park again and got a family of insects in his hair but I can't see wings! Old snotty mum, Heidi, over there, says he should be off school and I should tell the office but he got it here, I know he did. He certainly didn't get it at home." Rose could not help but look at Mel's own hair for signs of insects. Mel added illogically, "Of course, if I had girls, this wouldn't happen. It's boys, you know, always bobbing around banging heads, never still for a moment, probably find the whole lot of 'em have it. I would just leave them in his hair, to go away by themselves, but apparently they just keep multiplying, annoying little wotsits!"

Rose wanted to tell Mel to do something, for God's sake, before the whole school was contaminated but smiled politely instead and changed the subject,
"Isn't it the cake sale next week?" Mel nodded as she enthused,
"Cake sale for the new playground equipment next week, Friday, after school, make sure you make a note of that!"

"Hi Mummy!" Anna tugged at Rose's arm. Rose lent over and kissed her on the cheek. *Thank goodness, now I don't have to talk to Mel any more.* Anna's eyes looked eagerly into Rose's, "I got a certificate for my calligraphy. Miss Brown said it was the neatest, most accurate lettering she has ever seen. Aren't you proud of me?"

"Of course I am, darling. I knew you'd be the best. I haven't forgotten how hard you worked to make sure your letters were perfect. See, I told you hard work always pays off."

"Do I get a prize at home?"

"Nice try, Anna! We'll see. I'll talk to Daddy about it. Maybe, we could go swimming at the weekend to that new pool with the outside bit." Anna looked pleased with this.

Rose drove straight to the supermarket. She hated having to take all three children with her but she had not managed to go earlier. Stale bread and one can of beans would not make a family meal.

She ran through the list in her head with military precision: milk, bread, fish fingers, frozen chips and peas and eggs for Rob and her. A tub of ice cream for pudding would be enough. She lifted Evie into her buggy, making sure she was strapped in tightly. Anna and Thomas ran ahead to look at the comics. Rose hoped they would not return nagging her to buy one, or to get sweets, as she willed herself to concentrate and get this job done quickly.

"I need a poo," announced Thomas as he sidled up beside her. Rose ignored what he had said; hoping it would go away, but he repeated it again, then again. "I really need a poo." His hand was over the seat of his trousers.

Her heart sank. How was she going to manage this? She had just put her shopping on the conveyor belt. There was always something. Thomas repeatedly needed the toilet when they were out. He never seemed able to wait until they got home. Rose thought she might scream but managed to remain matter of fact,

"Off you go then. There's a good boy. You know where the toilet is. Be as quick as you can and remember to wash your hands. I'll be right here, waiting for you." Thomas looked unconvinced as he persisted,

"But it's a poo, Mummy. You'll have to come with me, to help me." Rose turned to Anna, who was back from the comics,

"Anna, please take Thomas to the toilet over there. I'll be along in a moment."

"No way," said Anna, "he's disgusting. I don't want to. Anyway, why can't he wait until we go home? That's what you always make me do!" Desperately, Rose hissed,

"Anna, please, I'll buy you sweets." While Anna thought about this, Rose turned back to Thomas and, in a barely audible tone, said closely to his ear,

"Please wait. I need to pay for these quickly then we'll be home in fifteen minutes and you can take your time in our nice, clean toilet." Thomas was not having any of this,

"But I need a poo!" Thomas yelled, apparently unaware they were in a public place, with people listening, even if they pretended not to be. Rose was saved by a patronising voice behind her,

"Do you need a poo and Mummy won't take you? I'll take you if Mummy can't!" Lynette, a mother of one, winked at Rose, "She's got too many of you, that's the trouble." Lynette scooped a furious looking Thomas off to the toilet. Rose felt sorry for him but knew it was no one's fault. She hoped this might teach him to wait until they were home next time.

Waiting in the checkout queue, Rose willed it to be over. Anna was doing her best to persuade Rose to buy her

'Chick Facts', a monthly magazine that consisted of six or so manically crammed pages of crucial secrets for girls, usually with a particularly small, sticky nail polish, in some vile colour, no one would buy on its own, taped to the cover. A packet of brightly coloured sweets, capable of making the calmest child wild, was also included. It was cleverly designed to entice the children to nag until their parents agreed to buy.

Rose said no automatically. Anna was not giving up, "But, all the girls in my class have this. You're so mean. You're the only Mum who is too mean to buy it just because you don't care about me or my nails."

Not wanting to argue in public, and knowing Anna would not give up without causing a scene, and noticing that the man in front of her had just had his credit card declined, Rose gave in. She was stuck in this queue, there was no sign of Thomas and now Evie was starting to whine, and wriggle around, in her buggy. Anna looked momentarily triumphant before doing round and round the garden on Evie's palms. *Worth the double standards to get through this*, thought Rose wryly.

"We had a bit of an accident," boomed Lynette with a red-faced Thomas standing uncomfortably next to her, "Left it a bit late and bit of poo in the pants." Lynette said the last bit like someone had winded her trying, surprisingly for her, to be subtle. She gesticulated dramatically while explaining what had happened. She handed Rose a rolled up, damp pair of pants.

Despite wishing Lynette had put them in the bin, or at least a bag, Rose thanked her gracefully. She shoved the pants into a carrier bag she had to ask the cashier for. The cashier, who looked about seventeen and had so much foundation on her face, it resembled china, looked disgustedly at Rose before offering her a squirt of hand gel. Obviously, the girl felt Rose's hands should now be boiled. Rose graciously accepted. She rubbed the gel into her hands. She wanted to state that we all felt like that about poo and kids, for that matter, at your age but did not bother. The girl asked her how many bags she needed for her shopping and proceeded to swipe and chuck all Rose's items into the bagging area at super-high speed, while looking bored out of her mind. All this before Rose could even process that she needed to pack it up.

"That's £17.78, please, cash back?" the girl chanted. Rose placed the last bag on the handle of the buggy and turned to the cashier,
"Sorry, did you say something?"
"Cash back?" the girl replied robotically, staring at the screen in front of her as if she were speaking to it and not Rose. Rose wondered if it was literally telling her what to say to the customer. Before Rose could answer, there was a heavy thud as the buggy tipped backwards and hit the floor. Evie had managed to wriggle out of her harness and stand up and that, with the weight of the bags, had sent the whole thing flying. Evie was fine but the eggs had smashed all over the floor.

The cashier stood up and observed the mess with a distinctly uninterested air before pressing the button to activate her microphone, announcing,
"Cleaner to checkout five, cleaner to checkout five immediately." She made the immediately sound like a whole sentence; she said it so distinctly and slowly.

Mortified, Rose struggled to resurrect the buggy and firmly strapped Evie back into it, making the shoulder straps extra tight. Rose knew Evie was fine because she was smiling widely, with a glint in her eye, at the havoc she had caused. Rose collected up her shopping with one hand while simultaneously paying for it. She silently berated herself. What had she expected bringing a toddler and two tired children into a supermarket, on her own, after school?

As Rose turned the buggy to leave, having cleared up the best she could with her only tissue, she felt red-faced and hot. She was amazed at how many customers waddled past her, stepping, ceremoniously, round the slow-growing, gloppy mess. Some people tut-tutted as if Rose had wanted all this to happen and had done it on purpose. No one offered to help yet one brazen woman had the nerve to say to Evie,
"Oh dear, did Mummy overload the buggy? Lucky you didn't hit your head, sweetheart." The woman glared disapprovingly at Rose as she walked away, just as the store cleaner arrived, a fed-up-looking man in his fifties. He did not make eye contact with Rose, or anyone else, as he mopped up the mess with a dirty mop and a bucket full of black water.

Rose was about to shout after the stubby-looking, moustached woman to mind her own business when she was struck by a familiar, soothing voice,
"In a spot of bother again?" Will smiled. Before Rose could utter a word, he had control of the buggy, "Come on, let me help you." To Rose's relief, he wheeled the buggy towards the exit.

Anna and Thomas looked at their addled mother and followed quietly and curiously, wondering who this mysterious new helper was,
"Who is this, Mummy?" asked Anna quietly while

grabbing hold of Rose.

"Just a kind gentleman helping us," said Rose who could not help but smile.

"But you've always told us not to go with strangers and he's got Evie."

"He hasn't got Evie, darling, he's just helping take her to the car."

"Where are you parked?" Will asked.

"In one of the parent and child spaces over there, the silver one." Rose pointed.

"Nice people carrier!" He smiled.

'It's what you drive when you have kids." said Rose, defensively.

"Hey, I didn't mean anything by it!" Anna tugged at Rose's arm and hissed,

"How do you know he's not a weirdo about to kidnap her?"

"Because I just do, Anna, now be quiet or he'll hear you." He had heard her and reassured her,

"I'm not a weirdo, please don't worry, I just thought Mummy needed a bit of help. I'll be gone in a minute." He looked directly into Rose's eyes, "some ladies seem to be distressed more often than others," he winked. Both were conscious of the children listening. He skipped off calling over his shoulder, "have a nice evening."

Rose felt like that teenager, yet again. She dismissed her feelings, once more. *He must think me a right idiot who can never get my act together. I bet if he knew what I was like pre-kids, he wouldn't find it so amusing. I hate that he laughs at me. He's so gorgeous but I'm a married woman so why should I care what he thinks?* She was surprised how someone she barely knew could arouse such strong feelings in her. For the first time since meeting Rob, she had to admit that she fancied another man. She reassured herself that this was bound to happen at some stage. Just because she was married did not mean that she would never find another man attractive. She would not take it any further. It was all right. What she had with her husband, she would not compromise for anyone. Meeting Will would make a good story over coffee with the girls and that was all. Rose was flattered that she was still attractive enough for another man to give her attention. What she really wanted was for Rob to notice her more. They had got very caught up in his work, the house and raising children. She wanted him to see her again as the individual she was when they first met and that, in her mind, required some changes. But, certainly not an affair.

EIGHT

Satisfied with the chunky, leather steering wheel within his grip, Will eased his sports car into the garage. He carefully removed the bunch of keys from the ignition. He did not want to scratch the dashboard. He reached back to retrieve his bag. He placed it on his lap and sat still for a while, staring, blankly, at the wall in front of him. His thoughts ran untamed, *Why can I not get that gorgeous 'fox of a woman'... what's her name?... Rose? Yes, Rose, out of my head?* He hardly knew her yet she was so clearly etched in his mind, like she was still looking at him. Remembering the body those eyes belonged to confirmed how much he fancied her. She excited him. However, for Will, this woman would not be such an easy one to seduce, like some of the others before her.

His usual formula would need to be adjusted. He lived in a close, settled community now. People tended to stay for a long time. Everyone knew, or knew of, each other. This was very different from the greater transience of Dubai, which he was used to. The intensity of his feelings did not trouble him. What did was the clear reality of Rose's children. He had seen, and even met, them. This had not happened before. It made fancying someone else's wife so much harder. It was not enough to stop him, though.

It would clearly hurt the children, if they found out. In a small community, he would be regularly reminded of what he had done by the mere sight of Rose and her family. What about his reputation? None of this had ever bothered him before because he had never really viewed Dubai as permanent. Here, he wanted to stay. There would be no running away. He had begun to put down roots. He liked being settled, for the first time since his marriage to Stella. With the women he had met before, he had always been able to push any commitments they may have had to the back of his mind. He could claim he did not know they had husbands or children. They had normally given him a sign they were interested, anyway. Rose had not given him any such signs. He imagined she would not cheat on any of the life she had built with her husband and children. He just could not get her out of his head and accept this. Despite having all those kids, she still looked amazing. He had had a good look at her as she bent over in the supermarket to pick up the toppled buggy. What she was doing in a supermarket he did not know. Had she not heard of home delivery? Or dog walkers for that matter. *Possibly bored*, he thought, but bored was good and usually worked in his favour. It meant he had more of a chance of giving them a bit of excitement. Harmless flirting, of course, to begin with, until they were up for more. Always hopeful, Will told himself that Rose may not be off limits after all.

He pressed the key fob. The car beeped as it locked. He

caught a glimpse of himself in the car wing and admired his reflection. *Not bad for a man of my age.* He entered the house. Once he would have taken any intimate relationships with women seriously but that was a lifetime ago. Now he believed women were not to be trusted, even the pleasant ones. He had been deceived. Back then, he believed in true love, in the sanctity and commitment of a marriage. He had been happily married, albeit briefly, before he turned thirty, to Stella, his soulmate. He had believed they would spend their whole lives together.

They had met at a photography evening class. He noticed her from the minute he opened the classroom door. He found a place at one of the tables arranged in a large, U shape. He sat near her. She had black, shiny curls which fell down her back in a V shape, big, green eyes and clear, pale skin. She wore a dark, fitted polo neck which showed off her petite figure. He barely took his eyes off her. He noticed her unique mannerism of quickly licking her top lip, like a little lizard grabbing a fly, just before she spoke. If you blinked, you would miss it but Will had not.

"And if you would all like to introduce yourselves, just a name and perhaps why you're here to learn about photography then we'll start with you, sir." The teacher pointed expectantly to a man on her left who was sitting at the table at the start of the U shape. Will was surprised that there were so many people in the room all of a sudden. He had been so mesmerised by Stella, he had not noticed everyone else arriving.

Stella introduced herself confidently and, Will noticed, bashfully. She was, perhaps, uncomfortable with speaking in front of so many strangers. This endeared her to Will even more. He felt an urge to take over, to look after her. She did well.

"I'm here to learn how to use this camera." In front of her was an impressive-looking, black camera with a long lens attached to it. "My Dad gave it to me for Christmas. I've always been interested in photography. Um.. I'm an A level student, a mature one." She framed the last sentence by making an inverted comma sign, with both hands, in the air. She was clearly still very young, "as you can probably see, I suppose," she joked, before adding,

"As I didn't work very hard at school. And, this is my boyfriend, Petey, who's here to keep me company, and learn about photography too, of course." She laughed nervously while looking at him. He just about managed a weak wave before allowing his neck, and almost his head too, to retreat into his patterned jumper. Will thought to himself, *and that jumper must be what you got for Christmas,* wondering what she saw in Petey, as it was not obvious.

Soon, it was Will's turn to introduce himself,

"I'm Will and I'm twenty-six. I'm a property surveyor and work for Griffiths and Gage, here in town. I want to improve my photography, especially of properties, for obvious reasons. I bought myself a decent camera but I can't make sense of the instructions. It's like learning another language. I want to understand it all better. It's been an interest of mine for a while."

As the spotlight moved on to the next person, Will caught sight of Stella looking right at him. He winked at her and she smiled bashfully before looking down at her empty notebook.

With the introductions over, the tutor continued,

"So, we'll be spending tonight in the classroom. Then, from next week, we'll be out and about to experiment with taking photos, putting into practice what we have learned. Make sure you all collect a sheet on your way out tonight so you know where and when we'll be meeting each week."

Over the next few weeks, at the classes, Will observed that Petey seemed more keen on Stella, in a clingy, follow-her-round sort of way, than the other way round. She barely spoke to him but instead struck up a friendship with Will. Petey skulked around in the background, nearly always fiddling with his camera, apparently ignoring the teacher's guidance and Stella's keenness to speak to Will, he was pleased to note. To his delight, Petey dropped out half way through and, after missing two classes, Stella informed Will that they had indeed split up. Petey had never had much to say for himself, had been unemployed for ages and had given up on finding a job. Although he had spent most days cooking amazing meals for her, it was just not what she wanted, so she had finished it. Apparently, he had only enrolled on the photography course to please her. She had suggested they find a mutual hobby. They had still had very little to say to each other.

On the last day of the course, when they tried night photography, Stella suggested that she and Will keep in touch. They had exchanged telephone numbers. He had had to control his urge to punch the air. He was bursting with joy. He wanted to propose there and then, so sure was he about his feelings for her.

The fact Stella had mentioned exchanging telephone numbers first was a fantastic sign. It meant there might be reciprocal feeling there. In a bid not to look too keen, he waited three long days before calling her, despite wanting to as soon as he got home. A date at the local Italian restaurant was fixed. He would never forget the sweet smell of her perfume as she climbed into his car that evening, or the excitement on her face.

Their relationship progressed at lightning speed. They never ran out of things to say to each other and, within six months, Will had proposed. After two years of meeting, they were married. Both their families referred to them as childhood sweethearts, even though they had not met as children, but it was as if they had known each other all their lives. Will felt having Stella in his life was a cherished blessing. He experienced such strong love for her that it managed to cross over and become a physical feeling. His heart ached. He happily supported her as she trained to be a hygienist.

She finished her course and got a job at a dental practice in a town nine miles away from where they lived. It was a private, purpose-built surgery offering the latest dental procedures. She was delighted to have landed a job she really wanted. Will felt so proud of her as he waved her off on her first day. She would come home full of good stories about work, always citing how lucky she was to be doing something she loved.

About six months into the job, he noticed that she seemed more tired than usual, not herself, when she came home from work. She did not tell him as much as she used to. Often, she grabbed her gym bag saying she was going to relax in the sauna. Sometimes she was gone before Will had got home from work so they did not see each other until bedtime. Initially, he put it down to the honeymoon period of the job, and in some ways, their relationship, wearing off. She had been working longer hours than usual most days. When he commented on this, Stella was quick to point out that there was a social element to her job. She joined in, in order to get on and not be overlooked. This seemed plausible to Will but on the days Stella did not socialise or go to the gym, she started to go to bed early. She wanted to go out less with Will. He hoped he was imagining it, but she seemed less interested in him too. She never asked how things were going for him. He tried broaching this with her but she merely smiled weakly and said that she was just tired, was working hard and wanted a pay rise so she had taken on extra responsibilities. The practice was popular and growing. Indeed, this was true. There was a three-month-waiting list for her patients. The practice was advertising for another hygienist to join them.

Even so, something niggled him. He still felt this did not fully explain why she was always so exhausted and uninterested. Surely they gave her some breaks during the day? And, could she not catch up on her rest at the weekend? If she sometimes had to work on a Saturday, she was given time off in lieu during the week. If possible, she chose the day she wanted. Her bosses seemed very fair.

One morning, Will left for work an hour earlier than usual. There was a staff meeting before the office opened to the public. Will had had to return home, only five minutes later, to grab the laptop he had forgotten. He crept in expecting Stella to be enjoying an extra half an hour in bed. He did not want to disturb her. Having got the laptop from the kitchen, he heard what sounded like vomiting coming from the upstairs bathroom, followed by a flushing toilet and the shower being turned on. He knew he could not be late for his meeting.

He rushed back out of the house. As he pulled out of their drive, it hit him that she could be pregnant. This would explain the tiredness and some of the other changes he had noticed. She had certainly gone off sex. A big smile spread across his face. It was awesome. He might be becoming a dad. He felt a surge of excitement course through him. They had talked about starting a family but she had made it clear she wanted to establish her career first. He totally understood this. He was happy to wait. But babies did not always come according to plan. And, now that he was faced with the real prospect of one, he felt excited and, surprisingly, rather prepared for it. Perhaps she had not said anything because she was waiting for the right time. Perhaps she needed a week or so to get used to the surprise herself. Either way, he decided not to pressure her into telling him.

As he walked across the car park to the office, he decided he would try to get home a bit earlier tonight, cook a special meal for Stella and even try to persuade her to have a little glass of champagne. Perhaps, this would make it easier for her to tell him. If she refused alcohol, then she would have to tell him, really.

Will did manage to beat Stella home from work. This gave him a chance to prepare the table and unpack the food he had bought. He got out the mats that she only liked to use occasionally. He lit two brand-new candles, which he placed in the red, glass candlesticks they had been given as a wedding gift. He arranged the white roses he had bought her in the matching vase. Stepping back to admire his handiwork, he heard her key in the lock.

"What's all this?" She smiled as she dumped her bags

on the floor and gave Will a peck on the cheek.

"I'm cooking you a meal," Will replied nonchalantly with a small smile.

"Oh, lovely," Stella looked a bit confused but managed weakly, "Why?"

"Do I need a reason to cook my beautiful, hard-working wife a meal?" Stella shrugged,

"I'll get changed then." Will sensed a feeling of discomfort from Stella but dismissed it as being part of her sweet nature. She never liked a fuss. He reassured her,

"You do that while I cook our favourite, steak and chips with black pepper sauce and of course green beans. Vegetables, especially green ones, are very good for you!" He enthused while giving her a quick wink, "Here, take a glass of this with you." He handed her the champagne. Stella eyed him suspiciously before taking the drink from him,

"Thank you, how long have I got?"

"Twenty maybe thirty minutes, sound OK?"

"Yep," was all she called back. She was already half way up the stairs before Will noticed she had left the champagne on the kitchen surface.

He almost could not believe it when she reappeared, barely fifteen minutes later, with her hair up in a messy bun, damp, unbrushed tendrils around her neck. She wore no make-up, her old tracksuit bottoms and top, the one he was sure she usually only wore in bed on really cold nights. Clearly, her efforts were not set to match his. He was determined not to let his annoyance show on such an important occasion. He continued with the romantic evening he had planned for them, where she would tell him she was pregnant with their first child. She might be happier once she had eaten.

With both steaks cooked to perfection, the meal was ready. He placed the plates, carefully, on the table. She managed a slight smile and complimented him on how well he had arranged everything. She said the look and feel of the table reminded her of a restaurant, but she did not know why he had gone to so much effort, especially on a work night. The atmosphere changed to a heavy silence as they ate. It was half way through the meal that he had had enough. She was clearly uninterested in the evening and the effort he had made.

"You like the food? You haven't said anything about it." Will enquired trying not to sound terse.

"Oh, yes, sorry," Stella seemed miles away. "It is lovely, just how I like it. Is there pudding?"

"Yes, rhubarb crumble and the thickest cream I could find. I know it's your favourite."

"Great," she said in a way that sounded mildly enthusiastic, as if it had taken all her effort to sound just a bit excited.

"Look, Stella, you know I hate playing games. Be straight with me, what's wrong? You haven't been yourself lately and I want to know what's up."

"Nothing at all!" Stella looked like she had been caught, red-handed, stealing.

"You're not yourself, you're distant with me. In fact, you've been distant with me for a while now. Have I done something wrong? Or, not done something? I've been racking my brains to come up with an answer but I just can't think of anything." Will sounded desperate.

"Nothing's wrong..." Stella looked like she was going to cry.

"Please don't be upset, Stella. Look, I'm sorry, you're probably just tired or unwell and I'm overreacting. I'll get the pudding, hand me your plate." As he got up, the scrapping of his chair on the kitchen floor sounded louder than usual. He was aware of having mashed-up a stray bean underfoot but he did not care. He told himself to stay unruffled, not to lose his temper. She could be pregnant and pregnancy hormones, he had heard, could send some women mad. But, something took over. He could not take it any longer and, holding onto the kitchen surface for support, he looked right at Stella and just blurted out,

"Stella, are you pregnant? I heard you being sick this morning. I came back for my laptop. I'd forgotten it. I didn't have time to come up and see you as I was already cutting it fine. You know what Bob is like about timekeeping. Anyway, I know it's not ideal timing, what with your job and everything, but, really, it's fine. Actually, I'm quite excited about becoming a dad, that is, if I'm right."

Stella looked both mystified and miserable. She looked at Will, her eyes filling up with tears. He went over to her and put his arm around her. Tears fell down her face.

"Come on, love. It's not the end of the world. You'll still be able to work. It won't hold you back or anything. They have to give you your job back these days. Come here." He went to hug her but she pulled away. She got up from her chair using it as a boundary between them,

"Will, I am pregnant, you're right, but it's not yours! The baby is not yours! I don't want to be with you any more. I've had enough. We don't get on. It was a big mistake, this whole thing, this marriage, everything, just a big mistake. You can't pretend you haven't noticed anything different. I just don't want this." She was staring at Will, panic and desperation in her eyes, as tears kept coming, "You're a lovely, lovely man, really you are. I...I..." She sobbed, "I just can't do this any more."

Will clung on to the surface for support, fearing he might collapse. He felt sick. His heart was beating uncomfortably hard. He was struggling to get a proper, satisfying breath. He was aware of heat rising up his chest and neck. It was as if his throat was threatening to shut down, making him giddy. He managed to drop into a chair. She dragged one towards him and sat down, "Come on, Will, don't tell me you hadn't noticed anything. This can't be that much of a surprise. We're just not suited any longer." Seeing how shocked and speechless he was, she added more softly, "I didn't plan the baby. I didn't plan any of this. It just...happened."

He told himself to calm down. He would be all right. He had really not seen any of this coming. Was he that naive? He had thought he was a perceptive person. Many people had told him so, but this, ironically, had crept up on him with no warning at all. He could not calm down.

Suddenly, his shock flashed to anger. He experienced a frightening lack of control. He wanted to strangle Stella, jump off a cliff, go out and crash his car, keep running until he collapsed. He feared he would act some of this out. Adrenaline was coursing so aggressively, and dangerously, through his veins.

As Will recalled what happened later, something he would do hundreds of times, a monster within him did take over. He yelled at Stella so loudly to get her things and get out, telling her he never wanted to see her again. He did not care. In his delirious state, he walked into the door as he went to grab a bag, to throw at Stella, to put her things in. His knee-jerk reaction was to punch the door so hard that his hand went through it. His voice was hoarse. His throat was sore. He thought that it was damaged for good.

He remembered Stella looking terrified, confused and hurt before she ran upstairs to grab some things. Quickly, she returned and ran out of the front door, leaving it open. On hearing her car vanish into the darkness, he slammed the door shut so hard the whole house shook. He collapsed on the floor hugging his knees. He howled, hoping, somehow, to drift out of the world.

Once his sobbing subsided, he managed to drag himself up to bed. He climbed under the duvet where he cried hard again. He screamed into his pillow for fear a neighbour might hear him and call the police. He needed and wanted to be alone. He must have fallen asleep eventually because he woke at three in the morning with a tissue stuck to his cheek, fresh tears still trickling from his eyes. He had a thumping headache, the sort expected from drinking way too much alcohol. After using the toilet, he caught a glimpse of himself in the bathroom mirror. He looked like he had been punched a few times in the face. His hand would barely move.

Will did not turn up for work the next day or the next. He did not answer the telephone. This, being totally out of character, made his boss, Bob Griffiths, turn up on the doorstep. Will knew he would have to face Bob but Will would not go to the front door. From the upstairs window, with his sweatshirt hood up, keeping his swollen face in the shade, Will let Bob know he was in. Bob looked up at the window,
"Hi Will, are you all right? I don't like to bother you like this, mate, but it's so unlike you not to turn up at work or answer your phone. I was worried. It's not a problem. I can see you look pretty bad. Just checking

you hadn't fallen over and knocked yourself out, or been held up for all your money!" he joked.

"Sorry mate, I thought I left a message on the office answer machine. I must have dialled wrong," Will lied, "I'm so ill with food poisoning. I've had my head down the loo twenty-four hours a day for the last couple of days, and have been drifting in and out of sleep. I'll be back next week. I just need a couple more days to recover."

"No problem, Will," Bob shouted up, "You take as long as you need. No rush, mate, just keep me informed! We'll manage without you for a few more days. Is there anything I can do?"

"No thanks, Bob. Stella's looking after me," Will felt a lump in his throat again. Bob seemed to believe everything Will said. He had no reason not to,

"Like I said, if you need anything... " He waved up at the window. Will watched the car disappear. He sunk to his heels and burst into tears again, wondering if they would ever run out. As much as he wanted to, he just could not seem to stop crying.

NINE

Quickly, word got round that Stella had left. Everyone, who knew Will, found out what had happened. What no one realised, at this point, was that Will would never return to his job.

Stella never looked back. She had embarked on an affair with one of the dentists at the practice. He had separated from his wife, from what Will gleaned much later, almost as soon as Stella had started working there. She had become pregnant, accidentally she claimed. Will eventually accepted he would never know all the truth. She had been so careful about pregnancy not happening with him, adamant she was not ready to start a family.

He knew, instinctively, there was no way the baby was his. He never pushed for proof and, in effect, let Stella go. She wanted a swift divorce. To his distress and amazement, the union he had entered into, as a lifelong commitment, was so easily over for her. She would not take his calls, even at work. She sent a friend round to collect the rest of her things.

The inevitable letter, from her solicitor, demanding a quick divorce, duly arrived. Will could not be bothered to argue about anything. Amazingly, he still imagined the day she would return, even though he knew it was just a fragile hope.

Stella did have the decency to write to him herself, saying, again, that she had made a mistake and was sorry. She thought he should get on with his life. Marriage had come at totally the wrong time for her. She had rushed into it with, she now knew, the wrong man. She certainly was not putting anything on hold now, though, and wanted to marry the dentist as soon as their divorces came through. Stella would appreciate Will's cooperation.

At times, to him, it all seemed like a really bad dream. She was so matter-of-fact, he kept thinking he would wake up and it would all be right again. After all, this sort of thing did not really happen, did it? But, it did and it was.

Broken, he visited his doctor. Will feared he would go mad if he spent another night awake, always close to tears. The doctor prescribed sleeping tablets and antidepressants saying it would help him recover and see him through this difficult time. The doctor assured him this was a temporary phase. He called it reactive depression. It would get better with time. Feeling slightly better but still angry and desperate, Will decided to make one last attempt to talk to Stella, to try to coax her back. He turned up at her work but she would not see him. He ended up crying on the doorstep, fruitless, bitter tears. Her mind was made up. She had changed and moved on. The kind receptionist, who brought him a cup of tea, said he should do the same.

Unfortunately, he could not move on. He continued to bombard Stella with pleas to return, flowers, letters and, eventually, to his shame, threats that he would kill himself if she did not come back. She contacted the police. They were kind and understanding, when they came round, but made it clear that Will was to leave Stella alone or he would be arrested for harassment and, possibly, assault, if he so much as brushed past her in the street. He started to accept that it really was over and went, a broken man, to stay with his mother.

His life, as he had known it, had fallen apart. His sympathetic doctor signed him off work indefinitely. Will had lost the inclination to return anyway. After some time, his boss called a meeting. He would have to stop paying Will, he explained. Bob could not afford to keep Will's post open indefinitely. They came to the mutual agreement that Will would leave,
"I would employ you again, mate, but you need to get better. Look, it's none of my business, but you need to move on. No woman is worth falling apart over." Bob could not think of anything else to say, "Look, mate, I'm only trying to help." Will said nothing as he turned towards the door, unshaven and unkempt. He walked, slowly and dejectedly, out of the office.

His mother persuaded him to see his doctor again to find out if there was any other way Will could be helped. The drugs had numbed him but a frozen life was not what his mother felt he should settle for. He was put on the waiting list for counselling as the doctor suggested a combination of that with medication might get him back onto his feet. After a few months, it materialised.
In spite of Will's initial reservations about opening up to a stranger, the therapist turned out to be helpful. He gave Will his full attention. He listened. He did not

seem judgemental, bored or surprised with anything Will said. As part of Will's recovery, and taking into account his background, the counsellor suggested he find a new focus, something to make him look forward to the future. Will relayed this to his mother, who suggested property development. He could use his surveying skills and would be physically tired at the end of each day, possibly encouraging a good-night's sleep. He would only be answerable to himself. He could complete the project at his own pace. She said it would get him back into the workforce. It would build up his confidence and self-worth. With this more flexible approach, if he had a bad day, he could simply write it off, without the fear of letting anyone down.

He liked this idea and, with his mother's help, and his old boss's direction, found a small, Victorian, terraced house in need of restoration and modernisation. His mother encouraged him every step of the way. She helped him to enrol on a brick-laying course and a do-it-yourself type evening class that, to his surprise, he really enjoyed. He found himself appreciating the company of people again. He made friends, offering him new focus.

Initially, Will did find just getting up at the same time each morning a challenge but eventually he was up and out of the house every day by seven-thirty. His mother would cook him breakfast, at first. As he became better, she slowly withdrew, and did less for him. He noticed and was glad, even though he did not say anything. He wanted to make a full recovery. He never intended for his mother to be looking after a grown-up. He vowed, to himself, to make it up to her one day. She was his rock and not once had she moaned, or told him to pull himself together.

If there was a job he could not do, he made sure he learned as much as he could from the tradesmen who helped him. He did his own research, too. He relished the challenge. This house project literally saved his life. Within six months of starting it, he had almost weaned himself off the antidepressants. He no longer needed sleeping pills. He had toned up from all the physical work and looked well. He had found a buyer and turned a good profit, for a first property deal. Will was looking to move out of his mother's place.

He often drove past the house that he had resurrected. He loved the feeling of satisfaction he got from knowing that it had helped him get better. Other properties followed. He found he was good at fixing houses and it rewarded him well. When a friend suggested he manage some building work for him in Dubai, Will jumped at the chance to go. It felt right. He could not resist all that sunshine and tax-free money. He worried about his mother. He would be deserting her and felt, to some degree, obliged to stay nearby, as she had nursed him back to health. However, he need not have been concerned, because, when he told her about the offer, she was full of praise, support and admiration for him, saying all he owed her was to get better. Now he had done that, he was free to go. She joked that he was starting to get under her feet, anyway,

"I never wanted a mummy's boy, you know that, but I will miss you. I love you. Go and enjoy yourself and remember, it's black, leather handbags I like. Actually, sickly though this may sound, the only gift I really want from you is for you to stay well and be happy. Look after yourself, darling. You deserve a good life, a full life. Just keep in touch. Don't leave me wondering how you're getting on!"

He remained in close contact with his mother and paid for her to visit him twice a year as his way of saying thank you. She often dropped hints about females, as she called them, but discussing that with anyone, especially his mother, was a closed shop, as far as Will was concerned. The truth, which he never voiced, was that still, to this day, he wondered about Stella and the baby, the one that should have been his, secretly made behind his back, without him, so crude a reality, so final.

In the darkest depth of his depression following his marriage break-up, he had not, even to his counsellor, ever been able to voice how deeply Stella had hurt him. He wondered if he would ever heal properly. An unfortunate symptom of this was that, although he sought to have fun with and liked women, he never intended to fully connect with one ever again. This way, no one could hurt him. He never wanted children, as that would tie him to the mother for life. If some women were up for a bit of fun, then so was he. He enjoyed many short relationships and slept with more women than he cared to count. Once they showed any sign of clinginess, he was off. He never promised them anything. Will was a player, or, as one spurned lover had put it rather unflatteringly, a 'commitment-phobe'. Anyway, he was all right with that. What more could a man want? He had his mother if he needed any emotional support. She kept him company at Christmas. Besides, his counsellor had assured him that he could always return, at any point, if he felt he needed to.

Will dated most women two or three times then never had anything to do with them again. However, Luisa was one girl he had an on-off relationship with. He had to admit that he enjoyed her company, a lot. She made him laugh and showed no signs of ever wanting to settle down. Like Will, she had been hurt in a different way but with the same outcome. Her father had walked out when she was seven years old, never to be seen again. Luisa's mother had confirmed that he was alive and well. He just did not want anything to do with them at all citing some weak excuse like he had never wanted any of the responsibility of having a family in the first place. Luisa was certainly not going to risk this happening to any of hers and so had decided not to have any children. Her business was her baby. Luisa had her own property agency in Dubai and it was through work that she and Will had met. She liked the buzz of the property market and big money could be made. Luisa and Will could go weeks, even months, without contacting one another but were always able to pick up where they left off. They never asked each other what they had been up to while apart. Silently and mutually, they agreed to "no strings". Like Will, Luisa had no hang-ups about casual sex. To her, it was simply a human need.

Will enjoyed five years of managing building projects, in Dubai, before he started to become bored with expat life. He joked to his friends that there were no women left to bed and returned to the UK. A lot of the people he had hung around with had moved on too. Luisa was not enough to keep him in Dubai. When he told her he was off, he thought he had seen a fleeting sign of neediness in her eyes. He worried he might miss her. He always felt so relaxed in her company. She had suggested he stay and they live together as friends, with benefits, she had joked, although that had been after a lot of illicit alcohol.

He returned briefly to his mother's place before finding a new project. This time, it was a home for himself, a house with a large garden. He refurbished it with expensive wallpapers and carpets, designer furniture and an annexe for his mother. It was his turn to look after her, despite her still being fiercely independent. She had stopped hinting at females. She knew he was straight. She also knew that he was a womanizer; after all, mothers always knew these things. They never needed to be spelt out. All she hoped was that none of these women were married, as she really did not agree with that sort of messing around, breaking up families. However, she knew it was not really any of her business and she certainly would not make it such. She was grateful to Will for his love and loyalty to her. Everything was settled. She just silently wished he would marry again and have children, before it was too late. She did not like to think of him on his own, once she was gone.

He was blissfully ignorant of his mother's concerns. For him, life was as good as it would get right now. He decided to pay his old boss a visit at the estate agency. Bob was delighted to see him looking so well, back in the area once again, before informing him that Stella had moved,
"...Up to Scotland, as I understand it, just thought you ought to know," he paused, "so... it's unlikely you'll be bumping into her any time soon. Will, it's none of my business but you haven't come back for her, have you? Only...well, you look so well and she...well, you're worth more, to be honest. I'm fond of you. I don't mind admitting that." Will smiled kindly at him,
"Thanks for that, Bob." He paused, "but, really, a lot has happened since then. I'm very different now. Perhaps, with hindsight, we should never have married in the first place. It's all in the past. I really am OK with it all." Bob swiftly changed the subject, enquiring cheerfully,

"So, what now for you?"

"Well, I'm doing up the house I told you about on the phone. That's nearly finished so I'll be looking for some projects to manage. If you hear of anything..."

"Funny you should say that because I do know of a guy, Rob Clarke, moved down from London, wants to make his new place here more up-to-date and fancy, and he's looking for a project manager. He's an architect so has done all the design work but he just can't do everything, I suppose, so if you're interested, I could put a word in for you?"

TEN

Rob opened the front door,

"You must be Mr Chapman. Do come in." He offered his hand and they shook firmly.

"How do you do. Will." Rob naturally took the lead and showed him into the kitchen, "Would you like tea... coffee?"

"Coffee sounds good, please. Fantastic place you've got here, great location, so close to the village centre."

"Thank you," replied Rob, "it'll be much improved, once we've put our stamp on it. We want a more modern feel, you know, to make it a bit lighter... airier." Rob made two cups of coffee, "Milk and sugar are there, so help yourself. My wife sends her apologies. She would have liked to be here today, to meet you, but had a prior engagement."

"No problem, I'm sure there will be plenty of opportunities to meet in the coming weeks." Will took a sip of his coffee, "great coffee, by the way, thank you."

As Rob looked in the cupboard for some biscuits, Will took in his surroundings. He noted a small, dark, clean kitchen. The facia on the integrated fridge was missing and he could smell well-browned toast in the air. He hoped it would not cling to his suit. He was relieved when Rob suggested they go out to the hut, to view the plans and discuss details. Now Will had seen the kitchen, he tried to imagine it with light flooding in, highlighting a lighter, more contemporary wood, which he had in mind and, of course, the smell of fresh air. In fact, the only thing he would keep was the Aga. He would be keen to remove the outer wall with its small, mean windows and replace it with floor to ceiling glass doors to make more of the garden. He hoped the plans Rob had drawn up would meet some of his desires for this place but he knew it was ultimately Rob's choice and taste that mattered. Will was here to project-manage, not design, and had to make the right, first-impression so, for now, he would keep his ideas to himself. He wanted to see the plans and get to know Rob a little better before he suggested any changes.

The hut had sounded very much like a garden shed, to Will, but he was impressed with it. Rob welcomed him inside,
"You're probably surprised at how warm it is in here. The heater was one of the first things I put in. I hate being cold and am not one to sit with a hot water bottle on my knees, while rubbing my hands together every five minutes, willing myself to warm up. The cold makes my thinking foggy, freezes my bones."

Will shut the door behind him. On the walls, Rob had framed certificates showing his qualifications, and pictures of what Will assumed to be previous, completed projects, all very ordered and impressive. From the completed projects he could see, Rob was a clever architect. His drawings looked complicated and very detailed but clear at the same time and, in a sense, ordered, which was what you would expect from a good architect. Will noted a letter, on the adjacent desk, which he nosily swept his eyes over. Rob noticed this,

"As you can see, I've won the bid to draw up the plans for a new housing development on the outskirts of town. It'll provide around twenty new homes. All very exciting, although I'm aware not everyone wants more houses around here. Bob Griffiths pointed me in the right direction, after finding us this place, when we came down from London. I was looking for a pretty-large project to get my teeth into. I went self-employed, a little while ago. He recommended you to me too, as you know."

'Yes, dear, old Bob, Griffiths and Gage, no Gage any more but he keeps the name. We go back a long way, lovely guy, the best..." Will trailed off. Sometimes, thinking about his old life started to bring up uncomfortable memories. Rob did not pick up on this, thankfully, and continued,

"That's one of the reasons I need someone like you to help, because I want this place transformed as soon as possible. I'm not the sort of person to live in a house while making gradual changes as I go along so it ends up taking the best part of seven years to complete, and still needs decorating or the bath plumbed in. Those sorts of timescales are way too long for me. I believe in a full attack, quick, sharp and effective. Have I put you off?"

"No, no, not at all," Will was smiling, thinking how Rob was his kind of guy, decisive, no messing around or, by the sounds of things, cash-flow issues to contend with. Will thought how this project should be easy enough but he did not want Rob to know this or he could do himself out of a job. Rob continued,

"Of course, I need someone, like yourself, to manage all this for me as I plan to continue building my business and be able, periodically, to sit back and watch the domestic transformation take place, if you know what I mean." Will smiled,

"Well, it sounds like I can definitely help you. Let's see the plans." Will moved a large sheet of paper towards himself.

"Of course, take a seat. It's possibly clearer on the screen." Rob beckoned to the chair neatly tucked into Jan's desk. The men shuffled their chairs as close to each other as they could. Rob politely angled the screen away from himself a little more so Will could see properly. A file jumped to life. It showed amazing drawings of a super-house, the new buzzword used to describe modern, sleek, energy-efficient buildings, which included a lot of glass.

"You know we have deer in the garden? Rose, my wife, loves them, which is why I want this outdoor galleried area upstairs, off our bedroom, so she can observe them unnoticed, especially in the summer. They are usually here in the evenings." Rob continued,

"You may not know that this place used to be two farm cottages. I think you can still tell, in some ways. My aim is to make it seem like it has always been one, large property, to save and conserve as much of its originality as possible, while creating a comfortable, modern, family home. There's some spiel for you." Rob laughed, "Interestingly, the old farmhouse, in that direction, has just been granted permission to be revamped, in a similar way. It will be interesting to see what they achieve."

Rob continued to explain that he planned to extend the cottage as well as revamp it, build a separate, triple, heritage-style garage with an open-plan office above. Access would be via an external staircase. He planned to employ one or two more architects very soon so he needed space to expand. Will was impressed with Rob's plans and felt excited at the prospect of managing the process. He was, however, finding it hard to concentrate. He was sure Rob had said Rose. Wasn't that the name of the woman he had his eye on? He scanned the room for a photograph of her. There were none on display. Will needed to check,

"Did you say your wife is called Rose?"

"Yes, why?"

"Oh, no reason, just making sure I heard you right." *Oh, God, this is awkward.* Will smiled and quickly moved on,

"May I have a look around the inside of your cottage? I would like to see the rest of it. Also, would you email me these plans, please? If I may, I'd like to take some photos... if you're OK with that?" Rob was impressed with Will's enthusiasm,

"Please, do! I'll email the plans to you now... there, done! Let's go back inside."

As Will moved from room to room, under Rob's direction, he noted children's toys and paraphernalia everywhere. He felt what he thought might be a dead mouse under his shoe before realising it was some kind of spongy toy. Hopefully, that would reinflate before anyone noticed. This house was a mess. He really did not get the attraction of having children if this is what they did to a home. He was clever enough to realise it was probably best not to give this away to Rob,

"How many children do you have?" Rob announced, proudly,

"Three; two girls and one boy,"

"Bet they're lovely?" Will felt this was the right response.

"Most of the time, yes."

"So, you'll be living here the whole time while all the building work is going on?" Rob chuckled lightly, in response to this,

"Well, we haven't anywhere else to go. If it gets too horrendous, Rose's mother has offered us beds. She lives locally but we're hoping it doesn't come to that. I think once you leave home for good, it is best to keep it that way. With three children, it would be less disturbing to sit it out here, I think. We want to try to avoid moving out if at all possible. Do you have children?"

"No, not yet, maybe one day," Will lied. Rob smiled. Will returned to business,

"I'm asking all these questions about your plans as I had assumed you'd all be staying. As project manager, it would be up to me to make sure areas being worked on are cordoned off properly. I would request that you always have a working toilet and the necessities of a running sink plus a hob, microwave or oven. I couldn't guarantee a whole, working kitchen all the time. I would advise turning the Aga off. Parts of the home will be a building site, as, I'm sure, you know, but loads of people manage it. The temporary upheaval is always worth it for the end result. I would advise trying not to be too daunted by it all, you know, not to expect too much. That way, you may well not find it quite so awful."

"I'm sure Rose can take Evie, our two-year-old, to her mother's or friends, if she needs to be out of the way. The other two will be at school. Actually, while I remember, please make a note that I want a portaloo on site and a designated coffee area so the builders can make their own tea etcetera. I'm happy for them to bring a microwave but they do their own clearing up. Rose and I will have enough to contend with." Will noted this in his book,

"Well, I've seen enough for now. I think this is a fantastic project and I would be very keen to manage it for you. I will send you an updated estimate for everything once I get back to the office and have had a more detailed look at the plans. If I may, I'd like to have a quick look at the out-house, what's left of it, and the garden." Rob smiled,

"Of course, go ahead, knock if you need anything, otherwise I look forward to hearing from you. Rob offered his hand, again. Will shook it enthusiastically then clicked the front door shut behind him. *Rose, Evie, the two-year-old, three children, too many coincidences, definitely the same person.*

ELEVEN

"And shake that tambourine, Evie... yes, that's right, Johnny, shake your maracas and little Henry sit down on mummy's lap, please, that's right, sit down... and let's do it again!" The teacher appeared to grow in size as she took a dramatic breath, "Shake! Clap! Stamp and sit down and sing and wee goes the elf down the slide! She made a swishing movement with her arm.

The inane atmosphere Lucy the Lollipop, Rose wondered if the Lucy part was her real name, created was not Rose's thing. The mixture of mania and hyperactivity made her cringe. "Hurrah! Oh! Jolly good! What fun we're having and a wobble of the head and a clap of the hands and a stamping of feet and the ants go weeeeeeeeeeee too!" The room was alive with a heady blend of forced, organised joy and bemused, knackered-looking mothers. There was one father. He wore tracksuit bottoms, a zip-up fleece and glasses, all items that had seen better days. Felicity, who was with her fourth child, two-year-old Alfie, the fifth one happily maturing inside her, rolled her eyes at Rose and mouthed "oh my God". It made Rose laugh. Lucy saw this,

"See, Evie, Mummy's having such a great time making music with you!" Rose did not detect any sarcasm in Lucy's voice. She was so sincere. Rose found it hard to comprehend why anyone would want to do this job. Surely, Lucy did not enjoy it that much? Rose just wanted to leave. Here she was, shaking little bells in a room full of adults and unpredictable, dribbling toddlers. Still, she supposed, the children enjoyed it and someone had to do it. Lucy certainly took her role seriously right down to the two big red circles of lipstick painted on her cheeks. She had a thick fringe with no gaps. Rose wondered if it was clip-on hair as it was so perfect, like her porcelain skin. Rose felt she should be relishing every moment with Evie yet classes like this made her miss her old 'adult' world more than ever. She caught sight of Felicity,

"No Alfie! That hurts!" Felicity grabbed his fist, "don't twist my nose like that! I've told you before not to do that to me." There was a straight expression on his face but his eyes looked gleeful. He tried again. He was determined to get a glorious reaction out of his mother this time. He failed. Calmly, she picked him up, "If you won't stop, we'll leave."

"No! I want to stay!"

"You have one more chance. If you grab my nose like that again, we'll go home. Pay attention to what Lucy is saying and do as she says." Felicity looked more tired than usual. The baby was beginning to show. She was around Rose's age. Felicity seemed to find motherhood completely satisfying and was perfectly at ease with being at home full-time.

Felicity's husband ran a successful gardening business meaning that she did not need to work. Their eldest son, Tom, was twenty-two, and a permanent member of staff, along with four other men. Felicity had patience that ran beyond most people's limits. She made few plans for the future, the thrill of a surprise baby always present. She liked it that way. A well-meaning friend had pointed out, aghast by Felicity's loose approach to the future, something along the lines of, what on earth would she do when the last one left home, to which Felicity had sarcastically, and comically, replied, look after the grandchildren, of course.

Felicity and John had met at school. They had been a couple since they were fourteen. Both had done well at school but had chosen not to further their education. Instead, they had got married at nineteen, when Felicity had found out she was pregnant with their first child. Neither had any regrets. They took every day as it came and seemed happy for it. At first, John found work mowing lawns then maintaining clients gardens before being offered a permanent position with a local firm of landscapers. He could make the dullest garden into a haven. Having become so adept at gardening, the company sent him on a garden-design course at a local college, to 'dot the i's and cross the t's', they had said.

Eventually, John took over his boss's business and never looked back. Rose envied their simple, seemingly stress-free approach to getting on with life, not trying to control or manipulate it. They seemed unruffled by the uncertainties and surprises it could throw up.

"Come on, Evie! Clap those hands, rub your tummy and touch your toes! And mummy pay attention too," said Lucy winking at Rose, as the class drew to an end. Rose knew Lucy had worked out she was not into this class. Rose felt a surge of embarrassment. "See you all next week. I might have a helper with me by then called Percy Penguin! He's learning how to be a singing and dancing teacher too. He wants to see how we do it, so until then, bye bye!" Lucy waved both hands in front of her then started wagging her head too. Rose frowned as she imagined doing such a thing would give her a headache.

Were it not for meeting friends here, Rose was not sure she would bother coming back. Evie could easily watch this sort of thing on the television.

"Hey, Rose," Charlotte was calling over to her, "Lily's for coffee? The one on the high street? Felicity's already gone. Says she'll grab a table. I'm going to repark at the supermarket as I've got a big shop to do later. Should be there in ten minutes or so." Rose said OK. Charlotte, enveloped in her usual perfume, waved as she slid out of the room, a child placed on each hip. She was also around Rose's age and mum to twins Maisie and Maya.

Charlotte had been a solicitor for almost twenty years. She still joked that she would never get over the shock of her instant family. She had tried for babies for ten years and endured many fruitless IVF rounds before accepting she would probably not have children. She accepted a promotion at work and moved on. The twins had caught her by surprise.

She had yet to return to work. She wanted to devote every waking minute to the twins. Rose had wondered what Charlotte's husband must have felt about this massive change but he was, according to Charlotte, supportive and happy to leave her to it. He spent a lot of time travelling to and from Europe with his work, leaving Charlotte on her own. She said she had no problem with this as he was out of her hair and she really did not give two figs what he got up to, as they had never been a particularly clingy couple anyway. It was clear that the bulk of the twins care was down to her. In contrast, it did not seem like much had changed for her husband at all.

Rose kept it to herself but wondered if Charlotte was hinting her husband had affairs on his business trips. Rose noted that Charlotte kept up-to-date with her law. She had not ruled out going back, once the twins were older. She had a small business on the Internet selling advice and drafting letters for people on small legal matters. Charlotte claimed this was easy. She managed to fit it in around the girls. Rose thought Charlotte must share some of her frustrations of being at home, but had never made the time to find out.

At the coffee shop, Evie, Alfie, Maisie and Maya behaved beautifully after their energetic class. Rose and her friends were able to have an uninterrupted chat and Rose felt her spirits lift. Charlotte asked,
"Rose, what was it you said you did or do now?"
"I'm a full-time mum to my three, at the moment. I used to run the customer-service side of a friend's online shop. Before that, I was a buyer for Webster's, the department store. Now, I have an idea for running my own business in soft furnishings with a coffee shop."
Charlotte looked impressed,
"Would you like to do that soon or is it just a pipe dream?"
"I certainly wouldn't call it a pipe dream. In fact, I'd do it tomorrow if I thought I could fit it all in. Who knows... it's harder with three. I don't get a lot of time. I'd definitely like to try, though." Rose felt unexpectedly sad. Silence fell upon the group. Charlotte looked concerned,

"Sorry, Rose, I didn't mean to put you on the spot, it's the solicitor in me, always questioning people. It is really hard to carve out a role separate from wife and mother, once you have children. I think most women feel the same way, unless they're lucky enough to have a team of helpers. Most ordinary folk can only dream of that!"

Rose was glad to be able to talk to her friends about her ideas and plans and decided to elaborate. A quick sip of her cappuccino and she was off,

"No, Charlotte, you haven't put me on the spot. It's nice you're interested. It's just I find it so very frustrating sometimes being, you know, just a mum, having nothing else, nothing just for me." Rose became acutely aware of Felicity's presence and looked at her.

"Oh God, Felicity; me and my big mouth. I didn't mean to be rude. It's just me; it's my problem, my feelings around staying at home. I wish I could be like you but something, I don't know what it is, pulls me towards wanting to work again. I'll be honest, I miss it." Felicity looked concerned,

"I'm not that thin-skinned, Rose! I know you're not being rude. I am very different to you because I really do love being a full-time mum. I'd be sad if I had to go to work. I love all of looking after the children. I can't pinpoint why. Maybe, it's naivety, ignorance even, or perhaps it's because I've never really gone out to work. If you don't know what you're missing!" She laughed, "And don't look so worried, Rose, you really haven't offended me in the slightest! Your feelings are very valid. Motherhood is not a 'one size fits all' just like most jobs don't suit absolutely everyone. We're all different." Rose smiled at her,

"To be honest, I started to put out feelers a while back for my business idea, especially once we decided to move down here, but then took up my friend's offer of the customer service job, then Evie came along and the time has just gone."

"Yes, you sort of went backwards, to a baby, I mean." Felicity looked concerned, "I know what that's like but can imagine it's harder if you want to work too." Felicity could not help wondering to herself why Rose had had a third child at all but reminded herself it was not her place to judge.

"Mmm..." said Rose looking at Evie, "but I do so love being her mum," before tapering off into a barely audible voice and adding, "it's so hard sometimes, a bit of a thankless task." Felicity and Charlotte were still looking at her with concern. Conscious of this, Rose felt the need to explain, "Evie was very much wanted, you know. It's just, well... Felicity, help me out here... it's just such a long, and sometimes arduous, length of time before you even get them off to school. I don't think I'm as cut out for this as I once thought."

"Human nature!" laughed Charlotte while Felicity added,

"Why do we always want what we don't have? Sounds like what you need, my darling, is a proper day off, one where you can get your hair done, buy yourself a new dress and go out on a date-night with... what's your husband called?" Rose replied,

"Rob"

"Yeah, Rob."

"Yes," chimed Charlotte, "why don't you organise it? We'll help you. If you would like me to look after Evie one day, I'd happily oblige. Tomorrow is good because my in-laws are staying for five days, God help me, and they just love kids."

Rose knew they were right. She needed a day off, some fun and to stop being so sensitive about everything.

Charlotte turned to Rose, "So, how about it then? How about tomorrow? I can have her for the day and you can arrange a babysitter for the evening bit." Rose was warming to the idea,

"Thank you, that's very kind. I'll rearrange my mother to babysit in the evening." Secretly, Rose was thinking how ideal it would be to have the whole day to herself for her business idea. Charlotte added,

"By the way, I think your shop idea is wonderful. You should go for it. We'd be able to come and see you. You'd never be lonely or lose touch. My advice, for what it's worth, is not to give up on your dreams, girlie - God knows I didn't. You know, I had to wait over ten years for these lovely babies. Yes, I did!" she beamed at the twins and they whooped back at the attention from their mother, arms and legs waving around like tortoises limbs with their shells locked into the double pushchair. "Anyway, I must get going soon as I have to get my two M & M's home and grumpy, 'I hurt my back playing squash', hubby, some dinner for tonight as he's home for a change, in preparation for his parents. Waitrose do nice ready-meals don't they? Doubt he'll notice if I quickly bin the packaging." She laughed loudly as she started to collect up her things to leave, "Can you just keep an eye on Maisie and Maya while I pop to the loo?" Rose and Felicity nodded their heads as Felicity turned the pushchair towards them.

Once Charlotte was out of sight, Rose said quietly to Felicity,

"I don't think Charlotte's marriage is too good reading between the lines. She's never particularly endearing about her husband." Felicity looked surprised at Rose's comment, which made Rose, feel unfavourably disloyal to Charlotte, talking about her the minute her back was turned. Rose wished she had not said anything and was about to apologise when Felicity replied,

"You haven't met Charlotte's husband, have you? Very intelligent, well-educated, hard work, if you ask me, typical alpha male, maybe not our type but you know something, I think it works for them. I believe they're really fond of each other. Apparently, Charlotte was the one determined to have children and to do whatever was necessary to fulfil her dream of becoming a mother. Her husband was quite happy being childless. He's not sure what to do with girls. He's a man's man. He had hoped for a boy to take to rugby every weekend so he leaves most of it to Charlotte and doesn't seem to have a lot to do with them all. But, I do believe he loves them. You'll see. He'll hang around."

"Who knows what the future holds for any of us, I suppose!" Rose replied rather flippantly, desperate to end the conversation, "maybe I shouldn't have said anything. Charlotte is clearly so happy to be a mum after so much disappointment. It's none of my business really."

Felicity looked at Rose and burst out laughing,

"Oh, do stop being so serious. You take everything far too seriously! Maybe she really isn't too bothered about her marriage or her career any more, what does it matter?" Felicity looked at the floor, "by the way, she's coming back now. Don't say any more." Charlotte descended on the silence as Rose and Felicity busily packed up their pushchairs,

"Did I miss something? Everyone's gone eerily quiet!" Rose could not even look up but Felicity saved everyone's blushes,

"Of course you didn't. Are we all ready? Same time next week, girls?" The group of three began awkwardly manoeuvring pushchairs towards the door of the coffee shop.

Will appeared in the doorway, beaming,
"Hello again!" he said cheerfully to the top of Rose's head. She was aware of a vaguely familiar voice. She looked up and immediately knew who it was. "We must stop meeting like this." To Rose, he looked amazing. After wrestling with her thoughts, and reminding herself that she was a married mother, she managed a rather curt, weak hello. She managed not to smile, wishing to hide how she really felt. He looked amused,
"I assume you're leaving? If you move your prams back so I can get in, I can hold the door for you all, might make it easier for you to leave. That is if none of you ladies manage to wrap those big wheels round the doorframe and cause a pram jam. I've already tucked my toes in." An old man waiting to enter the coffee shop tut-tutted as if they were blocking the doorway on purpose. Will rolled his eyes behind the man's back, and smiled, as he held the door wide open.

Sharp Felicity could not help noticing something between Will and Rose. Once outside, she asked Rose who he was. Rose tried to act casual as she told Felicity that he was just some guy she kept bumping into. However, Felicity had read her mind,
"Just some guy you fancy the pants off! Ooh Rose, you naughty girl!" Before Rose could say anything, Felicity, despite her pushchair, had managed to dart across the road waving her arm in the air as a goodbye. Charlotte put on a mock-serious face,
"Oh dear, Rose, he is very attractive and definitely likes you, be careful, could be awkward if you bump into him again." Charlotte then started laughing so loudly that an

elderly lady hobbling past them, with a stick, sighed loudly. Charlotte lent towards Rose,

"Honestly, Rose, do lighten up, enjoy the attention, don't look so embarrassed but," again Charlotte pulled a face, "do be careful; if you keep bumping into him, he could be stalking you."

TWELVE

Rose and Rob arrived home at the same time.

"A good morning?" enquired Rob as he leant into Rose's car and retrieved Evie from the back seat. He kissed Rose on the lips, "you look well." Rose felt refreshed. She had enjoyed her morning away from the house, especially the coffee part. She had managed to duck into the local chemist, on her way back to the car, and buy herself a red nail varnish. As a small child, she had coloured in all of her fingernails with her red pencil. She smiled, to herself, as she remembered using up the entire pencil, repeatedly and patiently sharpening then meticulously colouring until the pencil had almost disappeared. She had been satisfied with her effort and the fact she had made the pencil so small. Since then, to her, red nails signified the epitome of luxury and good grooming. Rose still tried to emulate the feeling of that day each time she painted her nails. For some reason, it was never the same.

Rob was clearly bursting to tell Rose all about his meeting with Mr Chapman, apparently before she could even get out of the car and enter the house. Rob always expected Rose to be prepared for what he needed her for straight away. Even though this could be annoying sometimes, it was this drive, to Rose, that was an attractive part of him.

As Rob launched into the details he had discussed with Mr Chapman, Rose drifted into a daydream.

"Rose, are you listening to me at all?"

"Umm, yes, sort of, actually ... no. Rob, I know you're all fired up but I've just got here and..." Before she could finish, Rob had plonked Evie in Rose's arms saying the morning had gone well and he would catch up with Rose later. He hurried towards the house mumbling something about catching Jan before she left for the day.

Rose needed to take Evie upstairs to change her nappy. Rose glanced across to the kitchen and saw Rob had caught up with Jan in the kitchen. He was laughing heartily at something she was telling him. She was laughing too and stomping round the kitchen, in her four-inch-stiletto heels, acting, thought Rose nastily, like it was her kitchen. Jan looked especially glamorous today. As usual, she looked stylish and sophisticated, not at all like mutton. Rose was aware of her own jealousy. She had not seen Rob laugh this much in ages. He was normally so sensible with Rose and, of late, only ever seemed to want to talk about the house. Jan was now hanging onto Rob's arm still laughing and telling him something that was obviously incredibly hilarious when Rob caught sight of Rose,

"Would you like a cup of tea?" Rob called over.

"No, thank you! I'm taking Evie upstairs to change her nappy... Hi Jan!" Rose smiled towards her.

"Hi Rose! Gosh, is that the time? I'd better get back to work!" She tottered off with a mug in her hand.

By the time Rose came back downstairs with Evie on her hip, the kitchen was empty and silent like a room once a party was over. Like magic, Rob reappeared,
"I've got to tell you how it went with Mr Chapman."
Rose ignored this,
"Jan gone?"
"Yes, just this minute actually."
"You were having a good laugh."
"Yes, she's very funny, always so funny." Rob smiled. If he had noticed Rose being curt, to his credit, he did not acknowledge it, "Look, it can wait until later. You seem preoccupied and I've work to finish." He quickly retreated and, for some reason, Rose felt unsettled. Will popped into her mind again. She just did not seem to be able to forget about that man whom she hardly knew. Why he unsettled her so much she did not know and now she had started to feel extremely jealous of Jan. Rose had never even considered Jan competition but it annoyed Rose that Jan was the one making her husband laugh. Should she not have been filing or something? It was Rose's job to make him laugh. *God, what is wrong with me?*

Rob was back in the kitchen, yet again. He startled Rose. It took all of her mettle not to shout at him to go away and stop popping up everywhere when she least expected it. She felt crowded by him.
"I forgot to grab a tea." Sensing Rose's unrest, Rob tried to reassure her as he waited for the kettle to boil, "Jan's all right you know and ever so good at keeping all my paperwork in order. She's definitely an asset to me and she's always so positive."

"And flirty?" said Rose, immediately regretting what she had said. Rob looked upset,

"Oh, come on Rose, is that what is bothering you? You know I only have eyes for you."

"Look, Rob, I'm sorry, I shouldn't have said that," said Rose, "I'm being silly. I'm in a strange mood. It's me. This morning was absolutely lovely. I had such fun. I've made some good friends. I told them about my business idea and, for some reason, it has unnerved me a bit," she tailed off before adding, "It's just so frustrating at home sometimes because I have more than enough to do here, to fill my time, you know that, and it's not like we need the money. I just don't feel this is the right kind of challenge for me, any more. I feel like I'm wasting my life... my talents, even."

"But Rose, you're a fantastic mother. Not all mums who stay at home do it as well as you. Can't you just enjoy it and stop feeling guilty because every other woman with children has to work whether they want to or not?" Rob paused, "As I've always said, if it's a change you really need, then, get yourself some help and do it. Honestly, Rose, you do go round in circles and make your life complicated and dramatic when it needn't be." Rose just shrugged her shoulders. Rob changed the subject,

"Anyway, just so you know, Jan wasn't flirting or anything like that. I'll tell you what we were talking about. This should make you laugh. It's funny. Jan was telling me about Ed.

"I walked round our garden this morning, for a bit of fresh air, and Ed was standing, with a hot mug of 'God knows what' in his hand, staring into oblivion, through the gap in the bushes, partly in my direction. He definitely saw me but completely ignored me. He just carried on staring. I sensed the vibes of hostility, so carried on walking. Anyway, I mentioned this to Jan, as

I was interested to hear what she makes of Ed. She told me how unpopular he's made himself, over the years, around here. It seems almost everyone is wary of him. He's as prickly as a hedgehog.

"Apparently, Nicky is lovely, a nurse, and, seemingly, blind to his lack of charm. Personally, I doubt that. I'd say she turns a blind eye to it, more likely. Anyway, years ago, after Ed was made redundant, he was a commercial pilot, he asked the landowner, Mr. Cunningham, the one who owned the farm, the land that backs on to Ed's property, not ours, you know, on the other side where they're planning to build new houses at some point, if he could walk his dog on his land. Bear in mind, it's not a public right of way. Well, of course, this guy politely declined explaining that he couldn't allow people to walk over his land, especially with the crops growing and tractors reversing etcetera. Now, most people wouldn't have asked in the first place and most who did would certainly take no as an answer. The lovely Ed didn't like the answer. He decided to launch into a foul-mouthed tirade about how 'you people with land are so selfish you don't know you're born with the silver spoon', and so on. You get the picture. Ed carried on, like a child having a tantrum. He called Mr Cunningham all sorts of names as he let rip, exposing a massive chip on his shoulder. He just couldn't stop. He blew the whole thing out of all proportion and said he would go to the council and get them to put a right-of-way thoroughfare all over Mr Cunningham's land so he couldn't plant any more 'shitty crops'. Ed said all sorts of ridiculous things like that. Obviously, the landowner was not amused, but managed to appear unfazed. In the end, he just walked off. This may have been the end of it but, and, perhaps this was Ed's biggest mistake, Ed started boasting about what he'd said to various people in the village. He reiterated that he thought Mr Cunningham was a 'pompous, silver-spooned wimp' and wasn't even able to fight back, he was such a coward.

"Ed really believed that he had the upper hand. What he failed to realise was that he was bad-mouthing a very popular, well-liked man who regularly donated money to the church fund and village hall repairs. After his outburst, Ed took to standing at the fence every time the farmers were in the field. He would stare at them, boasting to the village that there was no law against that and that if Mr Cunningham hadn't been so greedy and selfish and just let him walk his dog on his 'bleeding acreage' instead of being a prat about it then he might be a bit more popular.

"Apparently, Nicky told him to grow up and let it go, that it was simple. The landowner didn't want him on his land so he should get over it and move on and walk the dog somewhere else. She was unaware as to how often Ed stood at the fence, staring. She was usually at work. Anyway, one day, Ed went too far. The landowner had had enough. Ed made a V sign at him, which he later denied saying it was the way he was holding his mug. Mr Cunningham appeared to ignore the sign and walked off. Well, next thing, he came back, driving his tractor with the sprayer on the back. He drove round the field a couple of times while Ed stood staring defiantly. Mr Cunningham, who, incidentally, is dead now, drove past a few times before moving the sprayer to the side and covering Ed in stinking muck. Just like that! It all happened so quickly and unexpectedly. Ed just stood there covered in greasy, stinking muck. It was even in his mouth. Ed was retching and spitting while Mr Cunningham carried on calmly spreading the muck over his field pretending to be oblivious to the entire incident!" Rob was laughing so much he had to grab the kitchen surface for support and Rose was laughing too more at Rob now than what he had just told her,

"That's shocking! I actually feel a bit sorry for Ed. Did he get into trouble? I mean Mr Cunningham?"

"No, how could Ed prove it wasn't an accident? Mr Cunningham acted like he hadn't seen him all along. Ed knew that he had gone too far. It stopped Ed staring but there's more. On that particular day, Nicky had gone to work, for a twelve-hour shift, and had taken the door off the latch as she thought Ed had his keys with him. He didn't. As she was working for an agency back then, and Ed took very little interest in where she worked, he had no idea where she was, or even the agency she worked for, so he was effectively stuck outside covered in shit! Oh, and the best bit is that Ed had run over the garden hose with the lawnmower the week before, so that was in pieces. Rumour has it, that there he was trying to clean himself up with the dribbling, cold garden tap and some old rag he found in the garden!" Rose shook her head but was smiling,

"Rob, you're mean laughing like that. Don't you feel just a bit sorry for him?"

"No and neither will you when you see the letter I got from him today saying that the least we can do, seeing as he's got to put up with the noise of our builders once they start, is to resurface his drive as way of compensating him. The man's mad, I'm telling you. We don't own or even use his drive!"

"Really? What a cheek! Does he think we are stupid?" said Rose. Rob shrugged,

"Some people take your breath away. You know he probably believes that we'll do it if he bullies us enough." Rob was wiping his eyes, "Seriously, though, Rose, don't talk to him. I did call round there earlier

after I read the note but only Nicky was there. She seems so nice, it's hard to believe they're a couple." Rob was more serious now, "Also, I forgot to tell you that last week I actually saw him leave a note on a parked car, at the supermarket, saying, 'learn to park' in capital letters. He likes his notes. OK, so one wheel appeared to be parked slightly on the line, but, I mean, why bother? I'm telling you; he's an angry man with nothing better to do, literally seething inside. One comfort is that, basically, Ed decided not to like us before we even moved in. We could have been anyone. Once we moved in, he decided to like us even less, once he realised he couldn't walk all over us. Shame really as we've always got on with our neighbours, in the past." Rose sensed Rob was worrying about it all,
"Yes but don't take too much notice of him. Ed's clearly very unhappy. It'll go way deeper than him not wanting us to get builders in. He could be depressed. I mean, he must feel quite isolated there, mostly on his own, with no job, and I get the impression Nicky tolerates him, rather than idolises him. We'll have to continue to tread carefully. We're doing everything by the book so we've really nothing to worry about." Rob agreed,
"I think Nicky seems a bit timid around Ed, really, you know like the eggshell thing. Must be hard work for her."

Rob appeared to drift into his thoughts. Rose changed the subject,
"Anyway, Rob, I know you were dying to tell me about your meeting with Mr. Chapman. Before I forget to ask, does this Mr Chapman have a first name? It seems old fashioned to keep calling him mister, or is that how things are done in the countryside?" She laughed as Rob replied,

"He did say his first name when he came round but I didn't catch it. I felt too awkward to ask him again, once the conversation had moved on. I think it was John or something but I'm not sure, definitely one syllable. Anyway, I started calling him Mr Chapman and he hasn't said, you know, actually call me John or whatever, and he calls me Mr Clarke so I've left it at that for now, a bit formal but he probably thinks I prefer it." He smiled, "Anyway, perhaps once you meet him and work your beautiful charm on him, we'll all be on first name terms. I think he sent me a letter so I'll dig that out and see if his first name's on it. Actually, are you free, in the morning, to meet him, at last? It would be after I've visited Ed. Mr Chapman has agreed to come with me to see if he can help smooth things over."

"Rob, would you mind if I met him another time? If you're happy with him then do go ahead. I'm sure I will be too. Only, I can't be there in the morning. I'm actually looking at business premises, just to see what's on offer, really." Rose was playing it down. She noticed a fleeting look of disapproval in Rob's eyes, which he quickly checked,

"Really? You kept that one quiet. No problem, Rose. It is short notice. Anyway, I must get on with my work." He pecked her on the cheek and skipped off back to the hut.

Rose had an hour before she had to leave to collect Anna and Thomas from school. Time to take Evie round the garden before they left. Evie loved being pulled around in her red wagon, an early Christmas present. Evie loved to sit in it and grab as many leaves as she could along the way. As Rose approached the bottom of the garden, which was not visible from the house or even the hut, Evie had fallen silent. She had managed to recline and was staring at the sky, following the moving clouds. Rose was enjoying the fresh air and peace.

"Hello!" came a barely audible voice, "Is that you?" It was coming from the bush in front of Rose.

She stopped and answered the female voice. Nicky revealed herself. She was not usually that friendly. Rose had often caught a glimpse of her moving stealthily away from the bushes as Rose approached. She wondered if Nicky was aware of the letter that Ed had sent. Perhaps she wanted to smooth things over. Even so, it was possible that she was even behind it, Rose thought. She would be cautious,

"How are you?"

"Very well, thank you," replied Nicky, looking uneasy. She started to back away. She did not seem to be in the mood to chat. However, Rose reminded herself that Nicky was the one who had approached her. Rose preferred openness. She decided to tackle Nicky head on,

"Rob has mentioned the letter that Ed wrote to him." Nicky looked genuinely surprised then guarded like she knew, instinctively, that it would not be pleasant news,

'Letter?... I'm not sure about any letter." A worried look sprawled across her face. Clearly she did not know what Rose was talking about. Rose decided to enlighten her,

"Ed wrote Rob a letter about your drive being resurfaced." Nicky looked confused,

"Is it?" she replied, as if it was the first time she had heard anything of the sort. Rose paused then continued,

"Never mind, just tell Ed that Rob's planning to drop by about it, in the morning. Will Ed be at home?" Rose looked down, not enjoying Nicky's apparent discomfort at all. Nicky replied,

"Yes, he should be home. I'll tell him. I think I'd better go now."

"Yes, me too. I've got to do the school run. Nice to see you." Rose proceeded to tug the wagon back towards the house. It seemed heavier than before, having sunk into the lawn during its stop. Churned-up mud was stuck in its wheels.

That was awkward and weird. Nicky was hanging around almost like she was waiting for someone. Maybe, she was hoping to catch me after that letter to test the water and lost her bottle, but then she appeared to know nothing about it. She's very loyal to Ed. I suppose living with him would be enough to test a saint. Evie was growing impatient with the slow speed of the wagon. She demanded to be pulled faster. Rose completely forgot about Nicky.

THIRTEEN

The car park was well signposted. Rose walked through the tunnel that linked it to the shops. They overlooked the town below. She was struck by how clean the tunnel was. There was no litter or graffiti. It even smelt faintly of perfume.

The appointment with the estate agent was at quarter past ten. Rose, having purposely arrived fifteen minutes early, observed the charming, crooked cottage in front of her. Access to the rear garden was through a wrought-iron gate, similar to her mother's. It had large, bay windows on either side of the front door. A cobbled area, at the front, marked the property out from the neighbouring businesses. Rose imagined rolled up displays of fabric, in the windows, with candles and ribbons. She would enjoy creating seasonally cosy and fresh displays to entice her customers in, were she to go ahead with her business. A snowy scene at Christmas, with an antlered-deer model, adorned with glitter, glimmering under the spotlights.

Certainly, Rose felt an immediate attachment to the place, yet she tried to remain impartial. This property was not somewhere to live. Falling in love with it would not be enough. It had to be practical. She had still to see inside. Even so, she was willing it to feel the same as it did from where she was standing now.

She nipped round the back to look at the garden. She wanted to do this alone, without the estate agent. Rose did not want to look to anyone else to bolster her, even advise her, at this initial point, and she certainly did not want to hear anything negative about this place, no matter how helpful any comments were intended to be. Rose would trust her own instincts. She always felt inhibited by estate agents as, in her experience, they asked too many questions. They followed you around, indeed only doing their job, yet, always trying to gauge how serious you were, trying to find out as much as they could about you without asking, outright, the obvious questions like, have you actually got the money. Rose needed to trust her gut feel. Explaining her business plan to a stranger would take her mind to a different element, different thought patterns would come to the fore.

Rose lifted and pushed the old gate open. It shrieked like a stiff swing. She noted it would need lifting. She scuttled down the path. She stopped to absorb the view over the town below, roof tops, cars moving like ants, a church spire and tall trees standing like columns. The warm, autumn sun, low in the sky, shone onto the terrace. Rose imagined her customers sitting at metal, bistro-style tables, possibly in all weathers, were she to add an awning and heat. *Oh, wow, if this isn't a sign to go for it then I don't know what would be.*

"Mrs Clarke!" Rose jumped and let out an embarrassing squeal. She turned around, knowing it must be the estate agent, recognising his voice from the telephone,

"I'm Ben! How do you do? Sorry if I startled you!" As Rose offered her hand, he popped a key with a blue plastic key ring attached to it between his lips and shook her hand. His left hand was full of papers. As he turned towards the cottage, he mumbled something about startling her, clearly feeling awkward that he had. Ben seemed flustered and in a hurry. What struck her most about him was that he looked like a man with a boy's face. Was she really old enough to be his mother? Ben was set to show her round,

"Amazing, isn't it? Shall we?" Ben gestured towards the front door, dangling the key in front of her face.

"Yes please, the outside is certainly amazing!" Ben cut in enthusiastically,

"Yes but if it's a shop you're after then the inside will probably be just as important."

"Well, yes," murmured Rose deciding not to elaborate. He swished the post aside with his foot before struggling to grab a few letters that had got stuck under the front door preventing it from opening fully. He looked red and flustered once he'd cleared the obstruction but carried on regardless, "I don't know how well you know it around here but this is less than a five minute walk from the main high street, if you use the pedestrian cut through, and, of course, this is a well-known area of town. The opticians' next door is well established and Baldock, the chemist, on the other side. It's the only chemist in town if you don't include the one in the supermarket. They sell perfume, and stuff like that, so people come here all the time. Rose looked out of the window at the hairdresser flanked by the toy shop and sweet shop. There was no other coffee shop in the precinct. This appeared to be the only available unit.

The inside was clean, dry and cold. It needed some altering, for what Rose had in mind, but nothing major. A partition wall, a couple of white toilets in the customer area to replace the green ones, some paint, blinds and a blanket of heat, and she would not be far from opening.

Ben brought Rose back from her thoughts,
"Of course, you know this used to be a coffee shop and only stopped being one quite recently because the owners died, really close together, apparently. I think there was no one to take it over. I'm not sure how popular it was though as the couple were elderly and a bit slow and grumpy, so I've heard. You can see it's a bit dated. The thick net curtains in the windows weren't exactly enticing people in!" He laughed. Rose did not as it felt disrespectful to laugh at someone else's business now they were dead. Sensing this, Ben quickly pulled himself up, "Is it a coffee shop you're after?"
"Well, yes, but I want to sell fabric too and run classes, sewing classes."
"Oh, nice." Ben smiled, clearly unimpressed, but, remembering his sale, tried to feign enthusiasm. "My mum would love all that sewing stuff, I'm sure. It's surprising but we haven't had any interest from the well-known names yet. Although, I think that they prefer to stick to the town centres. We do have loads of interest from private people, like you, so it'll be snapped up soon." Rose thought he was probably exaggerating but she knew she would have to make a swift decision. She believed her idea would work. She would market her classes and fabrics first. She knew there would be demand. Ben had silently been trying to make the connection between coffee and fabric. He suddenly looked even more enthusiastic, like he really could fix this deal, "oh, I see, selling fabric with a coffee shop out back sort of thing. What a good idea. I don't think

anyone else is doing anything like that around here at all!"

"Yes, my priority would be the regular classes. I'd build the coffee part around that." Ben marched towards a corner of the room to remove a large piece of peeling paint. He looked gleeful and smiled, like a mischievous boy, before apparently remembering that he was meant to be selling the place not pointing out its faults. With a straight face, he said,

"Of course, the family who have inherited this want to let it out at first while they decide what to do. Apparently, there's a house to sell too, about fifteen miles from here. It has tenants in it for the rest of the year. Two brothers are the beneficiaries, I believe. One lives up North and the other America. I think they'd sell it if the right buyer approached them though. Perhaps, you could rent this first then, if it all works out, buy, just a suggestion, of course. Shall we look at the other rooms upstairs?" Rose looked up at the ceiling, which appeared sound, before replying,

"Yes, please." There was a narrow staircase, towards the rear of the building, hidden, to the side of the kitchen area. Rose imagined serving coffees and cakes behind the counter with the staircase, to her right, out of view from the public. Upstairs was a bathroom, a very small open plan kitchen area and two bedrooms. The previous owners had lived above their coffee shop and used the second bedroom as a sitting area. Rose imagined using one room as an office and storage room for surplus fabric with a sofa in it for her children to relax when she had to bring them to work, on odd occasions, if they were ill or it were the holidays, and she was unable to make alternative arrangements for them. The other room could be a staff room. It was ideal. Viewing this place felt like completing a quick jigsaw, for Rose, it all worked so well.

Ben started to dramatically look at his watch and roll the keys around in his hand. *Time's up*, thought Rose. She was not going to keep him any longer. She wondered if the next person, or people, would be as nice as her.

"Well, thank you, Ben," Rose held out her hand to him, "I shall have a think about this. I am definitely interested." Ben looked pleased,

"And it doesn't need much doing to it."

"No, although, I would want to change a fair bit. I'll get back to you either way." She left Ben to lock up.

Rose drove to a tucked away coffee shop. She had never bumped into anyone she knew there. None of the customers ever looked familiar. She needed time to think. She almost forensically examined the cottage details in front of her. She pored over the room measurements and layout and thought about the cost. She would have to ask Rob for the deposit. She knew it would not be a problem. She was ready to discuss it with him now.

Rose arrived early at the school to collect Thomas and Anna. She arranged another appointment to view the cottage. She hoped Rob would have a look with her. She also confirmed their reservation at Versanios for 8.30pm. Her mother was babysitting and as Charlotte, who was looking after Evie, would also feed her, all Rose would have to do was put her to bed before she and Rob went out. Rose's mother would sort out the other two.

Anna and Thomas came running out of school and hugged Rose,

"Where's Evie?" enquired Anna.

"She's with Charlotte, my friend, the one with the twins. Now, tell me, would you both like pizza for tea?"

"Yes, please!" They both eagerly nodded.

"How about Emmanuel's?"

"Yes!" Thomas punched the air.

"Can we have ice cream and drink lemonade?" Anna asked, expectantly. Rose pretended to think about it,

"Oh, I think that should be all right!"

Rose was about to pull away, in her car, when there was a knock on the window. It was Mel,

"Wind down the window," she mouthed at Rose. *Not you*, thought Rose but had no choice but to do as she was told. Mel seemed unaware of Rose's feelings and was very keen to tell her something of significance,

"I was dropping off a few leaflets, about my make-up parties, earlier, in your area, and Rob opened the front door, just as I was about to put one through your letterbox. Your cleaners, from that local firm, were there. Rob said, quietly of course, that he was having to hang around, as, he came in from that hut thing you've shoved him into in the garden," Mel snorted a laugh before continuing, "and found them looking in the kitchen cupboards, for coffee they claimed but they'd only been in for half an hour. I'd say they were looking for cash. He didn't send them away, though, as he said the house needed a good clean and you're too busy. Poor Rob's not happy, thought I ought to warn you. Must say, you are lucky having cleaners considering you don't work!" Before Rose could say a word, Mel continued, "Personally, I don't clean, better things to do. It wrecks my hands. I have lovely hands, and nails, used to be a hand model, you know! I could still do it but there's not the time. I still like to look after my nails. You look tired. Has Evie been keeping you awake? Actually, where is she? Gosh, we are a lady-of-leisure today! Bye! Have a good weekend!" Mel was gone as quickly as she had appeared. Rose had been unable to get a word in. She was now fuming. She thought she looked all right today but was used to Mel putting her foot in it, apparently blissfully unaware of what she was like or blissfully unable to care. *How dare she say I look tired. Perhaps next time you look in the mirror, you can trim your long, black, nose hair*, thought Rose bitchily, in retaliation, as she pulled out of the school. Anna piped up,

"I didn't know you shoved Daddy into the hut. I thought he liked working in there."

"He does, Anna. I think Mel is mad and doesn't know what she is saying but we mustn't tell anyone we know this or she might get upset, OK? Thomas? Anna?" Rose looked back at their faces in her mirror as they both agreed, in unison, while still looking confused.

Thomas and Anna were ravenous and silently ate their massive pizzas like they had not eaten for a week when Thomas asked,

"Why don't you work, Mummy?   All the other mummies do."

"I look after you and Anna and Evie," said Rose, stiffening.

"Yes, but we are all growing up. What will you do when we are grown up?"

"Oh, I'll think of something, Thomas, don't you worry. I might go back to work sooner than you think." Thomas smiled and went back to munching pizza before adding,

"I don't want you to work. I like you looking after me."

"I like you being at home too," said Anna, "Sophie has to go to a club after school and sit on a smelly bean bag and read a book or do homework then she goes home and eats cereal, like it's breakfast, then her mum puts her to bed and goes to work again on her computer. She says her mum is always working and hardly sees her and her Dad is always away, working in other countries. I wouldn't like that. I much prefer coming home."

"No, I don't suppose you would like that. Not everyone is as lucky as you though, you know, Anna, but I probably will work again soon. I like being at home but I like work too. It's hard to do both well but I may have found a solution so we can all be happy. You'll see. You mustn't worry because I'll always try to be around for you when you're at home and I promise you won't have to sit on a smelly bean bag after school. Now hurry up and finish because we've got to collect Evie. I'm going out with Daddy tonight. I'll need time to get ready."

"Will you wear the scary, red lipstick?" Thomas said.

"What do you mean?"

"You know, the scary one, like blood. You always wear it when you go out with Daddy.

'Oh, don't you like it?"

"I love it! You look like a vampire." Unaware that was not exactly the look Rose tried to create, Thomas took another mammoth mouthful of pizza as if he had said nothing out of the ordinary.

Back home, Rose managed to get the children into bed half an hour before their normal time. Rob came into their bedroom as Rose was getting ready,

"So, Mrs Clarke, what time is the table booked for at Versanios?"

"8.30pm, I booked a taxi for 8pm so we should be able to enjoy a few drinks without worrying about driving. Mum should be here soon. I'm amazed how easily they all went to bed tonight."

"Yes, that's a result! I'll leave you to get ready. You look beautiful!" Rob kissed Rose's forehead.

At dinner, Rose decided to tell Rob all about the cottage. "I saw a property today." Rob cut in before Rose had a chance to take a breath, a habit of his which Rose normally ignored but which really annoyed her when she was trying to tell him something of such importance to her. He started to rant,

"Oh my God, don't tell me you want to move again instead of doing up the cottage. I've put so much work into the plans and what with the council and finding a project manager...."

"Rob! If you would just listen and let me finish. I told you, yesterday, I was viewing that property for my business." She could see he was using all his might not to butt in so she continued, "It's the one on the hill above town, where you get your eyes tested. You saw the details. As you know, my business plans are nothing new. And, I think I might be ready to do it sooner than I may have initially thought."

"Yes, yes, I know it.", Rob looked impatient and Rose thought she noticed a look of panic flicker in his eyes as, for him, Rose doing her own business was no longer appearing to be safely in the future, making Rob face the reality of possible disruption to his current, rather settled, cosy life.

Rose took another sip of her red wine which went down like soothing cough mixture before telling him all about her business idea, the property, how she had thought it all through including, of course, how it would fit in with the children and running a home.

"It all sounds great, Rose, in theory, anyway, but, really, what about the children? Seriously, how will it all work if one of them is ill or you're called to the school suddenly because they've had an accident, been naughty...I don't know. It just all works now." He looked genuinely concerned. Rose had had enough,

"It all works now, yes… and forgive me for saying this and I don't wish to argue with you, but it all works perfectly...for you... not me, any more." She looked at him, straight into his frightened eyes, "Rob, I love you and I love our children but I feel stifled by it all. Please be happy for me. I have a good business brain. I won't let anyone down, I promise. I want to do this. You get one life and I want to live mine not try to pick up the pieces once the kids have left home and I'm bereft with nothing to do but wait for them to come home with a bag full of dirty washing. This isn't about money, of course, it's about me!" Rob looked surprised as he took her hand in his,

"Goodness Rose, you're a passionate one! Of course I'm happy for you! It's just I thought we had Evie especially because you wanted to stay at home and be a full-time mum because you felt you were pushed or pulled or whatever back into work with the other two and I'll be honest, I don't want to have to interrupt my working day to collect the children from school or babysit Evie because she's ill and it's not working for you." Rose gave him one of her 'don't mess with me' looks,

"You are their father and sometimes parents have to make sacrifices. That's a fact. Your reasons are weak and you know it." She paused. "This is about change and dynamic though you are, you hate it, just like everybody else. You know I'll make all the necessary childcare arrangements. Surely, a happy mum and," she paused and started again, "Just be excited for me!"

Rob paused as the waiter brought their meals to the table. He topped up their wine glasses and as he walked away, Rob replied,

"Look, Rose, I'm sorry if I don't sound as enthusiastic as you would like me to." He took her hand in his again, "I do really want you to be happy and fulfilled. It's just all happening so quickly. Of course I never expected you to stay at home for ever, just a bit longer, maybe a couple of years more, but I know you're so capable. I'm sure you'll make this work for all of us. I just don't want you overworked if I'm honest, Rose, but you have my blessing. I'm pleased for you, really I am." He smiled as he gestured to the plates in front of them, "Let's eat." Rose smiled back. She knew his concerns were genuine and knew that, in a year's time, he would be so used to her working again that he would, literally, have forgotten what it was like before. Her mind was made up.

FOURTEEN

Rob and Rose returned home with an air of renewed intimacy. They planned to stay up late. As they crept into the house, they found Cathy cradling a hot, shallow-breathing Evie. She was restlessly dozing, wearing only her vest and nappy,
"I'm sorry," said Rose's mother, "Evie woke up crying at around 9pm. I knew you'd be back soon so I didn't call. I've given her some Calpol. She has cooled down slightly but I think you're in for a restless night." Cathy looked forlorn as she delivered the news.

Just as Rob and Rose climbed into bed, it became clear that Evie's illness had night plans. She kept crying and coughing like a seal. She was grabbing her ears and just could not settle so, with Rose's blessing, Rob moved to the sofa downstairs. There was no point in both of them being exhausted. He lay awake, mulling over Rose's, rather, he had to be honest, unwelcome news, about her business. Why couldn't she stick to the original plan and be happy at home? It was what she had always wanted and really why he had agreed to a third child.

He was feeling sorry for himself, sorry that the evening they had enjoyed had abruptly ended. His thoughts moved to Ed, who really had no good reason to dislike them. Rob knew he had to try and smooth things over with him, for all their sakes, but part of him simply did not see why he should be the one to take the first step. Rob aggressively tossed and turned. He felt so frustrated. His eyes settled on a dishevelled 'Care Bear' poster, the bear eerily smiled out at him, lit by the moonlight, "Who the hell stuck that there, for God's sake?" *As for the children*, Rob thought, *they have just taken over. I can't get five minutes alone at home with Rose, even at night.*

It was no good. He flung off the sleeping bag and tiptoed into the kitchen to get a Scotch. It would calm him down and, hopefully, promote sleep. He sat back on the sofa, swung his feet up and arranged the sleeping bag back over himself. As he sipped his Scotch, he tried to be objective about Ed, as he continued to debate the situation in his mind. What made someone so prickly and difficult to approach? Could he, should he, handle Ed differently? Why did Nicky stay around if he was that bad? Could it be they'd just got off on the wrong foot and let their egos get in the way? Rob came to the conclusion that no one could, or would, ever, justify resurfacing a drive, for any neighbour, as a kind of compensation for probable, future, building noise. Surely, any sane person would not even have the nerve to suggest such a thing? Honestly, the sheer brazenness of it all. Rob vowed to go round there first thing in the morning, and sort things out once and for all. The drink was kicking in nicely. Rob felt calmer now as sleep, thankfully, took over.

He woke early, surprisingly refreshed for a night on the sofa, and a late Scotch. He downed a strong coffee and had a shower, next to the back door, the one they referred to as the gardener's. He did not want to disturb anyone too early. Rose would not have got much sleep. He had remembered to put in earplugs so he had not heard Evie crying. He went out to the hut and worked for a little while before calling in on Ed and Nicky. He wanted to catch them before they started their days.

Armed with the letter, and to save himself having to go the long way round, Rob managed to squeeze through a gap in the fence, behind one of the laurel bushes, at the far end of Ed and Nicky's garden, out of sight of the house. With any luck, Ed would think he had walked round the long way, if he used the front door. Probably, Nicky would not care.

At the front door, Rob paused before he rang the bell. It was early but he was certain someone was up. He could see all of the curtains were open and could hear a radio. He watched Nicky walk towards the door, through a narrow, glass panel, which ran the whole length of the front door. The property was a converted barn, and reminded Rob of the ready-to-assemble, timber-framed house-kits from Germany.

She opened the door and invited him in. He hesitated. A padded pod-chair, on the end of a long rope, hung from one of the beams, in the exposed loft space. It rocked in the draught created by his entrance.

She smiled cheerfully at him, revealing perfect teeth. He estimated her to be of a similar age to himself and Rose. He guessed that Ed might be older. Nicky was wearing shorts with a wrap-around, ballet-style cardigan that framed her ample chest perfectly. She appeared shorter than Rob remembered. She was plumper than Rose but not fat, he thought, just perfectly in proportion. He realised he had been staring at Nicky for a little too long. She met his gaze and smiled again before he spoke,

"Um...Hi Nicky, may I speak to Ed, please? You know, it's about the letter. I said I'd call round. You said he'd be in this morning."

"I'm really sorry, Rob, but he's not here. I expected him to be, but, well, he's not. No, he's gone up to London to stay with his brother, Graham, went last night for a few days, last minute lads thing for a birthday, you know, Brick Lane curry and lots of beer." She smiled, clearly trying to lighten the atmosphere she sensed from Rob. He now felt hasty, even rather stupid, at having rushed around here so early, and on his own. He should have waited for Mr Chapman to come with him, or even handed it over to him, completely. How Rob wished he could remember his first name. Nicky shivered,

"Look, it's cold outside and you're letting all my heat out so would you like to come in and maybe have a coffee, or are you just going to stand there on the door-step? Either way, I'm shutting the door before I freeze."

"Oh, um, yes, OK, I'll come in, just for a bit. I do have work to get on with so I haven't got long." As he followed Nicky towards the kitchen, his eyes wandered over her bottom. It was perfectly rounded, in his mind, just the right size. He wondered how he had not noticed before. In fact, she looked as gorgeous from behind as she did face-on. She gestured towards the kitchen table,

"Take a seat and I'll put the kettle on." She paused, "that is, if you want coffee?"

"Yes, I do, please." Rob felt like he was dreaming, the house was so quiet and peaceful, a real oasis away from the busy, hectic family life of his home, where there was always noise. In the hut, there was the almost-constant ringing of phones and chat from Jan. She would fill him in on some of the clients she knew, some of whom she had gone to school with.

Rob would normally have made his excuses and left before he had got to the coffee stage but something about Nicky had lured him in. He was particularly struck by her calmness and the peaceful air she had about her with the absence of Ed. He imagined her to be totally unflappable and an excellent nurse. It was hard to imagine she ever got stressed or cross enough to throw anything across the room. Actually, she was so attractive that he resisted the urge to get up from the kitchen table and grab her. He silently chastised himself, telling himself not to look at her like that again, to remember he was a married father-of-three.

Nicky turned around,
"Do you take milk and sugar in your coffee?"
"Just milk, please. You have a lovely place here. It's so peaceful."
"Yes, it is lovely. It used to belong to Ed's mother but, sadly, she died quite a while ago. She left it all to Ed. He had nearly always lived with her. Graham, his brother, has a successful portfolio of buy-to-lets in London which she guaranteed the mortgages on, back in the early days, so, I suppose, she felt she helped him then, and that he didn't need any of this place. Apparently, Graham was cool with it all. Ed's updated it a bit and after I moved in, we furnished it with our own stuff so it felt more like ours, but it's hard to think of it as ours sometimes when his mother lived here for so long, and was the one who converted it. We have no mortgage, though, which is good as Ed doesn't work much. He does bits here and there for Graham and that's about it. He used to be a pilot, you know, but he was

made redundant ages ago and well," she tapered off and looked anxious before changing the subject, "I remember your house was owned by old George, who we never heard a peep out of. You have a lovely place too, nice and big. Bet it'll be amazing once you've finished it."

Rob was not sure how to respond. A quiet, old man as a neighbour versus a busy family of five, working from home, must be quite a change, as neighbours go. Rob sensed Nicky felt she might have said too much so thought it best to get back to the reason he was here, "Lovely coffee, thank you," he smiled as he took another sip, "anyway, the letter, the one Ed wrote to me, suggesting resurfacing your drive as a gesture of goodwill, well, in response, really, it's a big ask and very presumptuous. I'm not sure why he thinks we should even consider it, to be honest." Nicky looked concerned, "I know, Rob. I know. I know it's an unreasonable request. Ed has a habit of blowing things out of proportion. He feels easily threatened by change. I'll talk to him." Nicky looked uncomfortable and embarrassed and Rob felt he had said enough, "I really must go, Nicky, thank you again for the lovely coffee." Nicky did not seem to want to let him go, "Did you say you're an architect?"
"That's right, I am. I do contract work for my old company as well as my own projects as I recently went self-employed. I plan to expand and employ another architect quite soon, more in the future. Also, my brother and I have talked at length about property-developing together. He does it for a living now. He's a chartered surveyor which comes in useful."
"Yes," Nicky paused, tailing off, "Look, I really am sorry about Ed and that letter. He shouldn't have sent that to you or even considered it." She exhaled loudly,

"sometimes, he doesn't think. I don't want you to get the wrong idea about him. He just gets a bit stressed. He found it very noisy when they built the houses over there as he is in most days and he used to enjoy walking the dog there as the land lay dormant, if you like, for two years, after Mr. Cunningham died, until his family sold it and the tall fences went up. I think he feels a bit uneasy about more building but we can't even see your house from our garden and I imagine it won't take longer than a year, will it? And, I do keep reminding him that it won't be constant banging and sawing. Long before you came here, and long before Ed's mother died, the only way to access your house was by a shared drive, the drive that is now ours. It wasn't until the council granted your property permission to make a drive onto the main highway, at the front, that the owners back then relinquished their rights to use our drive. It meant both properties became independent of each other and both became worth more on the market. So, that may help you see where Ed is trying to come from, but that was a long time ago and he shouldn't have said anything. Again, I am sorry."

Rob stifled a wry smile at the thought of Ed getting what he wanted, in the end, and resisted the urge to say but I heard that Mr Cunningham did not ever want him to use his land, when he was alive. Clearly, Ed has no respect for the wishes of the dead. *How utterly selfish*, thought Rob before stating, "We've been estimated eight months or so for the work. Look, I really want us all to get on so, here's my card if you or Ed need to call me about anything. I'd better go as I could sit here all day, it's so peaceful, but I must get back to my work. Do you mind if I go home through the fence-gap in your back garden?" She smiled and said,

"What? The same way you arrived earlier? Of course not! Maybe, I'll see you there soon?" He felt embarrassed. Was she flirting with him?

He was unaware how much his visit had unsettled her. As she shut the back door, she felt a sense of exhaustion run through her body. His visit had reminded her how difficult Ed could be. He was constantly complaining or moaning about something, a symptom of his deep-seated unhappiness and frustration about having never being able to find employment, as a pilot, again, following his redundancy. His latest moan was complaining about neighbours, always going on about them not clearing up leaves or mess of some kind and failing to tidy up trees, fix fences, going on about pompous, posh, city types who 'splash their city-made cash' in the countryside. Ironically, he liked visiting Graham, his brother, in London. Graham lived a luxurious, city life yet Rose and Rob were, in contrast, both originally from the countryside, anyway. Basically, Ed was not fussy who, or what, he vented about if it made him feel better, even if it was only for a while.

Rob, now back in his own house, having felt too tired to return to work, remembered how Nicky had held his gaze. He lay back on the sofa he had just spent the night on. What a washout his date night had been. He could not remember the last time he and Rose had got near uninterrupted intimacy. He must have drifted back to sleep because he was suddenly aware of Thomas's face so close to his, he could barely focus on him,
"So, you're not dead, Daddy. I thought you were. Have you seen this Lego model I made last night before I went to sleep? It has two doors and lots of ammunition for the baddies and that's where they make tea and that's the toilet and that's where they sleep and... wait a minute. I

must have dropped it. The alien has gone. Wait there while I get him." Thomas turned around to run before stopping and looking right at Rob, "Hang on a minute, Daddy. Where's Mummy? How come you're here?"

"Well, Evie was poorly last night and was up a lot so I decided to sleep here." Thomas ran off to look for his alien without any response just as Anna appeared in the doorway,

"Mummy is cross. She says she's tired and that you can get my damned breakfast." She had a cereal bowl and spoon in her right hand and hair that looked like she had rubbed a balloon all over it,

"Poor Mummy," said Rob. "Right then, we'd better get you some breakfast. Come on." He got up and went into the kitchen.

Anna was tucking into a bowl of *Coco Pops*, like she had not eaten for days. Some were jumping ship onto the floor but Rob could not be bothered to mention it as Anna had apparently already been on the receiving end of Rose's tiredness. He decided to make fresh coffee for himself and Rose. He had actually briefly dreamed about Nicky just now and found this quite disconcerting. They had been in a field of long grass together on a hot day. Nicky had been impressively illuminated by the sun. She had appeared glowing and sexy. She had nothing on underneath her see-through, white garment. She had smiled at Rob and beckoned him to follow her.

Rob heard a thud then crying. He rushed to the bottom of the stairs to find Thomas in a heap. So full of energy, and always in a hurry, he had missed his footing, as he often did, and his shin was bleeding. It already had visible swelling on it. As if to make it worse for Thomas, Lego was scattered all over the hall floor, obviously something Thomas had been eager to show

Rob. Rob felt so sorry for him as he scooped him up. Thomas sobbed into his shoulder, shaking his leg, shouting ouch every couple of seconds.

It only took one child to be ill or upset and the whole house went into disarray. Rose really did play such an enormous part in holding it all together, thought Rob, yet he felt so neglected, as her husband. He yearned for the days that they used to have before children when, apart from work, the rest of the time was their own. They could please themselves and each other, and, yet, Rob would not swap his children to have those days again.

Thomas's sobs eased off and he explained, between deep, solemn breaths how he had only banged his shin, in the same place, two weeks ago. It had only just healed. The Lego took him hours to build and was now in pieces. He had made up the design so there was no way of putting it back together in the same way as before,
"I hate Lego!" exclaimed Thomas with a burst of anger. Rob felt helpless,
"I can try and help you design and make something later if you like."
"No, you won't be able to. It's too hard. It took me ages. Ouch, my leg hurts." Thomas shook his hands in the air as his body tensed with the pain. Rob picked him up again,
"Let's get you some breakfast and we'll see how you are after that." Rob eyed the painful-looking, blue bump on Thomas's leg, "You are a brave little boy, Thomas. You'll feel better once you've had some breakfast."
"Can I have chocolate cereal as I'm hurt?"
"All right but don't tell Mummy."

Rose appeared in the kitchen looking puffy and tired. Rob felt sorry for her as well,

"Did you get any sleep?"

"Not much, I think it's her ears. Once I've had a coffee and woken up, I'll take her to the surgery. Hopefully, they'll have something for her. She's just gone to sleep now which is typical as I have to get going." Rob handed Rose a mug and kissed her gently on the forehead,

"I would take her for you but Jan's in this morning. We need to do some important admin together so I can't really not be here. We've got to squeeze it all into a couple of hours as she's got to go by eleven. She has a dental appointment so maybe I can help you then, if you like? Ed's done a bunk after giving me that stupid letter. Actually, hopefully, by Monday, Evie will be better and you'll finally be able to meet Mr Chapman."

Rose nodded as she shuffled towards the sink. Rob caught Rose by surprise,

"You could say something and sound a bit more enthusiastic. I've been working my arse off to plan this and sort things out as well as working but you just seem so uninterested sometimes."

"For God's sake, Rob, I'm knackered...and, no, right now, I couldn't give a shit about the house or plans or any of that crap. I am sick and tired of broken sleep. It's all right for you sleeping on the sofa in peace!"

"What? Peaceful, on a crappy sofa? Yeah, it's great for me, just great."

"Go away, Rob, you're getting on my nerves."

"Mummy," it was Anna. She looked worried at the sight of her parents arguing and Thomas was staring at them too, his spoon poised, mid-air. Rob and Rose had forgotten the children were in the room. Rose just looked at Anna then at Rob,

"Daddy will finish giving you breakfast, won't you?"
Rose glanced at Rob, "I'm going to have a shower."

Rob plonked a plate of buttered toast down in front of
Anna and she peered over it asking,
"Why are Mummy and you cross?"
"We're just tired, Anna, just very tired."
"I don't understand. You and Mummy just got up."

FIFTEEN

Surprisingly, the doctor saw Evie quickly. She had been
marked down as an emergency. Rose struggled with
sore ears being classified as one but was not going to
argue.

She was so tired; she was barely able to function. The
doctor did not consider this. He proceeded to read aloud
something on his computer screen. She heard someone
speak but he could have been saying anything. He must
have been reading random information, from his screen,
about Evie. He looked expectantly at Rose before
saying slowly and sarcastically,
"This is Evie, yes? And she has sore ears, you say, yes?"
"Um… yes. She's been up most of the night with it."
"Well, glad we're talking about the same child, your
child, Evie Mary Clarke, yes? The one in your arms
here, yes?"
"Yes," mumbled Rose, wanting to smack him in his
patronising mouth.
 "Let's have a look then." The doctor reached into a
black, plastic case for an otoscope. "Yep, ear infection."

He quickly printed a prescription for Evie and handed it to Rose, without any eye contact, as he returned to face his computer. Rose assumed this meant the consultation was over and she was dismissed.

Evie fell asleep on the way home. Rose managed to carry her from the car to her cot without waking her, something that was not possible when Evie was well. Rose decided to return to bed herself and fell into a deep sleep. Unbeknown to her, shortly afterwards, Rob popped his head round the bedroom door. Jan had gone. Rob had fancied some time with Rose. Realising she was asleep, he had left to return to the hut. *Typical*, thought Rob as he strode back towards it. He was about to open the door when he decided to go for a stroll, around the garden, to clear his head. He still felt unsettled and frustrated. He knew it was not Rose's fault but she never seemed able to make time for him. He was growing tired of feeling neglected. He was not getting much in return for all his hard work.

He went right to the bottom of the garden. He did not like to admit it but he was really hoping that Nicky would be there, especially with Ed being away. Rob hung around for a bit, pretending to check the plants, which, in reality, held little interest for him,
"Hello! Is that you, Rob?" Nicky appeared from behind a bush.
Has she been waiting for me too?
"I'm glad it's you. As you know, Ed isn't back until this evening, if not tomorrow. I need to move a bench. It's not terribly heavy but I'm not sure I can drag it on my own. I don't want to damage it, or myself! Any chance of a hand?"
"Of course!" Rob literally jumped onto Nicky's land.

"I want it moved from here to just outside the back door. If we get some nice, bright, winter days, I can drink my coffee outside, in my puffa coat, of course, without the tree blocking any sun." She smiled, "I do love fresh air so try to be outside as much as I can. What about you?"

"Yes, fresh air." Rob was not really listening. He was mesmerised by her full, pink lips. The way they moved as she spoke. Rob and Nicky lifted the heavy bench. She was surprisingly strong. Even so, she would have had trouble dragging it on her own.

"Have you time for a coffee, again? It's milk, no sugar, right?"

"Yes please, I'm not really in the mood for work today and it's a bit grim at home, to be honest. Evie is terrorising us. I notice you don't seem to have any children," he smiled.

"No." Nicky, brightly and abruptly, changed the subject, "Let me get the coffee. You try out the bench and I'll be back in a sec." She returned promptly with two mugs of steaming coffee, and two chocolate biscuits,

"Just the coffee for me, thank you," said Rob.

"Oh, go on, don't be so boring, you look like you have space for a biscuit without it showing on that lovely, taut physique!"

Rob did as he was told and accepted the biscuit. The sun shone down on them. It felt so warm in contrast to the usual damp, cold, autumn weather. Nicky sighed towards the sun,

"To elaborate, on my response to your earlier question, about having children. Ed and I tried a while back but it wasn't meant to be. I miscarried one quite late and then had a stillbirth. After that, we didn't try any more, too traumatic. I decided to accept that children weren't part of the plan for me. Unfortunately, poor Ed took it so badly and found it really hard to move on. In a way, my job helped me. I love nursing. Ed, well... like I said, he didn't have that. I suppose I might not enjoy my job so much if I had children to juggle too, or I might have taken time off to look after them and found it really hard to get back into work. What I'm trying to say is I feel lucky, even without children."

"I'm sorry to hear you went through so much. I do know what you mean about taking time off to have children, though. I think Rose gets frustrated at home all the time, and not working. Sometimes, I just don't understand you women. I mean, Rose wanted to be a full-time mother and now says she's frustrated. She's going to start a business of her own..." Rob tailed off wondering whether he had said too much. He felt a pang of disloyalty to Rose.

Nicky did not comment on Rose. She wriggled her body a little, in an affected way, before saying,
"You seem like a nice guy. I must mention it again. I hope Ed hasn't upset you too much. He's always been a bit impulsive and often blows up over tiny things but he's OK. Anyway, what I really want to say is that I hope the letter he wrote won't 'tar me with the same brush' for want of a better phrase." She forced a laugh.
"Don't worry. I can see you're separate people. Actually, maybe, I ought to head back and do some work."
"OK, I'm going to do some ironing while watching day time TV." Nicky collected up the mugs, "thank you," she said sincerely.
"For what?" asked Rob. She had already thanked him for moving the bench.
"For spending time with me. It can be lonely here, on my own all the time." Rob felt awkward and before he could stop himself, said,

"I'm sure we can have coffee again soon." They held each other's gaze. Unsettling, unavoidable feelings hung in the air around them.

"Yes, I'd like that," said Nicky, "I'd like that very much."

Rob made his way back to the hut, quickly. It felt like an oasis, his space. As he sat at his desk, his heart raced, not just from the brisk walk but also from something deep inside; a new, heady arousal. He was aware he fancied Nicky. He was aware of how wrong it would be to act upon this. He vowed to make things right again with Rose.

There was a knock on the door. Rose appeared, with Evie on her hip. Both looked much happier,

"Hi Rob and hello Daddy!" Rose planted a kiss on his lips and placed a hot mug on his desk, "you smell of outdoors and you've got a twig in your hair." She gently eased it out as she laughed. "What have you been up to? Surely not gardening? Sorry about what I said earlier, at breakfast. I've just managed a power nap. I feel much better. Evie is too. The antibiotics kicked in fast. I've just given her another dose of Calpol."

"I'm sorry too. I didn't mean to be so selfish. It's just we never seem to get much time together." He felt a pang of love, or was it guilt, in his stomach as he focused on Rose's intense, trusting eyes. Her skin was soft and flawless, even with little sleep. At that moment, he remembered why he loved her so much, his intelligent, capable, willing and loving Rose. He kissed her firmly on the lips. Rose looked happy,

"Are you still able to see the coffee shop this afternoon? The agent is free at two." Rob had totally forgotten about this,

"Yes, yes two should be fine." Rob felt like the changes around him were gaining momentum, with or without him.

As it turned out, he really liked the premises. She was relieved the he did not point out anything negative. She had promptly gone ahead and secured a year's lease. He, too proud to give anything away, was secretly impressed with her ideas and the quick, efficient way she was executing it all. She made it look easy. Silently, he still felt like he had gone from being totally in control of his life, with everything nicely in its place, including Rose, it all suiting him, to being whipped up by this change. He felt like an uprooted tree. Even so, he knew he did not have the right to stop her. He would have to get over it.

SIXTEEN

While Thomas and Anna sat in the car, Rose rang her mother's doorbell. Rose handed Evie to Cathy, complete with backpack. She looked concerned,

"Oh, you look tired, Rose. Mind you don't overdo it swimming. Try not to underestimate the strain of what you are trying to achieve at the moment. Perhaps you'd be better off having a nap in the car while Thomas and Anna have their lessons?"

"Stop worrying about me, Mum," Rose laughed, feeling comforted by her mother's concern yet thinking how bizarre it would be to let go enough to sleep while the children were in the pool, even if they were supervised by a teacher. "I have got a lot on my mind but I'm a big girl. I'll cope! Evie is sleeping much better now. She slept through last night. It was bliss. That's already made a massive difference to how I feel." Cathy confirmed,

"You'll be back for Evie at 'six-thirtyish' yes?"

"Yes, thank you, Mum!" Rose walked away then looked back and waved at her mother and Evie.

At the pool, Anna and Thomas sat on the bench waiting for their lessons to start. Rose was still in the changing room. She favoured the privacy of a cubicle. She never felt comfortable stripping off in front of strangers. As she stepped into her swimsuit, she promised herself a new one. The fabric was thin from the chlorine and the Lycra no longer offered her the support she felt she needed. This made her feel self-conscious. She reminded herself that the hardest bit would be walking over to the pool edge. Once plunged into the water, she would be safe from any scrutiny, her modesty covered.

To her relief, there was only one other person in the half of the pool not being used for lessons. The man was a very fast swimmer. He punched his way, from one end to the other, like a searchlight. He swam like a preprogrammed machine. There was no sign of fatigue. She made a mental note to stay well away from his swimming zone. She did not want to get knocked by a stray leg. She, after a few lengths of front crawl, had to admit she was too tired to swim any more. The man-machine was still going. She tried not to stare at him as he breathed, like a whale coming up for air, whooshing and puffing.

She climbed into the hot, bubbling Jacuzzi, next to the pool, and enjoyed the soothing jets as they temporarily massaged away her busy mind. She closed her eyes. She was aware of someone climbing in with her. She did not bother to open her eyes. The noise from the motor, and from the teacher instructing the children, along with their squeals, made conversation virtually impossible anyway. She was drifting off when a familiar voice addressed her,
"I think we've met before. Yes, I know, in the supermarket the other day."

Rose knew, before she even looked at the face, who it belonged to. The voice made her tingle. How she wished she had bought a new swimsuit, re-shaved her legs and bothered to put some polish on her rough toenails. She opened her eyes. Will looked straight at her. She felt exposed. It was like she had been caught naked, under an unforgiving light. Luckily, the bubbles came up to her chin, affording her the coverage she felt that she needed. *Let's just hope he gets out before me.*

Knowing she could not pretend she had never seen him before, as it was obvious who he was, she acknowledged him. There would be no hiding. Trying not to stumble over her words, she said, as nonchalantly as she could, "Oh, yes, I remember. I was a bit harassed. It can be hard shopping with children. I'm just enjoying a quiet few minutes to myself while they have their swimming lessons. Do you have children?"
"No,' he smiled, obviously with no intention of elaborating on that. She noted his broad chest and well-defined muscles, as he had not fully immersed himself in the water. *He must go to the gym or have a job that involves physical work, to look like that*, she thought. However, she noticed his hands looked soft. His nails were well manicured, not just clipped out of necessity.

For goodness sake, get a grip of yourself; you're a married mother of three in an old, saggy swimsuit. He finds you amusing. That's all. What she did not know was that he was finding the whole situation amusing, not just her bashfulness. She had no idea that her husband had hired him as their project manager. Will thought it would be funny when they all met up, soon. He wondered if she would let on that she already knew him. He would only let on if she did. Rob kept referring to him as Mr Chapman. That was funny too.

Will knew Rob had not remembered his name. However, once Will had worked out who everyone was, he had purposely not told Rob his name again. Silly? Yes but all just harmless fun, as far as Will was concerned. It would all be worth it just to see Rose's face, when she twigged.

She looked away from Will, hoping her children would be finished soon. She no longer felt relaxed. She wanted to get out, to return to the safety of her changing-cubicle. The problem she had was how to leave this big bath without giving him full-view of her behind. *Maybe*, she thought, *he is a gentleman and will not look.* She doubted that. Would not most men sneak a look?

Will spoke,
"Looks like your kids have finished their lessons," he beckoned towards the pool. The children were hurrying towards Rose,
"Please walk," she called over to them making sure the water stayed around her shoulders, like a modesty shawl. They scrambled into the Jacuzzi. To Rose's relief, Will stood up, way above the water level, the vision of a perfect man. It took all of Rose's willpower not to gasp. The children grabbed back her attention,
"Can we get sweets, as we swam so well, pleeeeease?" Rose turned to them and smiled,
"Um, yes, OK, but we must get out now. If you get changed as quickly as you can, you can earn them."
"Ok!" they smiled and stood straight up, "Let's go, Mummy!" Will had disappeared, almost like she had dreamed his presence. The swimming teacher was busy gathering up the floats. Rose confidently got out. Anna and Thomas, having been reminded they were not allowed to run, waddled really quickly towards the changing rooms, like penguins. Rose knew they would

squeeze into a cubicle together. They liked to hide. She could hear them giggling at the end of the changing room. She kept reminding them, through the divider, to be good and to hurry up. They would only get sweets if she did not have to tell them off.

She and Will, in their respective male and female changing rooms, removed their wet swimwear and revealed naked bodies to themselves. They were unaware of facing each other. Just a prefabricated wall separated them. They were also unaware that each was trying to make sense of what had just happened, of the unplanned, uncontrollable, feelings that had been aroused in them both.

Cathy answered the door with Evie. Cathy commented on how much better Rose looked. She was grateful her mother could not read her mind.
"You may as well come in as I've cooked dinner for the children, only fish fingers, mind you, but it'll fill them up. You and Rob ought to get a takeaway tonight and then you won't have any cooking to do. I'd offer to babysit but I'm going round to Moira's house, down the road. It's our monthly takeaway and champagne night, chance for a good chat with the girls. David is going to fix the dripping taps in the kitchen, bathroom and outside. They all decided to start dripping at the same time. Anyway, with any luck, it might reduce my water bill," she laughed.

Back home, Rose persuaded Rob to get a takeaway. They shared a bottle of wine and watched a film. They got to bed at a reasonable time,
"You use the bathroom first, Rose." She did. Rob was hopeful for tonight. He went outside to make sure the hut was locked up properly and checked the children.

They were asleep. When he returned to the bedroom, he found Rose fast asleep too. He toyed with the idea of waking her up. He longed to be close to her. The decision was made for him. Almost on cue, Evie started crying and calling for Mummy. Rose woke up,
"I'll go," she seemed unconcerned with Rob's presence. She wriggled her naked body into her pyjamas and attended to Evie. Rose knew she was rewarding Evie's bad behaviour by seeing her but felt powerless to stop it. Rob, abandoned once again, lent back against the headboard. He exhaled loudly.

Rose cuddled and comforted Evie. Rose remained optimistic that it would not be long before Evie grasped the concept of sleep for good. Rose willed it to be soon. She had heard the horror stories at the school gate, tales about children never sleeping and disturbing their parents, during the night, up to the age of ten, and beyond. Some of these storytellers seemed to relish passing on little nuggets of awful news. "Finished the marriage" some would say, "drove me to take antidepressants, don't think I'll ever come off them thanks to her" while pointing at an angelic-looking child. It was time to make a stand against Evie's demanding behaviour. She was taking over, clearly waking up at the wrong times. It was time for Rose to regain control.

SEVENTEEN

Rose was grateful to her mother for coming round early, to look after the children. Rose was to finally meet Mr. Chapman. She had promised Rob she would be there. This introduction was to be sandwiched between two meetings, she had lined up, with builders, who were interested in converting the coffee shop into exactly what she imagined. She felt both excited and edgy about it all.

Temporarily freed from her parenting responsibilities, she was able to spend longer in the shower. She conditioned her hair and shaved her legs. She applied her make-up and blow-dried her hair. She looked fresh and professional. She felt determined as she put on her flattering, black, wrap-around dress with long sleeves. It hid all the bits she did not like which she had decided she needed to. High-heeled, black, court shoes, which she had invested in pre-children, still looked amazing on her. She had missed dressing up for work, yet anyone who had ever worked with her knew that she was no doll. She went far deeper than a good figure in smart clothing. Already, her guilt about leaving the children was starting to creep in. She continued to remind herself of her entitlement, as should be the case with every parent, to a life, separate from the home and family. Guilt, in these circumstances, was wasted energy. If allowed to spread, it could eclipse her plans. She was exercising her choice. She had chosen to stay at home full-time, and, now she would work too.

She was admiring herself in the mirror. Rob came into the bedroom,
"Wow, you look amazing. Rose is back and she means business," he joked, "You look like you're in full, negotiating mode. By the way, I have to say that is still my favourite dress. You really do look gorgeous, Mrs Clarke. I wish we were going off together for the day, not seeing our project manager. Are you sure you'll be OK on your own with the builders, for your meeting?"
Rose gave him a withering look,
"Don't try and put me off. You know, full-well, I can hold my own."
"I'm joking. Go for it."

The meeting with the first builder, Mick Jones, went so well that she made up her mind to use him. She still met with the other one, as arranged, out of courtesy. Mick seemed to understand what she wanted. She was satisfied with his air of efficiency and eagerness to respect and accommodate what she said. He would send her a quote, by the end of the week, he promised. The meeting with him had been so thorough, and easy, that she had lost track of time. She checked her mobile in the car, before driving home. She read a message from Rob saying Mr Chapman would be arriving in ten minutes time and where was she? That was fifteen minutes ago. *Damn*, she thought to herself, *Rob is not going to be happy*.

She sensed his irritation, at her tardiness, once she entered the hut. She mumbled an apology. In fact, it turned out to be a blessing that Rob was busy silently fuming, over her supposed lack of respect for his time, and his baby, the house project, because it took all of Rose's might not to audibly gasp when she saw Mr. Chapman.

"This is Rose, my wife; Rose, Mr Chapman." As Rob introduced them, she saw mischief in Will's eyes. Rose offered her hand,
"How do you do." Will broke the silence that had engulfed them before it became awkward, "please, no more Mr Chapman, call me Will, everyone else does." He winked at Rose when Rob was not looking. Neither Will nor Rose let on to Rob that they had met before. She needed to collect herself, after this surprise, do something. She was relieved to see no sign of any cups,
"Would you like coffee?" directed at Will.
"Yes, please,"
"And you, Rob?" He looked fleetingly bewildered. He was eager to get on with the meeting but realised that if Will wanted coffee then he needed to politely agree, and not rush things. Will, clearly, was not bothered by her lateness and Rob, for some reason, suddenly wondered if Will fancied his wife. Rob had noticed the look of appreciation, on Will's face, when she arrived.

She returned, armed with coffee and a plate of biscuits. She thought about saying something, to Will, like haven't we met before, but did not. Instead, as she handed out the coffee, she explained why she was so late,

"I really must apologise again for being late. I had a meeting with a builder." Having got their attention, she continued, "for my business, not this place. This is our home and Rob's place of work... very much his baby, really. I'll just be picking the wallpaper and soft furnishings," she laughed, trying to lighten the atmosphere. Although Will smiled, neither man looked that interested. Certainly, their reaction was no match for the excitement she felt about her day so far. They all turned to the screen. Rob had uploaded the home and office plans.

She could tell he was still annoyed with her. He covered it up well. He said, cheerfully,
"I'm glad you two have finally met. Hard to believe, but, getting all of us together, at the same time, has proved very difficult indeed. Anyway, let me grab a pen and I'll give you a quick overview of the bits I've changed since you last saw them." As Rob turned his back on them, Will winked, again, at Rose. She felt uncomfortable. She should feel furious that he was doing this behind her husband's back, but she did not. Instead, she felt like a young girl again, alive and carefree. Her heart skipped before the guilt of liking someone, other than her husband, took prominence.

Will was their project manager and probably a playboy. No obvious sign of a partner, at his age, for someone so seemingly eligible, to Rose, usually indicated that. She reminded herself that although things were awkward, at the moment, marriage was to be worked at. She loved Rob and would not do anything to sabotage the family they had created together. They had children together. In her book, that meant you fought hard to make it work. She dismissed any feelings she had for Will as just those; feelings. They would pass as quickly as they appeared. She would be professional, enjoy the meeting and ignore any more winks.

Rob had laid out the paper plans. He had made a miniature model of how their finished home would look. She was impressed. Suddenly, it all seemed real. She felt rueful that this was the first time she had seen all this. Rob was always trying to corner her, to have a look, but she had never found time to.

"Wow!" exclaimed Will, "I love the kitchen, airy, double aspect, well thought through. The full length glass doors... just amazing." Rob looked pleased as he explained,

"The plans have been accepted subject to one little window being shifted along a bit on the side of the office building. Pointing to the outdoor staircase to the office, Rob confirmed, "That was Rose's idea." He looked proud of her, his earlier irritation having evaporated. 'I think we can start as soon as the council rubber stamps it, which should be soon."

"Yes," replied Will, "do you have anyone in mind for the kitchen?"

"Well, no, not yet." Rob and Rose said in unison, looking at one another.

"OK," said Will, "Why don't you come and see what I've done with mine. A reasonable, local company designed and fitted it. It's everything I imagined it would be. This is my address. He handed Rose a business card, "Come by, any time, for a look. If you like it then we'll take it from there."

Rose found Will professional. He knew what he was talking about. Like Rob, she had every confidence in him overseeing the project. It was encouraging to know that he was a chartered surveyor too. Rob smiled a thank you towards Will,

"There's just one thing that has been bothering us. You should know about it. Our neighbour, at the bottom of the garden, Ed, yes Ed, is, shall we say, somewhat prickly. I have mentioned him before. I suppose no one likes change but he can be a bit, well, odd really, perhaps even aggressive, in his approach. He wrote this. Remember you said you'd visit him with me. I, actually, tried to see him, on my own, which probably wasn't the wisest move. Luckily, he was out. It might be better if you see him alone, you know, he might be less prickly with you. Rob handed Will a letter, "I know it's ridiculous but I just want you to know what Ed's like. I've spoken to Nicky, his wife, about it and she has agreed to talk to him, so he probably won't push it."

Having looked at the letter, Will said,
"In my opinion, it's curt and presumptuous. Perhaps he's a freeloader, you know, everyone owes him something or perhaps he's mad. Either way, his request is entirely without grounding. I'd ignore it. If he persists, we'll have to bang out the standard 'sorry we can't help you' response, and, I'd be happy to use my letterhead for that." He smiled confidently, "I'd like to have a more thorough look at the office plans, if I may?"

As Rob and Will discussed the layout of the offices, Rose started to daydream about her new kitchen. Soon, she found herself listening to Will's voice. It sent a tingle through her body. Rob noticed her lack of concentration and commented to Will that Rose was tired at the moment. She tuned back in as Rob was explaining their lack of luck in finding a good cleaner. They wanted a reliable, local person, not a firm where you never really knew who was going to turn up,
"People here seem very guarded about their contacts but particularly, we've noticed, with cleaners, so different to

London. Of course that's probably because good cleaners, there, are two-a-penny. Down here... different story." Will looked amused,

"Well, you've been asking the wrong people. Rarely do I guard my contacts, otherwise I'd probably never gain any new ones. I have an excellent cleaner; Josie. In fact, she's cleaning mine and my mother's place this morning. I shall ask her to call you, if she wants the hours. That is if it's OK with you. I would rather mention it to her first than just hand out her number. She'll definitely call you if she's interested. She is very reliable. I'm sure she'll call as I happen to know that another family she cleans for are relocating to Dubai, at the end of the month, so I would imagine she'd be delighted to take you on." Rose had to confirm what she had just heard,

"You live with your mum?" She blurted this out, regretting it straight away. He looked surprised, then amused, by her sudden question. She had pictured him in a bachelor penthouse, not taking his relationships with women very seriously, waiting for the woman of his dreams, someone like her, to come along. She realised how ridiculous and fantastical this was.

"My mother lives in a self-contained annexe, within the grounds of my house. She has a footpath with a little gate, straight onto the pavement, outside. We are, actually, able to come and go without each other noticing, most of the time. Like I said, you're welcome to come and have a look at any time. I'm proud of my property. I oversaw all the renovations. And, for the record, before you jump to conclusions, I'm hardly what you might call a 'mummy's boy'." She saw amusement in his eyes. He was enjoying her embarrassment, "Well, I must be off. Lovely to meet you, Rose, ... Rob." They shook hands. Will confirmed, "I have my copy of the plans so I'll have a chat with the builders and we'll take it from there. Any problems or questions, do call me."

They watched Will pull away in his car. Rob said to Rose,
"God, Rose, talk about putting the poor man on the spot, about his mother. Did you have to say that? He's probably got some sad story about why he's single, or he might have planned it all that way. It may not be what you or I would want but each to their own. There you were, rubbing it in!" Rob laughed, "We could go through many possible scenarios, or he may, simply, want to live with his mum." He smiled sarcastically, "Who knows? And, who cares?"
"Trust me, Rob, he's a playboy. They usually end up living with their mum, or on their own."
"How can you be sure?"
"Women know these things. Look, I've got to go. I'm meant to be meeting another builder in fifteen minutes. Too late to cancel now." She grabbed her bag, kissed Rob and left in a puff of perfume and femininity. Rob wondered, again, how life had become one big rush. He was sure the car wheels had spun as she sped off. Any time they might have, as a couple, had definitely disintegrated or been put on what felt like permanent hold. Rob made himself a cup of tea, but, instead of taking it to the hut, decided to walk around the garden sipping it. It would be lovely to bump into Nicky.

Across town, Will sat at his desk, overlooking his neat, secluded garden. The expensive company that turned up regularly, to apply the magic spray, kept the lawn weed-free. His mother efficiently tended to the roses. Will loved to admire the view, yet, had no desire to garden.

He had added his glass office at the same time as the annexe. Inside the office, it felt like being outdoors. Light sensitive glass ensured it never got too hot. Following his depression, he had promised himself that he would never sit in the dark again, both literally and metaphorically. He sat, often, with his eyes closed, his face turned towards the potent sun. Sometimes, it would duck behind a cloud, reminding him that he could never completely control anything, neither should he try to.

He was familiarising himself with the Clarkes' plans. *Rose*, he thought again, *what a coincidence, a small world*. The situation was an awkward one. Obviously, he fancied her but now things could get complicated. He had a professional level of loyalty to Rob, who had hired him, and, really, that loyalty applied to Rose as well. Will could not sabotage the deal. This building project was going to be a profitable one. He would enjoy it, and take pride in it.

He thought he had sensed tension between Rob and Rose. Will had picked up on a particularly unsettled vibe from Rose so, perhaps, she would be up for some fun. Could there be much passion left in the marriage, after all those years, and kids? He knew most people stayed together for the children. It was all over the papers. One thing bothered him, though. He had never considered himself as a blatant home-breaker, despite the long list of women he had conquered. That is what he would be, if he went after Rose. For now, he would have to make do with looking at her pretty face and body, while he came up with a plan.

He liked Rob. He was easy to get on with, and, Will loved the design, and ideas, Rob had come up with. It really was a shame that Will felt the way he did about

Rose. She stirred something in him that he had not felt since leaving Dubai, and his on-off relationship with Luisa. Perhaps, he wondered, he was starting to yearn for a stable relationship, or, maybe, he was just missing the comfort of Luisa. A quick affair with Rose would be heavenly. Even so, he reminded himself that he did not want to gain a name here for running off with other men's wives.

As he had nothing pressing workwise, he planned to mooch around the gift shop in town, for his mother. Christmas was looming and he hated a last minute rush. He wanted to take time choosing her gift. She was his closest friend. Sometimes, he did wonder about finding a soulmate, someone he could trust as much as his mother, and someone with whom he could enjoy an exclusive, intimate relationship. Recently, he had even caught himself wondering what it would be like to be one of the men he often did projects for, with a wife, whom they remained exclusively loyal to, and children, mirror images of themselves, and to have that cosy familiar feeling of spending most evenings in with each other. Will did not think this was his destiny. The closest he had come to being this exclusively involved with someone, since Stella had dumped him, was Luisa, in Dubai, and she did not want to get married and have children. She had made that quite clear.

He put the Clarkes' plans away and, before switching his computer off, clicked on the email icon,
"Well, think of the devil!" Will said out loud to himself. A message from Luisa Ronson was waiting in his inbox. He clicked on it,

'Hi Will,

How are you, my old friend (with the best benefits)?! Hope the rain and the cold, and the grey skies, back in the UK aren't getting to you? I've been sunning myself by the pool...actually, if you fancy a few days in the sun over Christmas, you're welcome to come and stay, but if you prefer the cold and wet, I understand! Actually, if you don't come, perhaps you'd meet up with me in January? I'm booked into the Mandarin Oriental and plan to meet my sister for some serious sale shopping!!!

Let me know what you think.

Love always,

Luisa xx'

There was a knock at the door. Will's mother, Joan, popped her head round the door. She was wearing her familiar uniform of fitted black trousers, black, suede, wedge, court shoes and a long sleeved, black, cotton tee-shirt. Her clothes always looked new. Her white-grey hair was cropped short. On most women, of her age, with this haircut, the word harsh would come to mind, but, on her, it looked sophisticated. It enhanced her elfin features. Tortoise shell, framed glasses, red lipstick and a pink, chunky, beaded necklace completed a style that few women could carry off,

"Sorry to disturb you. May I pinch a little milk?" She did not see the point in buying any for one cup of tea as she was off to Wales today to visit Lyn, her sister.

"Yes, of course, help yourself. I'm just reading my email. One from Luisa here. Anyway, I'll talk to you later." Will returned to his email thinking she had gone. In fact, Joan was still hovering in the doorway,

"Why don't you invite Luisa, she is the one from Dubai isn't she, to stay here?"

Will knew his mother was being nosey. It was almost as if she sensed that he might be tiring of his bachelor lifestyle,

"Don't poke your nose in! Thank you for your suggestion, mother, but I think I can run my own life so take your milk and please go away!"

Joan smiled warmly at her son. She reminded him that she was off in an hour and aimed to be back in a few days. Will turned around to look at his mother,

"I'll lift your case into the car for you."

"Thank you, darling, but I've already packed the car. Just remember to feed my cat!"

"Of course I will! Maud will be fine and remember to give Aunty Lyn a kiss from me and don't you two go drinking too much red wine. Here, take this." Will extracted a large note from his buttery-leather wallet, "buy yourselves a decent bottle then you won't get a hangover."

"Oh Will, you don't have to give me money, heavens!" She hid her hands behind her back,

"But, I want you to take it, you proud, old bat!"

"I should wash your mouth out; thank you."

Will got up, hugged and kissed his mother's velvet cheek and wished her a safe trip, before staging a mock 'get out of my office' gesture by holding his hand dismissively in the air. As Joan turned to leave, she waved the note in the air above her head,

"I shall tell Lyn that you are encouraging us to drink! By the way, don't let Luisa slip through your fingers."

EIGHTEEN

An enthusiastic eruption from Rob broke into the early morning lethargy,
"Yes and yes and yes! All permission has been granted."
Rob laid the letter out on the surface in front of him.
Rose, Anna, Thomas and Evie were startled by Rob's sudden outburst. Anna and Thomas sat at the breakfast table looking at their father with their spoons poised mid-air. "The council have 'OKed' everything! Looks like the building will be starting early next year, as planned." Rob kissed Rose firmly on the lips, "not long now, Mrs Clarke, and we shall have our dream home. Yes!" Rob said this again in the way some people might once their winning football team had scored another goal. Thomas got up from the table and jumped up and down. Evie let out such an enthusiastic whoop-of-joy that her highchair looked like it might topple over.

"That's fantastic news," said Rose, feeling jubilant that the work would soon be under way. Rob would start to get results from his hard work. She still saw it as being his project, even though he always referred to it as theirs,

"I'll try to finalise a start date with Will and the builders today," he said. She was not terribly bothered when they started, but, sooner, rather than later, was preferable,

"Sounds good to me," she said, getting up from the table to bin most of Evie's porridge, and stack the bowl and spoon in the dishwasher. Rob continued,

"Can you look at Will's kitchen tomorrow morning? We can go together. It's just, some kitchens can take months to come, once they're ordered, and it would be helpful to know what we want."

"Yep, I can go with you tomorrow, no problem. The kitchen is one of the most exciting bits for me. I'll see if I can get someone to watch Evie, for a couple of hours, otherwise, we'll have to take her with us, which won't be ideal, as Will lives in a child-free zone." Rose laughed, "I'll have to strap her firmly into her buggy, if it comes to that."

Rob was not listening. He was sipping coffee while looking at an article, in the newspaper, on the surface in front of him. She could not be bothered to repeat herself. Instead, she quickly sifted through the remaining post, next to him. She recognised his mother's handwriting on one of the envelopes. This probably meant that her mother-in-law would be coming for Christmas which was fine. Liz was an easy house guest. Often, Rose almost forgot she was there. Ironically, Liz often told Rose that she hoped she was not getting in the way.

"Open this, please, Rob. I know the writing. It's from your mother. Bet she's coming for Christmas." The rest of the post was fusty-looking bills. The envelopes looked like they had travelled far. Rose tapped the pile of letters and bills on the work surface, a couple of times, to create a tidy pile, to deal with later, just as Jan breezed in, engulfed in expensive-smelling perfume. Her high-heels clicked loudly on the tiles. Rose still felt groggy. It seemed too early to be so glamorous and alert,

"Hi everyone! Beautiful day isn't it! Frosty and sunny! Wonderful! OK if I grab a coffee? Then, I'll be out of your way, off to the hut. Looks like you two need to rush!" Jan looked over at Anna and Thomas who were mesmerised by this catwalk figure in their kitchen, eyes wide, fluffy dressing gowns pulled up under their chins against the cold air that had gushed in when the front door was opened. Rose gestured to the kettle,

"Of course, help yourself! Gosh, you're right. Look at the time! Hurry up Anna and Thomas. Go and put on your uniforms. We are in a rush now. Breakfast seems to have taken too long today. Thomas, your hair will need wetting down, at the back." She turned to Jan, "That's lovely perfume." It was permeating the room, replacing the smell of food and waking-up. Rose welcomed the intrusion of it. Jan looked delighted, her eyes shined,

"It's one of the newer *Chanel* ones! One of my few extravagances!" Rob, still not listening, cut in,

"Rose, I've just had a message back from Will. Tomorrow morning is fine to have a look at his kitchen, so, I said straight after the school run, if that's OK?"

"Yes, that's fine. What did your mother say, in the letter?" Rob looked a little bit sheepish,

"She's written to confirm she's coming for Christmas. I did invite her, over the phone, last week but she always prefers to write, with her answer."

"Really? You didn't think to mention it to me first?" Rose replied tersely, surprised at herself.

"Well, she's always welcome isn't she? She is my mother." Rob shot her a glance. Jan, sensing the tension, made her excuses and clicked away, towards the hut, to start work, with a mug of coffee in her hand, held up so high it looked affected, like she was carrying something valuable.

Rob leant towards Rose,

"Do you have to do that in front of Jan?"

"Do what? You should have asked me first. After all, I'm the one who makes up the room for her, cleans, shops, cooks. I don't mind. It's just nice to be considered."

"For God's sake, Rose, she nearly always comes here for Christmas. It's no big deal. You, yourself, always comment on what an easy guest she is."

"That's not the point here, Rob, and you know it." Evie started crying so Rose picked her up. Rob looked beaten but was not prepared to back down,

"Look, Rose, I don't want to argue, OK? Perhaps you're taking on too much with this business. I mean, look at Evie, she's crying and Anna and Thomas aren't even ready for school. That's your job. How will you cope, with more to do?" Rose hissed at Rob determined not to rise to the bait,

"Quite fine, thank you, Rob." She looked at him defiantly before adding, "Just remember, I do appreciate being asked before you invite guests to stay here, particularly now that I shall be working, just like you, and still doing the bulk of the housework. Unless..." she paused, "unless, you want to prepare the room, the sheets, the extra food, and so on, at the last minute, on your own." He repeated,

"Rose, she's my mother and you've never minded before." He looked hurt. Rose started to feel guilty,

"Look, Rob, I'm sorry, OK? Your mother's always welcome here; you know that. I would just appreciate being asked first. I want you to communicate with me."

"OK, no problem..." He added, "And you know, Rose, I really do want you to do this business. I just don't want you to over do it. I really didn't think my mother staying would be a big deal. I can cancel her if you prefer."

"No, don't. I didn't mean anything, just forget it." Rob kissed her forehead,

"I'd better go. It doesn't look good, in front of Jan, for the boss to be idly chatting." He started towards the back door, "By the way, I forgot to tell you, Nicky's hurt her wrist. She tripped over something, in the garden, I think. I can't remember exactly. I only spoke to her briefly. I wouldn't put it past Ed to have pushed her but that's just me being nasty. I don't trust him. It's not broken but she's off work for a week, at least. It could take six weeks to heal completely. Anyway, she said the good thing is that Ed has offered to write all the Christmas cards and is really looking after her well, even cooking. I wonder if he'll send us a card."

Coincidentally, despite it being late November, a Christmas card had been delivered, from Ed and Nicky, on Rose's return from the school run. His writing was quite a scrawl. She noted that he had written love, in the card. She wondered if he actually meant it, or had just written it, routinely, as the thing to put in cards. Perhaps Nicky had stood over him, telling him what to put. Rose put the card on the windowsill, where she expected to have a whole row of them soon.

The following day, when Rose's alarm woke her up, she found Rob lying rigid, next to her, his head firmly pressed into the pillow. This was unusual because, whereas Rose relied on an alarm, Rob always woke up naturally, and earlier than her. He would sit bolt upright, reading, or would go downstairs, before she was even aware it was morning. For a second, she wondered whether he was breathing. She nudged him,

"Are you OK? You're normally up by now." She put her hand on his shoulder, expecting him to turn over and smile. He did not,

"Not really, it's my tooth. It hurts so much. He put the palm of his hand to his cheek. I've been awake all night. I hope I didn't disturb you?"

"No, you didn't. I slept really well. Sorry," she paused, "I'm not trying to rub it in. Which tooth is it? Is it really bad?"

"Yes, I think it might be the same one, where I had the abscess, years ago, so bloody annoying, and, so damn painful." He turned towards her. She saw a red patch on his cheek, as he took his hand away. It looked like he had been slapped. She grimaced at it,

"Have you taken anything?"

"Ibuprofen but it's not touching it."

"Shall I ring the dentist?"

"I've done that. I got up earlier, left a message on their machine. You were fast asleep. They should ring me back, as soon as they get in. If I haven't heard anything, in half an hour, then I'll go over there. I'm sure Mr Zuki will fit me in." Rob smiled before flinching, and rubbing his cheek, forlornly, "You carry on, you've got to get the kids off to school. I'll get up in a minute and go downstairs."

'Would you like some ice or a cup of tea?" enquired Rose, "you know they won't turn you away, if you turn up. It's an emergency. I'm sure they'll fit you in." She stroked his hair as he replied,

"No, thanks, I don't think I could bear to put anything near my mouth. I've had some water. Even that hurt." He looked like a wounded, little boy, his eyes sad. She felt sorry for him as he lay on the edge of the bed, gripped by pain, "Rather than postponing, would you mind going on your own to look at Will's kitchen, this morning, please, Rose? I don't want to slow anything down, at this stage, as everything is moving well. My tooth will be fine. The sooner we crack on with ordering products, and materials, for the house, the happier I'll feel. We have similar taste. Perhaps you could take some pictures so I can have a look later."

"Yes, of course, don't worry, I'll go. It's fine. You just concentrate on getting better. You do seem to be in awful pain."

"I really am, yes. I get tiny moments where I think it might be easing off before another pain-wave literally crashes in my mouth."

"How are you going to drive like this? Surely, Will can wait until another day so I can take you in? He's got our business now so he won't be bothered."

"Actually, Jan's offered so I'm OK. When I texted her this morning, before you woke up, to let her know where I'd leave the key, so she could get in, and to tell her what work I need doing, she offered, so I took her up on it, very sweet of her."

Yes, thought Rose, rather nastily, *so kind of her, and while she's getting paid too. She must be an early riser, like you.* Rose smiled, trying to sound as unbothered as possible, "Yes, that really is sweet of her. She's so kind." However, Rob, in spite of his pain, must have picked up on a hint of sarcasm in her voice, which she had been unable to hide, because he sat up on the edge of the bed and turned to look right at Rose,

"You don't really like Jan do you? I know she's a bit brash and overly bubbly at times but she's a good worker, extremely efficient, and she's friendly, and there's not many people as nice, or as nicely turned out, as her who would want to work in a hut and have to use the loo and kettle in someone's house, and in all weathers!"

"I know all that but, well, it's not easy for me either."
Rose retorted. She was aware she had unintentionally
raised her voice. It would have been wiser not to say
anything. Rob was furious,
"Oh, it's all about you isn't it? Do you ever think that
you're not the only one having to make sacrifices here,
not the only one who finds things hard?"
"Don't be so ridiculous, Rob, she's your secretary. I
hardly know her so how could I say whether I like her or
not. She's just an employee of yours." Rob was now
wincing with the pain and Rose felt bad for arguing.
Anna appeared at the bedroom door,
"Why are you shouting at Daddy, Mummy?"
"I'm not, darling. We were just talking passionately."
Rose smoothed down the fluffy hair on the back of
Anna's head and guided her towards the stairs, so they
could go down for breakfast.

Rose poured cereal and milk into bowls. She felt guilty
for what she had said to Rob, but, also angry. He was so
readily cross with her but then pain made most people
moody. She knew she should keep any criticism of Jan
to herself and not voice it to Rob, but her reaction was a
symptom of her true feelings. Carving out time for her
business, even with her mother's help and support, was
going to be very hard. Seeing Jan breeze in and out,
with purpose and responsibilities outside her job as a
mother, in her nice clothes with her hair and make-up
finished to perfection, made Rose feel sidelined. What
really bugged her was that Jan then got time to spend
with her husband, even flirt with him. Rose rarely got to
spend any time alone with him.

She reminded herself that this was not Jan's fault.
Nothing had really changed about Jan since Rose had
known her. Jan had always dressed up and flirted a little

with Rob, and this had never bothered Rose in the slightest, until now. Really, it was Rose who had changed.

The doorbell rang. She let an exuberant Jan in, "Where's the patient then?" She squealed. Her feet, in slightly lower shoes today, confidently clacked across the hallway, as she called upstairs, "I'm here!" Rob came carefully down the stairs as if he had a problem with his leg, not his teeth. At that moment, Rose was pleased that Jan would take over because she was able to say what Rose was thinking, "Oh dear me, you are in a bad way. You can't even walk properly." Rob ignored this, "Mr. Zuki just called. He can fit me in straight away, thank God." Jan looked visibly shocked as she noticed his red cheek, "Oh my, I didn't realise your face was that swollen, you do look bad. Well, let's be going then. Bye, Rose!" Rob followed Jan through the front door, muttering goodbye to the floor, just before he crossed the threshold, clearly still annoyed with Rose, and drained from the pain. She wanted to run and hug him, reassure him she really did love him, but she did not. He would be back to normal soon, once the dentist had sorted him out. She could not help thinking, though, as she retrieved a dusty, child's sock from behind the front door, as she closed it, that Rob's irritable mood ran deeper than just his bad tooth.

Outside, as Rob climbed into the passenger seat of Jan's car, and dejectedly slumped into it, he reiterated how he could not thank her enough for this.
"No problem," she smiled. I've got a few errands to run in town so when you're finished, if I'm not waiting for you, give me a ring and I'll be there right away, to take

you home, that is, if you haven't got anything too pressing in the office, and are expecting me to return, while Mr Zuki pokes around in your mouth?"

"I have got work for you but it can wait. I'll pay you for this morning, of course."

"Oh, don't be silly. I'll make up my hours another time. I'm a friend this morning not an employee," she laughed, "I don't suppose you got much sleep last night."

"Not enough, no." Rob was trying not to look at Jan's legs. Her skirt only just seemed to cover the top of her lap as she sat in the moulded, driver's seat. It took all his might not to stare. Instead, he looked out of the passenger window. He followed a robin along the grass verge.

As Jan drove, Rob did not like the silence. For some reason, it felt particularly uncomfortable today so he asked Jan,

"How are things with you? I mean generally."

"Well, I'm still single and still alive," she laughed. "What would you like to know?" Jan glanced at Rob who bashfully shrugged. "I'm only joking, giving you a hard time. Everything is well with me, can't complain," she smiled. "I've taken up salsa with my friend, Julie, which is a laugh, although, I doubt we'll last the full course. Dancing is not my thing." Jan continued, "My son, Fred, is doing well. As you know, he works hard at school and seems to get the grades, which is a good thing. Mum's well, and, more of a friend now than a mother, can't really ask for more than that."

"Yes, it's good if they work hard, the children..." Rob tapered off, his toothache was hell and he was starting to feel even weaker from the pain. Jan glanced over and saw him wince,

"We're almost there. My grandad used to put cloves in his teeth, if they hurt. He swore by them but then I never remember him having a cheek as red and puffed up, as yours!"

"I'll remember that for next time, God forbid this ever happens again," Rob tried to smile but any movement hurt. Jan pressed ahead with their chat,

"Rose seems busy." Rob replied with raised eyebrows,

"Yes, she is, three kids is a lot and she's got a fixation about starting her business, right away. I don't get it. Personally, I think she's got enough on her plate but she seems to enjoy being constantly busy. She needs to be. She gets bored easily."

"Well, she's always struck me as being a clever, capable lady, probably enjoys the challenge. Maybe being at home isn't enough for her any more. I'd say go for it. Why shouldn't she do a business? Come on, Rob, you should be encouraging her. One day the children will leave and then what? Rose might not have the same level of motivation to start something then and she'll only regret it. It can be pretty boring looking after kids. You need adult conversation and that's something kids just can't do. I had my moments with Fred, if I'm honest, and I love him dearly. I found spending long periods of time with him so boring. I'm not sure I could have done it again, twice more, like Rose." It was Rob's turn to speak,

"I hear what you're saying, Jan, but it's not like we need the money and it was Rose who wanted to stay at home full-time with Evie. She felt she missed out a bit with the other two, as she had to go back to work after they were born. We were pretty much starting out back then but I'm established now. I'll be honest. I don't really get it."

"She looks after you well, doesn't she?"

"What do you mean?"

"Well, I would imagine that someone as efficient as Rose is doing all your washing and ironing on time, cleaning, preparing all the meals from scratch, seeing to the kids if they wake up at night and so on. Oh, and not to mention trying to be that sexy wife you married all those years ago, on top of it all. Come on, Rob, no wonder you don't want that to change!"

"That's not fair!"

"It's a little bit true though, isn't it?"

"No," Rob protested, "It's not."

"I know it's none of my business, and I hope you don't sack me for saying this, but, I mean what I say about encouraging her. Surely, you want a fulfilled, happy wife not some frustrated showpiece, at your beck and call, allowing resentment slowly, and poisonously, to build up. People change their minds all the time. Perhaps being a full-time mum has worked, until recently, for Rose. Now, it doesn't." Rob said nothing so Jan continued, "Evie was planned then?"

"That is a bit direct, Jan."

"Sorry, you don't have to answer that. It's just I was going to say, even if she was, because obviously you have a fairly large gap between her and Thomas, perhaps Rose has outgrown the mummy bit sooner than she expected to. It can be a long four or five years before they start school. Look after Rose. You'll both be happier if you're both fulfilled and able to grow as individuals. There! Lecture over!"

Rob did not know what to say. It all made sense. He had not realised how perceptive, and wise, Jan was, or how much she had absorbed of his family life, from her toilet and tea trips.

Jan eased the car into a space right by the door, pulled up the handbrake and dropped the keys into her bag,

"Well we're here now, not long and you should be out of your misery."

"Thanks, Jan." Rob looked sincerely into her eyes. Jan looked back,

"No problem,"

"Er... I meant for the lift, of course, but also the advice. You make a lot of sense. It'll give me something to think about in the dentist's chair."

NINETEEN

The front door, at Cathy's house, had swollen with damp,
"Oh dear, not much of a slick welcome if I have to wrestle the front door open, is it? I only hope I can force it shut again once you've gone or it really will be cold in here." Evie ran straight into the house, as if it were her home, without even looking back at her mother. "Thanks for this, Mum. I don't know what I'd do without your help. Here's her bag. I shouldn't be longer than two hours. Can't David do something with the door for you?"
"I'm sure he will, Rose. I don't like to ask him but he'll notice as soon as he gets here." Cathy popped her head outside to look at Rose's car, "You're on your own?"
'Yes, Rob's had to go to the dentist, thinks he may have an abscess again, poor thing. I must hurry. It's been one of those mornings. I'm only just going to make it on time." Evie had come back to the door. Rose pecked her on the forehead.

"You look lovely!" Cathy called after Rose as she got back into the car,

"Isn't your mother beautiful? I'm not sure how she drives in those shoes, though."

"Beautiful," exclaimed Evie with glee as she wriggled out of Cathy's arms and ran towards the kitchen, "I paint, I paint!" She was already yanking up the sleeves of her jumper, revealing chubby arms covered in perfect skin. *How can I resist?* Cathy thought, as she started to get the paint and paper out,

"You must wear an apron or Mummy will be cross."

"Cross," Evie enthused. "Mummy and Daddy shout today," she put her hand to the side of her mouth, "like this!" Evie let out a loud shout. Cathy knew better than to enquire further. Evie was starting to repeat everything she heard. She carried on bouncing herself on and off the chair until everything was ready.

Rose pulled up slowly onto the smart drive, outside Will's property. The entire place was neat, like those featured in country-living articles. Everything was well kept. There were no worn out patches, on the drive, or peeling window frames. It resembled, exactly, the way she wanted her home to look, once the work was complete.

She straightened her dress and encouraged her hair from behind her ears. Her habit of smoothing it back was impossible to break, even though she knew it looked better left to fall naturally. Will swung open the heavy, oak door, with ease, just as she reached up to press the black, silicone bell-button. He greeted her cheerfully,

"Hello there, not bad service?" he laughed. Rose was surprised that he had come to the door so fast. Had he been watching her? He must have read her mind, "I've got CCTV. It's really handy because my office is at the back of the house and the camera alerts me by email every time someone comes onto the property. A useful deterrent for those who might be up to no good," he winked.

Rose smiled. A couple of super-quick glances meant she had clocked the leather-soled, slip-on shoes, tailored trousers, slim-fit shirt, open at the neck, no tie and the familiar, manicured finger nails. He shut the front door, with barely a sound. He seemed more attractive to her than she remembered. This time, she noted his warmth, and a more relaxed demeanour. He was, clearly, much more at ease, in his own property. It was pleasant to be in an adult setting so different from her home. This place was untouched by reeling children, business talk from Rob and Jan, clacking around the kitchen, oblivious to the fact she was invading what Rose classed as private, family space.

Rose cast her eyes around the hall, noting all the doors were shut. She fought to keep a smile off her face as an image of mess and mayhem, behind those doors, came to mind. She imagined a sea of mess rushing out, flooding everything in its wake. Of course, the hall was neat, clean and neutrally painted. It felt like a five star, boutique hotel. The rest of the house was likely the same. The grand, gold, throne-like chair, in the corner of the hall, next to the plain mirror, that covered one wall, looked sturdy, and regal, not at all vulgar or out of place, as it might look in her family home. The luxurious, cream rug matched perfectly. There was not one fingerprint on the walls. She wanted to stand there and absorb it, for a moment, as she might the first spring sun, warm on her face after the greyness of winter.

She was glad she had dressed up. Her wedge-soled shoes were the right choice. As she walked around, she did not have to face the embarrassment of tiptoeing, for fear of digging up Will's wooden floors with sharp heels. She had expected expensive flooring, and the place to be show-home standard. She was not disappointed. She half expected a uniformed member of staff to appear, offer to take her coat and make coffee.

Rose and Will shook hands. His intense gaze weakened her. The last thing she wanted to do was come across as a stereotypical, token, pretty wife with nothing to say for herself. Not many people knew of her business plans or pre-children life. She had met builders with ease and confidence, so she could do this,

"Rob sends his apologies, toothache, really bad toothache. He's at the dentist now." Will replied,

"Sorry to hear that. Please pass on my wishes for a speedy recovery. Bad teeth can be a pig." Will had already turned around before Rose could say more. He did not appear concerned by the absence. She followed him down the corridor. He smiled back at her,

"Coffee?"

"Yes, please," she smiled, hoping she appeared more at ease than she actually felt.

"Here it is, my amazing kitchen!" Will gave her a cheeky smile as he stroked the button on the coffee machine. It started making promising noises. He gestured towards the stools, near the island, "sit down." Rose chose one. "First impressions?" he enquired. Rose, feeling more relaxed, replied,

"Of you or the kitchen?" She could not believe she had just said that. He looked momentarily taken aback, before laughing, "well... both, I suppose, although I thought you came to rate my kitchen, not me."

"Yes," Rose felt bashfully crippled. A strong, sensible question about the kitchen was required, "This is a lovely kitchen. I've always fancied an island like this in the middle of mine, a focal point. I like the fact the units are tall and attached to the ceiling so the dust can't settle, out of reach. How high are they? I mean, do you think something similar would work in our kitchen?" Will looked up at them,

"I think your ceilings may be lower, but, I may be wrong. You have a big space for your kitchen. We can make pretty much anything work. The company that did this, and I recommend them highly, are excellent. I know what I'll do, I'll measure the height of these then you can check at home. He handed her a cup, "help yourself to milk and sugar...oh, and a biscuit."

She was losing interest in the kitchen. It seemed unimportant. He was far more interesting. As he reached up, to catch the top of the tape measure onto the unit door, his shirt eased out of his trousers revealing taught flesh. She resisted the urge to hop off her stool and grab him.

"That's just over two metres thirty." He turned towards her. She stared at him. "Are you all right? You seem miles away."

"Do I? Sorry, I lost my train of thought. Do you think they're too tall?" She sprung off the stool. She could not stay any longer, "I must go." He seemed disappointed,

"Don't you have time to look round the rest of the house?"

"Yes, er... no, I mean no, I have to get back to collect Evie and so on." A momentary silence fell between them before Will said,

"No problem, another time, maybe," he smiled. "Ring me if you think of anything you want to ask me later on." Rose nodded and made her way towards the front door and tried to open it,

"Oh, it's locked." Will reached past Rose and up for a key on a hook above the front door,

"Sorry, habit," he smiled and for some reason, forewent the business-like handshake and leant over to kiss her cheek. Somehow, Rose turned at the crucial moment and they ended up pecking each other on the lips, pausing, then, losing all sense of themselves, kissing again, with open mouths, lingering over each other, before Rose suddenly broke away. She ran from the house, muttering sorry, retreating quickly, in her car, with far less of the care, or stealth, with which she had arrived.

She pulled into a secluded lay-by. Her mother would notice something was up, if she went straight there before calming down. She needed to return to her normal, unflustered self. It was just a kiss, a mistake. She had turned her head at the wrong time, or he had. It did not matter. Best not to mention it again. It would be fine. It happened to people all the time. It meant nothing. All marriages endured hard times; no one ever said it was easy. It would be impossible to stay married to someone, for life, and not fancy someone else, even a tiny bit, at some point. She loved Rob and he loved her and soon the lustful side of their marriage would be back. Everything would be back to normal.

"Have you got time for a coffee?" enquired Cathy as she wedged the door shut. Evie had jumped into Rose's arms,

"Yes, please, Mum."

"What's the house like?"

"Um, the house?"

"Yes, the one you just saw, your project manager's one?"

"He's called Will, Will Chapman. His house is lovely, of course." Rose could feel panic, or perhaps guilt, rising in her chest. Her neck was red, with histamine. Her mother eyed her, suspiciously,

"Did the meeting go OK? He was all right this man you saw, this Will?"

"Mum, of course he was, and, the meeting went well. I'm just tired and out of practice of dealing with people on my own, that's all. Life, for me, always seems to be all or nothing. I've taken on a lot. How's Evie been?"

"Lovely! You know Evie! She painted again, and loved it. She chatted away." Rose looked momentarily alarmed, "Evie is starting to repeat everything, though, Mum. I'm going to have to really watch what I say around her." Cathy eyed Rose,

"Don't take this the wrong way but you are looking after yourself and…erm, you know, everything is OK with you and Rob? I know it's none of my business but you must nurture what you have, Rose, guard it carefully, just don't overdo it with everything else. You know what I mean."

"Mum, I'm fine. We're fine. Stop worrying. I'm a grown woman!"

"I know you are. You've got a good marriage and lovely children. All the rest is secondary. It's people who count." Conveniently, for Rose, the discussion her mother seemed so keen to have came to an abrupt end as Evie pulled a pot of red paint off the kitchen surface all down herself, the side of the kitchen unit and across the floor.

Rob and Jan, and Rose and Evie, arrived home at the same time, around lunchtime. Jan dropped Rob off. She did not come inside, as she had to rush off to tend to her mother's dog. She would drop by later, Rob reported. He looked a lot happier. The dentist had cleaned out the infection and given Rob antibiotics. He would go back, in a week's time, for the rest of the treatment, once the infection had gone. Rob rolled his eyes,

"Going to be expensive but the alternative is a missing tooth."

"Well I'm glad you're in less pain now and that they are actually able to fix it." She stroked Rob's cheek. "Can you eat anything? I'm going to have a sandwich. Would you like one, or maybe soup would be better?"

"It's still a bit numb," said Rob, "so I'll have soup, please. I had a weird experience just before Jan pulled in. The sun was low, shining right in our eyes so she could barely see anything ahead. At the last minute, someone ran across the road in front of the car! She narrowly missed them but they must have seen us coming first. Anyway, I leant over and beeped the horn but they didn't even look round which was odd. When I looked back, this man was waving his fist at us, even though he was the one who ran in front of the car. The creepy bit is; I'm sure it was Ed. Why would you do that and then wave your fist? He really doesn't like me, you know."

"There's nothing you can do about it, Rob. You can't make someone like you if they don't. Some people do take an instant dislike to others, for no good reason. I think it's like the opposite to when people immediately gel."

"I suppose so. He is weird though, that Ed." Rob retreated to the sitting room where Evie had fallen asleep. He turned 'Peppa Pig' down, sat in the armchair and fell asleep himself. Rose poked her head round the door, a bowl of warm soup in her hand. She noted how attractive and familiar Rob looked, as well as relaxed, and at last free of pain. As she returned the soup to the pan, leaving it on a low heat, for him to have once he woke up, she thought, wistfully, *never, ever much time together.*

TWENTY

Christmas skated by, as usual. Considering the long build up, the day itself was always over far too swiftly, for Rose. This year, the whole thing had got in the way. It had slowed Rose down. She would have liked to postpone it until the spring. And, there was still another week before the children went back to school.

As the door bell rang, Anna and Thomas hurtled down the stairs, Evie shrieking behind them. She was too slow and uncoordinated to catch up but desperate to join the whirl of excitement.

"Granny, Granny, it's Granny!" They all shouted together. Thomas had already upturned a plastic toy box, to stand on, to enable him to unlock the front door. Cathy was taking them to see a Christmas show then for burgers and chips. While Thomas and Anna wrapped up warmly, Cathy updated Rose on the classes,

"I've managed to rustle up enough interest in the sewing classes to run two a week now so we'll need to book the village hall, while your place is being finished. We don't want these interested customers to have to wait too long. It should be a smooth transition into the new premises, after that. Anyway, we'll talk about that later! Come on, my darlings, let's get going." They left in a puff of chaos. Evie ran to the window to wave at them. Rose felt sorry for her being left out,

"Don't worry, Evie, your turn will come. It would be a long time for you to have to just sit. Would you like to do some playdough?"

"Oh, wow! Yes!" Evie danced with excitement.

As Rose set out the cutter shapes for Evie, her mobile vibrated on the kitchen surface. It was a text from Charlotte,

"Fancy a couple of hours at the play centre? Felicity is coming. Let me know. Charlotte xx" Rose texted straight back,

"Would love to thanks. Just Evie and me. See you in a little while. xx"

While Evie poked and prodded the playdough, Rose sifted through the mail. One car magazine for Rob, three bills and one letter, again addressed to Rob, caught her eye, in a cheap-looking, small, brown envelope. The writing on it was shaky and, on closer inspection, made her think it might be that of an elderly person. Even so, the writing looked vaguely familiar but she could not match it to anyone she knew. Resisting the urge to rip it open, she noticed the London postmark. She chucked it on the surface, with the other post. Rob would collect it later.

After a couple of enjoyable hours of chat, with the girls, while the children played, she made a quick supermarket dash. She planned something easy, like eggs and soldiers, for Evie. Steak and chips for Rob and herself, with a bottle of wine, once the children had gone to bed.

Rose was battered by the wind and soaked by the rain, while wrestling Evie out of her car seat. Rose managed a difficult stretch, while holding the car door, to stop it hurling into the adjacent car. She stepped in a puddle. Her ballet pumps squelched with every step. The dripping trolley, from the leaking covered area, was too wet to put Evie in. Rose struggled with the stiff-wheeled trolley, with one hand. Her handbag swung off her wrist, digging in like a wet rope. She gripped a struggling-to-get-down Evie, in the other arm, and headed towards customer service for something to dry the trolley with. By now, her hands were red-raw from the wet and cold. *I would turn around and go straight home, were it not for the fact we need food.* She stood at the desk, dripping and trying to hang on to Evie, who was now wriggling like an eel. She was managing to make herself streamline, starting to slip out of Rose's arms. She gripped Evie tighter,

"You're hurting me, Mummy, hurting me a lot. Ouch!" A few customers looked over in her direction. Rose could feel herself getting uncomfortably hot, what with Evie's heat and the store's heating. *Oh my God, I will hurt you in a minute, if you don't stop wriggling.* Through clenched teeth, Rose warned her, "stop wriggling, Evie, or I won't buy you any nice pudding." Evie wanted to know if it would be a chocolate cookie. Rose said yes and Evie stopped trying to escape.

The customer-service girl appeared not to have noticed them standing there. She seemed to be doing a very important job of reading a plastic-coated folder, while ignoring Rose, the customer. She was about to rouse the young girl from her plastic page, when another member of staff came rushing over. She had a lovely smile and an eager-to-help air about her,

"May I help you, madam?"

Not a plastic-page reader, thought Rose. "I just need something to dry this trolley with, please. It's too wet to put my daughter in."

"Oh, there should be a roll of paper-towels out. Where is it, Gemma?"

"Umm, I don't know." She returned to the plastic page.

"Hang on," the older woman, whose badge read, Glyn, looked under the counter,

"Here it is!" As she handed Rose some blue paper, she looked wistfully at Gemma,

"Best keep this on the desk as it's pouring outside. That way, the customers aren't left waiting when you're busy!" This was said in a sing-song voice, as if she was speaking to someone who was slow on the uptake. Glyn gave Rose a knowing smile as she whizzed round the desk and helped her to dry the trolley. She turned to Evie, "you're gorgeous, aren't you?" Evie giggled, enjoying the attention. "There you are, nice and dry. Here's some tissue for Mummy, who looks a bit wet!" To Rose's dismay, the tissue proved to be slightly water resistant. Rose plonked Evie into the seat.

"Thank you," said Rose who was now cold. She steered the trolley towards the chilled section and came face to face with Will,

"Hi Rose, raining out there is it?" He looked amused.

Great, thought Rose, *just what I need*. Will was not soaked and had obviously missed the shower. To her relief, he appeared to have decided to act like the other day had not happened.

"What about this one?" A well-groomed, pretty lady sidled up to him, with a bottle of expensive-looking, red wine in her hand. Realising Will was talking to Rose, the lady immediately smiled then looked to him to introduce them, which he did,

"This is Luisa, a friend of mine from Dubai, and, this is Rose, a client of mine." The two women shook hands, more on Luisa's cue. She was warm and friendly but Rose wanted the ground to open up and swallow her because, while Luisa looked perfect, Rose felt that she herself looked like someone who had just had a bucket of cold water thrown in her face. She was shorter and curvier than Rose, petite. Luisa wore an expensive-looking dress in red, which suited her perfectly. She wore smart, black, high-heels that Rose guessed to be designer shoes. A tan, leather bag perched on the wrist of the arm holding the wine. Her nails were manicured in the latest black-red colour and her blonde hair hung around her shoulders in thick waves. Rose half-expected Luisa to snub her soaked self for managing to be stupid enough to get caught in the rain. Instead, Luisa charmed her,

"It was forty degrees in Dubai a couple of days ago! I'm beginning to wonder why I came here, to this, and I'm so wearing the wrong thing, as you can see. You're sensible, and wearing the right coat, which is lovely, by the way. It is stylish, and practical." Luisa barely paused for a breath, "I love clothes and have spent the week in London, with my sister, enjoying the sales. I did buy a raincoat, should have brought it with me today. Silly of me. Actually, Will, why don't you get the car and pick me up at the door, otherwise I'll ruin these shoes." As Will said goodbye and did as he was told, Luisa smiled and winked at Rose, "Well, I'd better pay for this, nice meeting you!" Rose watched as Luisa tottered towards the tills looking out of place amongst the other waterproofed customers.

Back home, Rob opened the envelope with the shaky writing. He was not expecting anything from London. Sometimes, the estate agent sent them information about their flat but that was always addressed to them both. Anyway, Rose dealt with that. This did not look like it had come from another office, or anyone official, as those envelopes nearly always had printed labels on them and looked smart. In fact, this envelope reminded Rob of the sort his cash wages used to be put in, when he did his student jobs.

A scribbled note, on the sort of paper you might expect on a purpose-made shopping list pad, thin, easy to tear off, read,
'<u>Rob ClarkE</u> (underlined with such force, the paper had almost ripped)
You will <u>nEvEr</u> ChaNge. Take a lOOk at <u>yoursElf</u>. You think your so wonderful but <u>No</u> one around here likes you. Your such a <u>priCk</u>.'

That was it. For a moment, Rob thought it must be a joke but then he could not think of anyone who would write such a stupid, childish note in the first place and then actually send it. In fact, it was not funny at all. He felt anger rise within him. He sat right back in his chair and put his hands behind his head. *What the hell?* He said aloud,
"Unbelievable!" He reread it. Without doubt, it was intended to be spiteful. What coward would write that to him, without the guts to own it? Did someone really think about him enough to write an anonymous note like this? He looked closely at the envelope. The address was correct right down to the postcode so it was from someone who had his address, or knew exactly where he lived, but he could not think of anyone who would do it. He felt unnerved.

As he stared at the writing, it started to look familiar but he just could not place it. It would be satisfying to remember. The mixture of capitals and lower case letters could be a give away. Rob smiled to himself as he stared at the letters again and again thinking that someone might have gone to some length to mask their handwriting, even more cowardly. Rob was well-liked and the only person he could think of who did not like him, basically for no good reason, was Ed, his neighbour, but Rob did not think even he would do this, even if Rob had refused to resurface his drive.

Oh well, thought Rob, *I know I'm a good enough person. I won't let a bully like this upset me*. Rob decided not to tell Rose about it straight away. It was his problem. He would wait until the morning and show it to Jan, see what she had to say about it. She was level headed and thick skinned. He would call it a day as far as work was concerned. He slipped the note into the bottom drawer of his desk, under some files, locked up the hut and dashed through the rain, into the house.

Rose was just coming through the front door as Rob locked the back door. She was struggling with shopping bags, Evie draped over her. Rob took Evie from her. She was relieved to be home, "Thank you! We're soaked, got caught in the shower in the supermarket car park, the really heavy one. It was like a waterfall! Evie is OK but I'm going upstairs to change. My feet are wet and cold. I'm damp all over. I hate this weather but I did get us some lovely food. Once the children are settled, we can have a meal together."
Rob was feeding Evie soldiers dipped in egg, by the time Rose came downstairs. Sometimes her husband surprised her. He could manage so well, and, yet, be so

helpless, on other occasions. She took a sip of the hot tea Rob had made her, in her favourite mug. She joined them at the table,

"That's it! I knew there was something I wanted to ask you. Who was that funny, almost mouldy, little brown envelope from today, the one with the scraggy writing? Just being nosey, it didn't look very professional, or even friendly, for that matter." He got up from the table to put Evie's bowl in the dishwasher,

"You are so nosey," he smiled.

"No, I'm not, just curious! OK... and, maybe, a little nosey. It's just you normally get such professional, slick-looking letters or, of course, bills, maybe the odd card. This was different, that's all. It stood out." She looked right at him, "so, come on, do tell!"

"Nothing exciting, it was a cheque from a client I did a sketch for, a while back," Rob lied. "How about you open a bottle of wine and enjoy a glass while I put Evie to bed? We can cook together once the other two are settled. They should be back soon."

"Oh, sorry, I forgot to say, I spoke to Mum just now. She's keeping Anna and Thomas for a sleepover tonight."

"Even better."

As Rose sipped the smooth wine, she tried to dismiss the nagging doubt, at the back of her mind, that her marriage had lost its shimmer. She felt ambivalent about the evening ahead. What had happened with Will did not help, because she still desired him.

TWENTY-ONE

Evie followed Rose from room to room as she tidied up. It seemed later than ten-thirty in the morning. Rose felt a sense of relief, as she always did, that the house was in a good-enough state. She put the kettle on and picked up the post that was waiting on the mat. Sifting through it, she found nothing exciting. There was another letter for Nicky Turner. Surely, the postman had noticed? Their addresses were quite different, apart from the postcode.

The wrong post was often delivered, when their usual postwoman was absent. It was not a massive deal but Rose felt obliged to take the letters round. It seemed unneighbourly to put hem back in the post box, to complete the circuit again. Rose remembered how, years back, she had had to pay significant interest on her credit card bill because one particular neighbour, at the time, had literally sat on it for a month. Eventually, the neighbour had sheepishly appeared at the door with it, claiming she had only just noticed it in a pile of post. Rose thought it might actually be against the law to keep post like that. She imagined it would be very difficult to prove.

It was inconvenient dropping letters round to Nicky because although Rose had noticed a small gap in the hedge that bordered her garden, she felt it was presumptuous to assume it was all right to use it then appear at the back door. Nicky, probably, would not mind, but, Ed might and, anyway, Nicky might be dusting in her underwear. Someone appearing at the back door would be the last thing she would need. After all, they did not know each other that well. This left the option of driving, or walking, all the way round to the front of Nicky and Ed's house.

Rose's thoughts were interrupted by Evie tugging at her leg,
"Hey little Vi Vi, what do you want? Am I ignoring you? Let's get you a snack." Rose eased Evie into her highchair, "Would you like a drink, my love?" Evie clapped her hands then covered her eyes,
"Peek a boo!"
"Where's Evie gone?" said Rose as she reached into the fridge for some food. She loved these simple, little moments with Evie.

Evie turned cranky, while eating her snack. She tried to rest her head back, in her highchair. Rose decided that she was either tired or sickening for something, yet again. Rose put her in her cot where she fell asleep straight away. Rose checked the listening monitor was plugged in, in Evie's room, and took the coordinating piece with her, out to the hut. She could see Rob and Jan inside. Rob looked up first and beckoned Rose in.

Shutting the door behind her, Rose looked over at Jan,

"Hi Jan, how are you?"

"Very well, thank you." She looked well turned out, as always. Rose liked Jan's perfume. Rob probably did not notice it, as he was used to it. He had a habit of not noticing much, after a while, thought Rose, dryly,

"Rob, would you mind if I left the monitor in here? Evie's asleep. She's very tired. She'll be out for at least half-an-hour. I've locked the back door so she is safe. I'm going to walk this letter round to Nicky. The postman delivered it to us, by mistake."

"Sure," Rob smiled as he accepted the monitor and placed it on his desk. "I'm not expecting any calls so it shouldn't be a problem, even if she does wake up."

"Thanks, she really shouldn't do, she's so exhausted. I hope it is tiredness and she's not sickening for something." Rose raised her eyebrows and rushed off.

She was sure Nicky must dust and polish her front door. There was not a cobweb, or crispy leaf, in sight, on the doorstep, let alone any sign of weeds, in the crevices. A brushed-steel planter stood proudly next to the door. It contained a flourishing bay tree, adorned with fairy lights. She rang the bell. Almost immediately, Nicky came to the door.

"Hi Nicky, thought I'd drop this in. The new postman delivered it to us by mistake."

"Thank you, Rose. That's thoughtful of you. I must admit I usually just plop them back in the post box when it happens here." Nicky, realising what she had just said added, "Never yours, though, no, I wouldn't do that with your post... no kids with you today?"

"No, my mum has Thomas and Anna. They're not back yet. I'll be seeing them later. Evie's asleep. Rob has the monitor. I haven't abandoned her!" Rose laughed.

"I wasn't suggesting you had! Actually, I've just made a pot of coffee. Would you like one?"

"I told Rob I wouldn't be long. I'm sure a quick cup wouldn't hurt, though. Yes, please, that would be lovely," Rose struggled to wrestle her boots off until Nicky pointed out the iron earwig.

Nicky's house was immaculate inside. Rose had not been inside before. She had only ever spoken to Nicky through the bushes in the garden, or on a doorstep. The hall was impressive. The vaulted ceiling housed a network of beams. A skylight allowed light, from the late autumn sunshine, to pour down onto the flagstones. Nicky clattered over towards the kitchen, leaving a waft of perfume behind her, which Rose recognised as the same one Jan wore. Nicky wore kitten-heeled mules. Rose wondered how some women managed to look, and possibly feel, glamorous all the time, as she watched Nicky waft around.

The kitchen was beautiful. Imposing oak cupboards and a large, artists' sink matched the strength of the beams. A glass wall, at the far end, overlooked a terrace and what looked like a hot tub. Rose had never had Nicky and Ed down as hot tub types, whatever they were. Nicky always appeared to be in full make-up and Ed did not appear relaxed enough to sit still for long, especially, Rose imagined, outside in the cold. Nicky noticed Rose looking at it,
"Yes, I know the hot tub looks a bit naff but Ed plays rugby. It helps with the aching, after a game. Not the nicest thing to look out onto but it can be used all year round. I love sitting in it with a glass of bubbly on the phone to my sister. Talking of rugby, the whole team got in it once. Some of those men are fit. I was able to watch them from my bedroom window upstairs!" Nicky let out a laugh that resembled a snort, totally out-of-line

with the perfectly serene image that Rose had been building up of her.

"Oh, lucky you," said Rose without much conviction wondering how she had got away with that without any of them noticing. Nicky changed the subject,

"So, are you back to normal after Christmas?"

"Yes, it's nice to have this week to relax before the children return to school. Rob's mother stayed. All went well. I've taken all the rubbish, you know, toy packaging and extra food waste to the tip so we're tidy and as back to normal as possible!"

"And, Rob's back at work?"

"Yes, already! He loves it though. It's never a chore for him." Rose smiled as Nicky handed her a cup of coffee, "He never takes much time off anyway. It's a way of life. He wanted to be an architect when he was still in nappies. It's a notoriously time consuming job as you probably know." Nicky nodded,

"You two been married for long?"

"Yes, ten years now, a fair length of time. And, what about you and Ed? How long have you been together?"

"Well, not many people know this, but, we were actually at primary school together but didn't really know each other then. We went to different secondary schools then I trained to be a nurse and Ed a pilot so we weren't really that aware of each other back then. We've only been together as a couple for seven years, actually. We met at a house party here in the village by chance. Some of our mutual, old primary school friends tracked each other down and decided to have a get-together. We were both there, hit it off and quickly went our separate ways again. Can you believe it? We actually came to nothing after that party, a few dates and that was it then a few years later, we literally bumped into each other in London, went for a coffee and ended up together properly. I moved in pretty much straight away mainly because I found out I was pregnant, unplanned needless to say. Sadly, I had a very late miscarriage. We realised how much we had both wanted that baby so I became pregnant again, planned this time, but endured a stillbirth. It clearly wasn't meant to be. We stopped trying after that, just too traumatic." There was a terseness to Nicky's voice before she fell silent.

"I'm sorry," said Rose, softly, then found she could not think of one more word to say that did not sound patronising. She was lucky, with her three. Thankfully, Nicky broke the silence,

"I've accepted it, really. It's Ed who's found it harder. It was almost the final straw for him. You must know he doesn't work, well, not much. Shortly before the stillbirth, Ed was made redundant. The airline he worked for downsized. Well, that's what they called it. They did say it was nothing personal but it's hard not to see it that way. There was nothing we could do really and he did get a generous pay-off. In fact, financially, we're fine. We have no mortgage on this place thanks to Ed's mother leaving it to him. He kind of had no push to get another job after that but unfortunately got depressed. He got out of practice and his confidence went until he no longer felt able to even try and go back to flying. I mustn't complain, though. He's done a lot with the garden and helps his brother out in London quite often, doing odd jobs like slapping up paint. His brother, Graham, is a property developer. He pays Ed well, which is good for Ed's self esteem. He's OK now. He's all right."

Rose got the feeling Nicky was saying this almost to convince herself. Rose felt sorry for her but despite Nicky's openness, she still found she did not particularly warm to her. In fact, for some reason, she was not sure she liked her at all. Nicky continued to talk,

"I'm older now and my chances of having children naturally are rapidly disappearing so no point dwelling on it. Ed hardly mentioned it after the stillbirth so we've sort of bumbled along together. We don't live in each other's pockets and that seems to suit us both. He's in London at the moment with Graham." Nicky changed the subject. Looking expectantly at Rose, she enquired, "you and Rob must be close, living and working at the same place?"

"Well, yes, I suppose we are. It's not something I give a lot of thought. We get on well but things change once you have children. It becomes much more about them. Time as a couple tends to come way down the list of priorities but we muddle along. That probably sounds very unexciting, mundane even, but... yes... we're OK." For some reason, Rose felt uncomfortable that Nicky had asked her again about her relationship with Rob when really it was none of her business. Rose finished her coffee and placed the cup carefully in the sink,

"Well, thank you so much for the coffee. I'd better go as Evie will definitely wake soon and I need to be there." Nicky was still looking at her, a serene expression on her face,

"Would Rob ever leave you?" Rose managed to cover up her surprise, and annoyance, at this question. She was not at all prepared for it and replied, with a laugh, to try to cover up how she really felt,

"Well, I hope not. After all, we've got three children together!" Oddly, Nicky persisted,

"And when they've all flown the nest?"

"No," Rose had had enough. She made her way towards the front door. Nicky smiled smugly. Rose resisted the urge to say something like if your marriage is a charade, don't assume everyone else's is or that other people's husbands are up-for-grabs. Rose was surprised at how defensive she felt. She realised that she could not stand this woman. She left promptly.

She gently opened the hut door to retrieve the monitor, "Not a murmur from her," said Jan before Rose even had a chance to say hello. Rob barely looked up. Rose, unnerved by Nicky, felt irritable. She stopped herself from saying,

"I gave the baby monitor to Rob, not you. I asked him to keep an ear out for Evie, his child, his responsibility, and none of your business. You're employed to help Rob not look after Evie. Butt out." Instead, Rose gracefully accepted the monitor back leaving Jan unaware of her thoughts. Evie was still fast asleep. Rose decided to leave her for another ten minutes and returned downstairs. Jan was boiling the kettle,

"I suppose you don't know what to do with yourself, when Evie's still asleep." Rose responded, curtly,

"I have plenty to do, thank you. I'm always busy. Hasn't Rob told you I'm starting my own business?"

"Rose, I didn't mean anything by it. I was being flippant, trying to be funny, sorry. Yes, Rob has told me about your business. I'm pleased for you. You're a bright, capable lady. I admire you. Three children, alone, must keep you busy enough. I only have one child and feel rushed off my feet with work on top," Jan smiled kindly, "I don't know how you do it." She clacked out of the kitchen, carrying two mugs.

"There's your tea," Jan placed the mug on the coaster next to Rob's screen,

"Thank you, Jan," Rob turned around in his chair, "could I show you something? I would appreciate your opinion." Rob produced the brown envelope, with the note inside, from his drawer, "I haven't shown this to Rose yet because she has enough to think about, at the moment. Frankly, I don't want to worry her. Do you think I should be worried or just throw it away? At first I wasn't bothered...," he tapered off, "well..., read it and tell me what you think."

Jan looked at the note,
"Oh, how childish," was her first response, "who on earth wrote that to you?" Rob was relieved to have shared the message,
"No idea. They didn't have the guts to sign it. As you can see, the postmark is London but I can't think of anyone I know in London who would send something so ridiculous. I know it's childish and I shouldn't take any notice. I'm a bit worried as part of me thinks that childish adults can be dangerous. Most of us have fantasised about sending nasty notes to people, or worse, but never actually act on it. It's like saying you could wring someone's neck. You don't actually go ahead and do it."
"Woah, Rob, take a breath, it's not a death threat. Personally, I would not worry too much about it. It'll be someone you know, for sure, as they know where you live. Everyone knows everyone's business around here so it's likely to be a local person, and, as for the postmark, it's only an hour to London, on the train, so that doesn't really narrow it down at all," she smiled, "anyone can travel."

Following a pause where neither of them said anything, Jan broke in,
"Trouble is, Rob, you've lived in the civilised and, dare I say, privileged world all your life! I used to get notes pinned to my flat door, frequently, when Fred was a baby, requesting I keep him quiet and stop him crying - a baby! Come on, I thought. The person who wrote them was too much of a coward to sign these notes or face me.

I used to pin them on the notice board, in the communal entrance hall, where everyone would see them, with my own note, asking the perpetrator not to be so cowardly and to sign any notes in future, or come and see me. There were six flats, in my building, and I didn't have time, or patience, to knock on all the doors, for them all to deny it. I have to admit, that, although I seem strong, I was really shaken by those notes. I felt that I was doing a good job as a single mum. I had accepted that a baby cries. It would pass, along with some of the hard bits of being a mum. I just expected everyone would feel the same way, or, at least, be a little tolerant. Anyway, I had a suspicion who it was so my dad, who was pretty handy, and his friend who was in the security business, wired up a camera to my spy hole. It ran for twenty-four-hours a day. We caught the culprit, late one night, pushing another unpleasant note under my door. What was most upsetting was that it happened to be the one person I had least suspected. It was a lady, in her eighties, called Nel, who lived in the flat at the very top of our building. She had always seemed so sweet. You know she called me dear and always cooed over Fred. She would tell me I was doing a good job, especially as a single mum, and not to worry what anyone thought, you know, about not having a husband. Looking back, she was the one truly bothered that I did not have a husband. I never really considered worrying about that."
Rob chuckled and commented, sarcastically,
"She wasn't at all judgemental then?" Jan continued,
"Actually, I was no fool. I knew people talked and judged. I had Fred, and, I know, in my heart, I did the right thing. I did my best. It was not my fault that his father deserted me. This woman felt Fred needed his dad and, in an ideal world, that would have been great, to have his support, and so on, but, we all make the best of what life hands us. I think because I was so young,

and alone, she hoped she could get rid of me, by unnerving me. It actually made me more determined to stay and stand up for myself. I'd had a baby out of wedlock, on my own, not committed a crime.

"Anyway, my father decided we would visit her, together. We wanted to talk to her with the aim of making peace, really. She was old, living alone, and we wondered if she felt isolated, and had got the wrong idea about me. We apologised for Fred's crying but pointed out that I never left him for long. We asked her if it bothered her and how clearly she heard it. After all, she was on the top floor and I was at ground level! She was as nice as pie and denied she had sent me anything. We told her about the camera and even then she still denied it saying how awful they were; the notes, I mean. She happened to be a fantastic actress and had I not been so upset it would have been almost amusing. I'll never forget her face when we told her that the evidence I had, on camera, of her pushing a note under my door, would be given to the police, if she sent me any more. She moved out a month later and, would you believe it, I actually felt bad about it. I worried I'd driven her out!

"So, perhaps the person who sent your note is closer than you think. I can assure you it's not me!" Jan laughed out loud, "most people know their abusers they say, well, the newspapers say that!" Rob laughed too, masking his uneasiness. He sat motionless, for a while, mulling it all over, again. Someone I know, he thought, and the only person he could come up with, still, was Ed. He certainly did not like Rob but would he really have the nerve to send an anonymous note? He sent enough signed letters, didn't mind putting his name to all those, did he, in fairness to him? However, he was clearly impulsive. He did not appear to always think things through properly, so he remained the suspected culprit. Rob needed a break,

"I'm going back to the house for a bit. Thanks for listening and telling me what you think. Please don't say anything to anyone, at this stage, especially Rose. I will tell her, just not right now. Have you much more to do, Jan?"

"A couple of standard letters, a few to file. I need twenty minutes or so."

"Well, I'll say goodbye now and see you tomorrow. Don't bother locking the door if you go before I'm back. I don't plan to be very long." Rob hoped Evie would still be asleep and that he might be lucky enough to catch Rose in a good mood. Maybe, they could sneak in some intimate time. He was disappointed. They had already gone out. He sent Rose a text, out of annoyance, if nothing else, something to the effect of where are you and is there anything for lunch. He had still not eaten. She promptly replied to look in the fridge. Rob smiled to himself and said out loud,

"Suppose I asked for that one." He sifted through the post and came across a letter, addressed to Nicola Turner, stuck to the back of one of his letters. *Rose missed that one*, he thought, as he saw Jan leaving, tottering across the drive, smiling to herself.

Still hungry and finding nothing appealing in the fridge, he decided to walk the short distance to the local pub, for a late lunch. He would drop the stray letter off on his way there. He would enjoy reading the newspaper while eating his meal.

He was about to push the letter through the gap at Nicky's place when the door swung open, almost knocking him off balance.

"Hi Rob! Another letter, for me? You know I don't mind if you just repost them, if they don't look urgent. I don't expect you to drop my mail round on an almost daily basis just because the sorting office can't differentiate between our houses! But, I must say it's always lovely to see you. Will you come in?"

Rob felt coy about going in. He was not sure if it was because Nicky was flirting with him, or, because she was dressed in a short, silk dressing gown. It looked like it could slip to the ground easily. He hoped it would. Trying not to think about it, he kept his eyes firmly on her face, and, fort the urge, desperately, to sneak another look at her curvy, reassuring, female form, accentuated by the silk. He, silently, berated himself. *God, get a grip, Rob. You're a married man, for goodness sake, and, she's your flirty neighbour with the weird husband. He would, more than likely, kill you, if he knew what you were thinking. Just walk away.* Rob's feet remained rooted to the ground. He managed to reply,
"No problem about the letter, Nicky, and no thank you to coming in. I'm off to the pub, for a quick bite." He turned to leave but Nicky was not giving up,
"Actually, I know you must be hungry, but, I need your help, if you've got five minutes? Ed's in London, again, for a couple of days, and, I really fancy a loll around in the hot tub. Trouble is I can't get the stuck, shed door open, to get the chemicals and tester kits, etcetera, out. I would need to test the water before I get in. I don't fancy chemical-burn, cocktail-bubbles in my hot tub, or, an upset tummy. Is there a chance you could use your lovely, manly strength to open the shed for me, *pleease*? My wrist still isn't quite right, after my fall, so I'm not prepared to pull too hard. I did ask Ed to leave it slightly open for me, before he left, but my relaxation obviously wasn't a priority for him because he forgot." She gave a

wry smile at the mention of Ed before she eyed Rob, willing him to agree to help.

"Of course, where is it?"

"Follow me."

Rob watched her shapely bottom, wriggling beneath the gown. He smelled perfume, in the air, in front of him. She wore the same one as Jan, yet Jan always had a calming influence on him. Nicky was making him jittery. His heart was racing. He prised open the door for her. She looked delighted,

"You must be much stronger than Ed. He always has trouble opening that door. It takes him a few tries. It swells with the damp. Just needs shaving, I imagine." She bent over the side of the hot tub to test the chlorine, the dressing gown barely covering her bottom. Rob noticed toned legs with unblemished skin. If she was wearing knickers, it was not obvious.

She turned to face him. He wondered if she had bent over on purpose. He knew that he should make his excuses and leave. He stayed. He did not want to leave. She did not want him to leave either,

"If you change your mind about the pub, you can have something here, only, I've got some sushi in the fridge and we could have a cuppa."

"I think I'll stick to my plan which is the pub. I'm quite hungry and sushi isn't really my thing. I should get going."

"Oh, surely you've time for a quick cuppa, in that case, let the late-lunchtime rush die down or you'll be waiting ages at the pub, and, possibly, without a seat." She stared right at him and he gave in,

"I'll have a quick coffee then, if you insist," he smiled.

She handed him his drink and sat down in front of him,

"I'm not really suitably dressed for sitting at the table. I'm starting to feel chilly. The hot tub should be ready now so I'm going to get in if that's OK?... Only, well, it was my original intention," she laughed. Rob quickly finished his drink and stood up,

"I'll go." He went to leave.

"No rush," Nicky laughed.

"Well, I don't want to hold you up and I'm pretty hungry." She ignored this,

"Actually, would you mind hanging around for five more minutes because, if the chlorine levels aren't quite correct, I may need to heave this bigger tester-thingy out of the shed and, like I said, with my wrist, I don't want to be lifting anything, putting any strain on it."

"OK, I can't refuse, when you put it like that." He exposed both palms of his hands in a 'you've got me' gesture.

Outside, the water in the hot tub turned out to be perfect. What happened next, when Rob went over it again, and again, as he sat motionless at his desk, later that afternoon, unable to concentrate on work, and trying to make sense of it all, was totally out of character, and not really planned in any kind of way, certainly not on his side. He should have left as soon as he handed her the letter. He had been weak. He had allowed his eyes to watch and his feet to stand firm before following Nicky.

With Rob watching, she had let the dressing gown flow off her body, like a ribbon curling, caught in a warm breeze. It had landed around her ankles. To him, she had resembled a naked cherub. He had been aghast at her perfectly toned body, firm nipples and a lower half completely devoid of hair. A tattoo, of some kind of bird, rested at the top of her leg. Normally, he hated tattoos but, on Nicky, it added to the attraction. Steam, from the hot tub, made the image before him seem surreal. Was he dreaming? Hallucinating? He knew he was not.

Nicky lowered herself into the hot tub. The water, on her skin, made her sparkle, enticingly. She looked over at Rob,
"I hope I didn't embarrass you just now but I much prefer going naked in this, so much more natural. Swimwear can be such a bore. Why don't you come in? You can leave your pants on." She giggled, "I've plenty of spare towels. I won't say anything to Rose. I certainly won't be telling Ed. He can get terribly jealous, bless him. Surely, there's no harm in two adults sharing a hot tub?" Nicky raised her eyebrows, in a hopeful gesture.

The urge overcame him. He wanted prohibited, decadent satisfaction. He told himself, men, up and down the country, justifiably, did this sort of thing, from time to time. It was a one-off. No one would know. Most British people had a terrible hang-up about nakedness anyway. He kept trying to convince himself, he was doing nothing wrong, even when Nicky kissed him, caressed him and moved his hand between her legs. Even as they joined, he still managed to justify it as servicing a need that was not being satisfied at home.

Caught up in their lust, Rob and Nicky were blissfully unaware that Will had decided to drop off a schedule. This was part of Will's strategy to get projects to run as smoothly as possible, especially with prickly neighbours. He liked to keep people informed. In his experience, communication was key, a face, as well as a name, people could relate to, always helped. Getting no answer at the front door, he let himself through the side gate into the back garden. He thought he had heard Nicky talking. He saw Nicky and Rob, in full swing, in the hot tub. Will backed away, as quietly as he could, before they noticed him. He was shocked by what he had just seen. He had never witnessed, so blatantly, two people cheating on their partners. Granted, Will was never one to stick with the same woman for long, and, had had many affairs, but Rose had run away from her chance the other day. Clearly, she was committed to Rob. Evidently, on his part, it was not reciprocal.

Alone and safely back in the hut, Rob continued to justify what he had just done, but he was finding it difficult. The experience was haunting him, his mistake pulling him down.

TWENTY-TWO

Rose scratched the sleep out of her eyes then massaged her temples. She had what she called a sober hangover. She had not drunk any alcohol and had slept well but she felt tired and groggy. The children had gone to bed easily, the night before, leaving the evening free for Rose to read her book. Rob had worked late. She had fallen asleep long before he joined her and now he was already up. Turning over to kiss him, she had fallen upon a cold space. An indent in the pillow was the only evidence that he had been in bed at all. It was unlike Rob to work excessively hard. Normally, he would lie in if he had worked late. She looked round the bathroom door, half-expecting him to be there but there was no sign of him. She went to wake the children up who had, as yet, to stir.

Rob had been at his desk since five-thirty that morning. He could not sleep. He was in the helpless grip of being unable to rewrite what had happened. He feared he might start hallucinating, so disturbed was he. At one point, during the night, he had drifted off but had woken up, gasping for breath. He was literally smothering in his own terrifying regret.

He knew no amount of worrying, punishing himself or trying to pretend it did not happen could put it right. His marriage promise was shattered. Unbeknown to Rose, he had thrown away her trust. He could not even share his feelings with her. There would be no antidote. He would have to cope with its punishing poison alone. Rob felt fresh panic at the thought of anyone finding out, of Nicky telling someone. He moaned as he put his head in his hands. The sweat and grease from his tired, unwashed face was now on his hands but he did not care. He felt completely dirty.

He knew Rose had been struggling lately. She had not felt as fulfilled as she wished. She was starting a business, for this reason. Instead of paying her more attention, and helping her, he had gone behind her back. Yes, it was only sex but it stood for so much more. Whichever way he looked at it, it was adultery, plain and simple. What he had done with Nicky was supposed to be exclusively reserved for him and Rose. He had been too weak to honour that as he chose to insult his wife.

The telephone cut into the silence. It made Rob jump. As he picked up the receiver, he was aware of his heart running in his chest. He managed to say,
"Rob Clarke architects, Rob speaking, May I help you?"
"Hi there, darling." It was Nicky. Rob felt giddy. He thought he might collapse should he get up from his desk,
"How did you get this number?" He hissed into the telephone.
"From your business card, of course! I'm not stupid, you know!"

"But... you're calling me at work and it's early, really early and if you start leaving messages, they may be picked up by my secretary. This is a work phone, Nicky, not a social one."

"Well, you haven't given me your home number and, well... I'm not going to call you at home am I? After all, you've got a wife and I wouldn't want to leave a message she might pick up." Rob felt heat rising inside him and bile at the back of his throat. Was this a veiled threat?

"Look, Nicky, about yesterday," Before he could say any more, Nicky cut in,

"Ed's staying in London for another couple of days now. Fancy a hot tub at lunchtime, or around then, if you can get away? I'm off work until tomorrow evening." Rob shut his eyes tightly and said nothing. Nicky continued, "Rob? Are you still there?"

"I'm still here. No, no, I don't think I'll be having any more hot tubs with you, not ever. I'm sorry, Nicky, but it was a mistake, my mistake. It's not you. You're lovely but I'm married. I love Rose and we have children and..., look, I'm really sorry." Nicky's tone changed and she replied coldly and slowly,

"Who the hell do you think you are? Meet me in my back garden today or I shall shout from the rooftops what we did together yesterday. You've got way more to lose than me and I won't be treated like some easy slag by someone who clearly isn't being looked after properly at home. I'm not asking you to leave your family but I know you enjoyed yesterday and I want to carry on." The line went dead.

Thank goodness Jan's off today was Rob's first thought, followed by a definite decision to see Nicky, before she got more angry, and demonstrated a total lack of discretion, or empathy, towards him.

Around lunchtime, Rob squeezed through the hedge-gap, making sure no one saw him. Nicky was already waiting,

"You came then." She leant up to kiss him. He turned his head away, much to her annoyance. Her perfume smelt too strong. She tried to put her arms around him, ignoring his reluctance. He grabbed her hands and put them by her side,

"Nicky, please, this is hard enough. I'm sorry but I don't want any of this." She tried, once more, to cajole him into doing what she would like him to, reassuring him that she would not tell a soul. It would be their secret. He stood his ground,

"Nicky, I love Rose, I really do." Nicky ignored this,

"You know, I'm not some sort of toy you can just cast aside because you got what you wanted."

"Look, believe me, please, Nicky, yesterday was a mistake. I enjoyed it at the time, of course I did, but I don't know why I did it. I wholeheartedly regret it. It's not your fault, it's me. You're lovely. But, I've cheated on my wife. I've got a fantastic wife and three kids. Why would I leave all that? I don't want to lose them, Nicky."

"You don't get what you need at home so you can't be that happy. You seemed more than happy in the hot tub, yesterday, and, if no one knows, but us, then how can it harm anyone?" She smiled, sardonically.

"It just does harm people, Nicky. It was a mistake and I want us both to put it behind us."

"How convenient, just forget it? You must be joking. How can you just cast me aside? I've never done this kind of thing before and I thought we were on the cusp of something special."

"Nicky, I'm sorry but no, we're not." Rob felt utterly hopeless and distressed by Nicky's response because she was right. He had taken full advantage of what she had offered. He could have walked away, yet, appallingly, he had not. Now, he would have to live with the isolation of what he had done, and, the knowledge that he was weak enough to risk losing everything of value in his life, for lust.

Nicky looked furious,
"You know what, I wonder if Ed might be right about you. He thinks you're a jumped up, little prat." Rob could see she was fighting back tears. Saliva escaped from her mouth and rested on her chin. She wiped it off with the back of her hand. Fresh anger flashed in her eyes. She let rip, "As I said, you can't just use people like you've used me. You can't have it your way all the time. If you don't want me telling anyone, then, I've got a rather hefty credit card bill that needs paying, about two grand, actually." She stared right into his eyes. The tears and anger had been replaced with a look of triumph.

He was shocked,
"That's blackmail. How dare you," he spat. She remained calm,
"See, I'm not so nice and easy now, am I? You can't treat people like this and expect to get away with it. So, give me a cheque, or cash, if you prefer, tomorrow and we'll say no more about it." She turned on her heel.

Feeling exposed, he retreated to the safety of his hut, in disbelief. However, he already knew what he was going to do and he was pretty sure now, too, who the poison-pen writer was. He focused on his idea for barely a minute before Rose appeared, Evie on her hip,
"Have I caught you at a bad time?"
"No, not really, I'm busy."
"I can come back."

"No it's OK, come in." He gestured towards an empty chair. Rose kissed him on the forehead,

"Are you sure you're all right? You were up very early and...late to bed." She narrowed her eyes as Evie wriggled down onto the floor, towards an elastic band ball, under Jan's desk. He said, as cheerfully as he could,

"I'm so busy and maybe a little bit tired. I haven't showered yet which is never a good look for me." He smiled weakly. Rose persisted,

"No kidding! You look absolutely awful. I'm not going to lie. Something is up, isn't it? Has someone let you down? Perhaps you should take some time off? Nothing's worth exhausting yourself over." He felt suddenly tearful. He tried to swallow his emotions but Rose knew him too well. A tear escaped from the corner of his left eye. She put her arm around him, "Rob, what is it? You can tell me, surely?" He whispered as he lied,

"I don't want Evie to see me crying. I'm overwrought. I've worked too hard. You know me, the perfectionist. I made a silly mistake on a plan that I thought was perfect. I'm upset and overwhelmed." The elastic band ball struck him in the back of his head. He spun round in his chair to see Evie standing in the middle of the room with both fists clenched, waiting for a reaction to what she had done,

"I sorry! I hurt you. Oh no, Daddy cry," she burst into tears. Rose scooped her up,

"Oh, Evie, it's OK. You just made Daddy's eyes water. He wasn't expecting it to hit him. That's why you shouldn't throw things. Come on, kiss Daddy's head better and we'll see him later." Evie reached down, from Rose's arms, and kissed the back of Rob's head saying,

"All better!" Evie was smiling now. It took all of his might not to cry fresh tears. His shame was raw. Rose stroked the back of his head,

"We all get overwhelmed sometimes. Perhaps, take the morning off? Anyway, come and have a coffee, once you feel ready. Love you."

Almost two hours later, a much calmer Rob was in the kitchen, boiling the kettle. Rose appeared in the doorway,
"You look a bit better." She gave him a hug. Evie's watching a DVD so I'm all ears if you need to talk."
They sat at the kitchen table. Rob spoke first,
"I'm sorry you had to see me like that, Rose. It all got too much for me. I've never been like this before have I?"
"No but you've never taken on quite as much as you have now either, Rob, so, maybe, you need to cut back a bit, take on less. As I always say, nothing is worth making yourself ill over."
"Rose, you're so kind. I also need to say that I'm sorry if I haven't been terribly supportive, or interested in you, lately. I really want you to be happy and you know you have my blessing, with everything you do. Do what it takes to make your shop work," he smiled and added, "I'm proud of you. You've got guts. I love that about you."
"Thank you, Rob, that means a lot. Aren't I lucky to have such a lovely husband? I still think there was more to your little melt down this morning, though. I know you too well, mister!"
"Well, actually, there was," Rob cleared his throat and Rose looked puzzled. "I need to talk to you about something but I don't want you to worry as it's nothing, means nothing to me. It was just like, the final straw, if you like. I'll be back in a minute." Rob came back, with the note.

Rose gasped in disbelief,

"Who sent that? No wonder you were so upset. Honestly, Rob, I never knew you took such things to heart. Clearly, the person who wrote this is an immature coward."

"I have a feeling it might be from Ed. Just a hunch. What do you think I should do?"

"I don't know. How can you be sure it's from him? Wait a minute," Rose got up from the table and went over to the cupboard, where she had put the pile of Christmas cards, until she found time to make a list of who sent them, so she did not forget anyone the following year.

"Voila," she declared, waving a card in front of him, "remember? Ed wrote the cards, this time, because Nicky couldn't, because of her broken hand, or whatever it was. Here's the one from them." She passed it to him. He was relieved that mentioning the note seemed enough to explain his stress away to Rose, "Yes, I do vaguely remember, now you come to mention it. Let's have a look." He laid the card and note out on the table, side by side. He immediately concluded they were from different people, "the writing, on the note, is much smaller."

"So?" said Rose, "anyone can change the size of their writing. I think it is the same person, you know, because look at the way those letters are formed. They're the same." Rose continued to draw comparisons between the two, before declaring, "I'm ninety-eight percent sure it's the same person, but, that tiny bit of doubt, with no proof, in my book, is not enough to accuse Ed. I just know, deep down, it's him." Rob looked forlorn,

"He must really hate me," before thinking, grimly, *how he would hate me all the more if he knew what I did with his wife yesterday.* "Do you think I should confront him over it?"

"No, ignore it, Rob. I'm sure he's harmless enough. Concentrate on yourself and leave him be. Also, there's a minute chance he didn't send it. He'll definitely deny it. No point, really."

TWENTY-THREE

Normally, when Jan was absent from the office, Rob kept on top of the administrative part of the business. He had been unable to manage, this time. No post was opened, nothing was tidied up or put away, and, despite the pristine filing system Jan had devised, he could not find anything. He was getting behind with work. There was, simply, no space in his head for it. He had stopped taking his fresh-air breaks too, for fear of Nicky jumping out from behind a bush.

I can't be here any more. I am tortured by what I have done. He dialled Andrew, his brother. Rob needed to get away. He would go and see him, for a few days. Rose would understand. He would tell her that he was going to help with some decorating, and, perhaps, for a game of golf. He did not expect it to be a problem for Rose. She was so remarkably understanding and trusting. Even so, she was clearly surprised. Normally, he planned these sorts of trips weeks ahead, but she was pleased he was to take some time off. Andrew always had a beneficial influence over Rob. She admired him for acknowledging that he needed to go. He had cited helping Andrew with some decorating, or such like, as the reason for the trip, but she knew it was more likely to involve drinking and re-runs of the rugby. She did not mind. It would be nice to have the house to herself, even though Jan would, probably, still come during the day.

Cathy had taken Evie to the park, giving Rose a chance to tidy up, in peace. As she loaded the washing machine, she came across Rob's blue shirt, her favourite. She always took particular care, when washing it. She knew he had worn it for two days, especially on the one when he had shown her the nasty note. It was unusual that he had been so upset. He did not tend to let people get to him. In fact, he was pretty tough. It was almost as if he had not been telling her everything.

As she checked the shirt for stains, she caught a whiff of perfume, different to Rob's usual deodorant, or, aftershave. She sniffed again, to be sure. As she put her nose closer to the collar, she was shocked to notice the unmistakeable smell of Jan's perfume. It was as if it had been directly rubbed into the fabric.

With her heart racing, Rose began to feel giddy. She steadied herself, trying not to jump to conclusions. Perhaps Jan had hugged him, which was all right. She was a tactile person. However, Rose questioned whether or not Jan had actually been in the office when Rob had worn this shirt before reasoning that he had probably actually worn it a few times, not just twice. He would often change, in the evenings, anyway, or afternoons, if he were not seeing any clients. That way, it was not unusual for him to wear the same shirt, on three or four occasions, before putting it in the wash.

Surely, if he were having an affair, he would not be stupid enough to get perfume all over his shirt, a bit obvious. Anyway, affairs happened to other women, not her. She had a strong marriage. She banged the washing machine door shut, added powder and switched it on. A nice, hot wash would get rid of everything.

She was reaching into the cleaning cupboard when she heard a familiar clacking, on the kitchen floor,
"Hi Rose," Jan said cheerfully. She looked smart. Rose felt self-conscious, in her old leggings and shapeless, white tee-shirt, "just making a tea. Would you like one?"
"Hi Jan, no thank you." Rose was aware this sounded a bit curt so she tried to counteract it, "You've been off for a few days, haven't you? Have you been up to anything nice?"
Rose could hear the edge in her own voice as she forced herself to be friendly. Jan looked solemn,
"Well no, not really, I thought Rob might have told you. I was very sick, literally vomiting, for one of the days. It wiped me out and is so annoying as I had planned to visit my friend in Plymouth but, no, instead, I was stuck at home, with my head in the toilet. Pesky bugs! I'm better now. Rob said he found it hard to manage without me. I'm glad about that because I like to think I'm indispensable! Actually, the pain with this bug was horrendous." Rose was surprised,
"Pain?"
"Yes, awful stomach cramps, I'd say as bad as labour, at one point! I thought I was going to be one of those women who give birth on the bathroom floor. You know the ones. They don't have any idea that they're pregnant, except I haven't had sex for years so it would have been a proper shock."

"Really?" Rose put Jan on the spot. She looked surprised, then bemused, at Rose's question,

"Um, yes, well no, actually, certainly not lately anyway but I'm, well..." Rose cut in,

"It's actually none of my business. I shouldn't have put you on the spot. You don't have to answer that."

"It's OK, Rose, don't worry. I'm not really looking for a partner. It's almost always been me and Fred and Mum, of course, helping. My last relationship, after my husband left, fizzled out long before my divorce three years ago. What I have now is enough for me really. Oh, and this job. I do like it here, Rose. It gives me a sense of purpose. I'm very fond of Rob, you know, and you Rose, you've both been very good to me. I don't feel you've ever judged me for being a single mum or anything like that. People around here can be very judgemental, you know, and a lot of men have seen me as fair game and I guess that might be because of the way I dress. I like to dress up and I like high-heels. They make me feel good, the same with make-up and doing my hair. This is how I present myself to the world, if you like. Of course, when I get home, and Fred's in his room, I like to put on my pyjamas, take off all my make-up and knit, yes, knit! That's what I do and probably why I won't meet anyone else. Perhaps I'm already too set in my ways and, well, I was never academic, or ambitious, like you and Rob, so this job, well... it's enough for me. I'd better get on with my work. Rob's left me plenty to do. He took off fast didn't he? Everything's all right?"

"Yes, why wouldn't it be?" Rose said, abruptly.

"Oh," realising she may have overstepped the mark, Jan smiled, "just asking! Don't clean too hard, Rose. It'll be dirty again, in a flash. Housework is always there waiting. The rest of life isn't."

Rose felt a bit ashamed, even arrogant, for thinking that Jan might be up to something with Rob. Rose also felt uncomfortable that she had, in turn, made Jan feel uncomfortable, by putting her on the spot. To Rose, she seemed wise and loyal, sensibly aware of her blessings and happy with her life. Rose wondered why she and Rob always seemed to complicate theirs. Jan would have to be a very polished, comfortable liar to pull off what she had just said, were it not true. Rose was sure she and Rob were not up to anything, so, how could such a strong smell, on his shirt, be explained?

She shelved her fixation with the perfumed shirt and threw herself back into the housework. Scrubbing the yellowing shower base to reveal a sparkling, white square was very satisfying. She had not realised how grubby it had become. As she scrubbed, she became more immersed in her thoughts. Nicky popped into her head, the perfume smell, Rob going off to London... *Nicky, oh my God, it's Nicky, she wears that perfume, the same as Jan.* Rose had got a definite whiff of it the other day when she dropped the post off. Surely, Rob had not... but then it made perfect sense. Rose just knew. She did not need any more evidence.

Tears streamed down her face. Something took over. She felt physical pain in her heart. She could barely breathe. The pressure of so many tears, stacked up behind her eyeballs. She felt trapped. She did not want to face what she was thinking. She wanted to scream but feared she would break. Finally, she grabbed a towel, and using it to muffle her sobs and screams, buried her face in it. She bawled into it until she had nothing left.

She managed to calm herself down. Her mother could turn up very soon with Evie. Cathy would know, for sure, that Rose had been crying. She did not feel she could talk to anyone right now about what she suspected Rob and Nicky might have done. She needed something to quickly de-puff her face. She splashed cold water on it and forced herself to lie for ten minutes with cucumber on her eyes. She layered on copious amounts of make-up, especially eye liner, in the hope of drawing attention away from any puffiness. She would blame any eye watering, or redness, on the make-up itself. She would pass it off as nothing. She willed herself to be brave.

TWENTY-FOUR

Andrew welcomed Rob with a sturdy hug and a cold beer,
"So, how are you, mate? This is an unexpected, but very welcome, visit from my favourite brother."
"Yes, thanks for agreeing to have me at such short notice," Rob took a sip of beer, from the bottle, "It's all getting a bit intense, in the countryside," he laughed, "I needed to get out, for a bit, and return to a more jovial pace of life."

Andrew eyed him suspiciously,
"If you say so, mate, you and Rose haven't had a row have you?"
"No!" Rob looked at the floor and shook his head, "I've taken on a lot and need a break, that's all. Rose is fine with it. She's busy, anyway, so she won't miss me. In fact, she's starting her own business, coffees and sewing or the other way round, depends how you look at it really."
"Sounds good, I'm sure she mentioned something like that to me a couple of years ago. God, you two never

slow down do you? You're like two townies whizzing around the countryside on rockets," Andrew laughed at his own joke, put his half-drunk beer bottle on the kitchen surface and continued, "Now, I've got to go back to work for a few hours so you're welcome to roll up your sleeves and help. It's two roads away, number ten." He dangled the key in front of Rob, "The sitting room needs painting. It's all covered, and washed down, and ready, but, if you don't fancy it and you'd prefer, you can mooch around a gallery for a bit. It's entirely up to you."

"I'm happy to do a bit of painting for you. I find it relaxing and I'd like to earn my keep!" Rob laughed and Andrew feigned offence, "God, you're not staying for that long, are you? Only joking, that sounds great." Andrew looked pleased, "My decorator's on another job and couldn't commit to getting it done. It's at times like these that I roll up my sleeves and just get on with it. However, I've got a meeting with my financial adviser. I'm hoping to raise the finance for my next project so I can go ahead before selling this one. Your help couldn't have come at a better time. By the way, before I go, two things, do you need any old clothes? And, where would you like to eat tonight, my treat?"

"I came prepared, brought some old clothes. The Indian, down the road, is always good, if I remember rightly. Well, the food was particularly good last time, when we literally crawled back!"

"I fear a drinking session coming on! Great, I'll book us a table. You're staying in there, same as last time," Andrew pointed to a bedroom door, "seven-thirty sound OK for dinner?"

"Yeah, great!"

After an exhausting day reaching up with the brush, not to mention a heavy curry and more beer, Rob went to bed physically exhausted, and tipsy. The fun with Andrew, his only brother, had enabled him to forget about his woes, for a little while. At times like these, Rob wished he still lived in London, so he was able to see more of Andrew, who was also one of his trusted friends.

Despite his state, sleep did not come easily to Rob and once it did, he jolted awake many times during the night, partly because of the beer, but mainly because he was plagued by his thoughts, dread, panic and regret, at what he had done. He kept replaying the conversation he had had with Nicky, before leaving for London. He had called in before driving away. Ed had been out so she had ushered him straight in,

"Had a re-think?" She had said, seductively licking her lips, like a lizard about to ensnare its prey, "I knew you wouldn't stay away for long. Our little secret, eh?" She had run her hands suggestively down the length of her body, waiting for Rob to make a move. Her expectation had danced in the air. This had made Rob angry,

"Look, Nicky, we both took advantage of something we offered each other. We both have to live with it and I don't wish to repeat it, not now, or ever. I've made my position clear, many times. I love my wife and would do anything to undo what I did with you, but I can't. Please, stay away from me, Nicky, and don't try to contact me again, unless you need to about our respective properties. Take note that I won't be blackmailed. I won't be paying you a penny. You say that I have a lot more to lose than you, but, arguably, you have way more to lose, bearing in mind your home. I know that Ed owns the house. You live in it and, from what I know, you haven't lived there for a very long time so walk away, Nicky. Leave me alone, and leave what we did alone, in the past, where it belongs."

She had folded her cardigan tightly around her and, with crossed arms, had looked straight at him,

"Well, Rob, I hope you've brought my money with you. What you say all sounds very plausible, and convenient, to safely leave it in the past. What I say, is, that I don't really love Ed, you're right. Well, I love him but am not in love with him. I am still his wife. He's miserable and annoying and yes, you're right, in a way, it suits me living here, but it suits Ed having me here too. I must point out, well, you've already lost more, because you've got to live with the fact that you regret you're an untrustworthy cheater. Not only have you cheated on your wife, who you claim to be in love with, but on your children too. Good luck living with that. Oh," there was a renewed flash of anger in her eyes, "you never know, as you're refusing to help me, your mistress, out financially, like any decent man would, you're going to be wondering, forever, whether or not I'll tell Rose, and whether or not I've told anyone else. You're always going to wonder. It'll kill you in the end."

"Well, that's a risk I'll have to take because you're really not getting a penny out of me," he hissed, "and, by the way, you are not, and never were, my mistress." He spat the last word and sped off, in his car, before she had a chance to retaliate.

On the way to Andrew's, before he hit the motorway, Rob had had to pull over his hands were shaking so much. Again, his heart felt like it was going to bump out of his body. He sat for half an hour staring ahead, not focusing on anything in particular, while berating himself for being so stupid as to think he could have a one-off, no-strings-attached, sexual encounter, with his neighbour, and still be free. What had he been thinking?

Now, lying in the unfamiliar bed, with no Rose to cuddle up to, he continued to punish himself, in the heavy darkness. He felt weak, thoughtless and selfish. His capable, vivacious wife; what had he done? Why had he neglected her so much? He had been aware of her crying herself to sleep, on many occasions. He had, callously, ignored this. He had done nothing to comfort her, had pretended he was asleep so it would all go away. She was strong but she was frustrated. She had been quite open about this, which was why, in her stoical way, she was taking action and starting her own business. He had done barely anything to help, silently and selfishly worrying about how this change would affect him. He felt so ashamed as he drifted into another restless snooze.

His phone woke him abruptly, intruding on another horrible dream where he was screaming and no one heard him. As it buzzed around, like a dying fly, on the table next to his bed, he reached over, squeezed a button on the phone, thinking he had rejected the call, and turned over only to hear Nicky's unmistakable voice,

"Hello, Rob, are you there? Hello? Hello?" Knowing she would only keep calling back, he felt it was best to answer,

"Hi Nicky, what do you want? I really don't have anything else to say to you."

"Well that's not a very nice way to greet a friend is it?" Friend sounds OK, he thought, thanking God it did not have the word girl in front of it.

"Is there something you rang me for, Nicky?"

"Well, you and I both know what I want you for but, you don't want to play any more, which is not OK, but, I can't make you have fun." Rob remained silent as Nicky continued, "Thing is, as you know, I've been expecting my credit card bill. It is two grand and a penny, exactly, as expected. You know nurses don't earn anything much, unlike architects." She trailed off, "Anyway, you have a good think about helping me. How are Rose and the family?"

"Leave them out of this, Nicky. It's over and I've already told you I'm not paying your credit card bill."

"Shame, maybe I'll ask Rose instead, seeing as we all know each other so intimately now. Yes, I might just have a chat with Rose." Rob spluttered down the phone, "You wouldn't, I mean, don't you dare."

"What, have a chat with her, why not? She seems such an understanding wife, and so trusting, don't you think? I'm sure she wouldn't question why I feel able to ask you, Rob, my special friend, and lovely neighbour, for two grand. Don't worry about the penny."

"Get lost, Nicky," he hung up and chucked the phone back onto the side, "Oh God, oh God, oh God," he said out loud, as he sat up on the edge of the bed, and ran his hands through his hair and down his face.

"Everything all right?" Andrew was at the bedroom door with two cups of coffee. He offered one to Rob. He exhaled loudly,

"Just a ghastly hangover, thanks for the coffee. It should help." He ran his fingers through his hair again, feeling more bewildered. Andrew nodded knowingly as he sipped his coffee,

"Fancy breakfast out? They do a mean one at Bellisi, a ten-minute walk away. The fresh air might help? After all, you didn't drink that much last night, you lightweight," he smiled.

"I know, I know. It must be the city smog clouding my brain."

"Very funny,"

"Yes, definitely yes to breakfast. Have I got time for a quick shower?"

"Sure, I'll hop in now, while you drink your coffee, then it's all yours. Let's aim to be out of here in half an hour... that sound OK to you?"

"I'll be ready," Rob smiled. His brother always liked to have a schedule to stick to. Time never seemed to run away when he was on it. He eyed Rob suspiciously,

"Are you sure you're all right, mate? Something's up, I can tell. You and Rose are OK aren't you? Only, you didn't say much about her last night. I get the sense you're peeved she's starting a business. Surely, you don't expect her to spend the rest of her life washing your shirts?" When Rob did not laugh, Andrew laughed, "That last bit was meant to be a joke."

"Not now, Andrew, please. I've got a bloody hangover. How many times do I have to say that everything's OK?" Rob almost shouted. Andrew, never one to back down until he had said his piece, bravely retorted, "Until you believe it yourself?" before gently shutting the bedroom door.

Rob's phone buzzed again. It was Will, thankfully,

"Morning, Rob, how are you?"

"Good...good," he said twice, the second time with more enthusiasm, "Just spending a few days in London with my brother, Andrew."

"Yes, Rose said, everything OK with you both?"

"Er...yeah, why do you ask? Do you know something I don't?" Rob laughed nervously. *If only you knew,* thought Will before realising that, perhaps, he should not have just asked that question. Will hurled himself back into professional mode, pushing the memory of what he had seen, in the hot tub, out of his mind,

"Oh, no reason, no reason at all," he laughed before continuing, "I'm ringing about a couple of things, actually. I did drop by this morning to run it by you face to face. Anyway, everything is going in the right direction. It's just Ed. He keeps ringing up the planners, questioning everything, like what colour the bricks he won't see will be, which is, reading between the lines, bugging them. So..., I wondered if you might want to think about writing yet another letter, which I can help you with, to Ed, clarifying what's been agreed, already, and what we plan to do with timescales, etcetera. In my experience, there are usually far less complaints and questions if you keep your neighbours up-to-date. If the communication is good then everyone feels like they count." As Will said this, he could not help thinking, *although that normally would not include jogging with their wife, in the hot tub*. He added, "and, I need to know whether you want me to order the opal or the cream kitchen-floor tiles. There is a minuscule difference between the two colours. I mention it because I like to be thorough. It's your call. Obviously, you need to decide soon as they'll be one of the first things to go in."

Rob felt faint. Right now, he could not care if Will ordered bright-orange floor tiles, or ran Ed over in his car, but he responded to Will politely,
"A letter? Yes, whatever it takes to shut him up. You write it, please. Just show me a copy before you send it. As for the tiles, um..., ask Rose. I don't know. If they're not very different then either should do." Will laughed,
'Rose said the same, said to ask you... "
"Ok, then, what would you order, if it were for your kitchen?"
"The cream as I prefer cream to white, it's softer. I think the opal is slightly more white."
"Fine, go with those, thanks Will. I must go now."

"Shower's free," shouted Andrew through the door, "Hurry up, I'm hungry, my stomach's rumbling!"

Twenty minutes later, Rob was still lying in bed, his back to the bedroom door. Andrew poked his head into the room,
"Oh, come on, mate, just get up!" There was no response from Rob so Andrew walked round to the side of the bed, expecting to find ear buds in Rob's hungover ears, Rob fast asleep. Andrew was shocked to find him, his face soaked, sobbing, almost silently, into the pillow.

TWENTY-FIVE

Rose missed Rob. Her suspicions, about what he might have done, would not go away. He might not wish to be or, indeed, may not be entirely hers any more. That thought was devastating. She ached for everything to be back to normal. She missed the way he clinked around the kitchen, especially in the mornings. He always left his worn socks draped over the side of the bath instead of putting them in the laundry basket. She could not bear to think that small familiarities, like this, could disappear from her life, because he no longer loved her.

Her business spurred her on. She would check the premises' progress today. The most fun bit was just around the corner. Choosing accessories, like bunting, tables and chairs, crockery and teaspoons, the frivolous bits and pieces.

The doorbell chased away her thoughts. She was surprised to see David. He sensed this and looked uncomfortable, as he forced his awkward self to make eye contact. He said, robotically, as if reciting from a memorised script,

"Hello, Rose, your mother sent me to get Evie. I need Evie, her changing bag, coat and wellington boots. We plan to walk in the woods, and Thomas and Anna, please. I shall drive them to school."

"David!" Rose said warmly, "Do come in, please." David looked awkwardly at his shoes and hesitated. Rose took over, "Don't worry about your shoes; Just come in. You're letting all the heat out."

"Oh, gosh, am I? I am sorry." He stepped inside, gently shutting the front door behind him. She called the children. Evie came first and Rose wrestled her into her coat before placing her in David's arms. He looked awkward like someone had handed him an unpredictable animal. He looked like he had something to say but could not find the words. Rose smiled encouragingly before he spoke, "Cathy says you've bought a coffee shop, that you're checking on the builders, this morning?"

"Yes, well I'm renting it to begin with. I'm going to offer sewing lessons, which Mum will teach. I'm going to sell fabric too. There's quite a demand for that sort of thing around here."

"Is there?" David said, bluntly, looking unconvinced, "You know, you could do a profession like accountancy, retrain. They take people like you, you know, older." He looked embarrassed, " I mean a bit older, not eighteen. That's what I'm trying to say."

"I'm sure they do," she smiled, "but, I want to do this, not accountancy."

"Mmm... professionals are always in demand. Cressida and Giles will always have work, wherever they are. You are bright, Rose." David was clearly unable to hide the fact he did not rate her decision.

"Thank you, David. I'm flattered that you think I have other options but I'm doing what I want to, what feels right. You know people will always need company, coffee and cake, curtains and clothes, the five 'c's'!" She was aware of sounding flippant so changed the subject, "Tell Mum I'll collect Evie this afternoon once I've got the other two. I'll put Evie's bag, and wellies, in the car for you. Thank you, this is such a help."

"I shall pass all that onto Cathy," replied David, stiffly. The children waved happily at Rose as they disappeared, in the car, round the corner.

Rose checked the house before slipping on her kitten-heels, and rolling lipstick over her lips, in front of the large mirror she and Rob had hung together, shortly after moving in. She grabbed her handbag, and keys, from the hall table. She opened the front door and stepped straight into Will, before she realised he was there.

"Steady!" he exclaimed, as he put out his arms and took a step back, "I didn't even get a chance to ring the bell!" Rose was stunned then embarrassed. She had let out a shriek as she bumped into him. Once she realised who it was, she found it difficult to recover her composure. He explained why he had called round, unannounced, "I wanted to run a couple of things by you, and Rob, but I can tell it's not a good time."

"No, it's not," she replied, curtly, "I've got to get to my shop, ...builders."

"Mind if I go through to the hut and talk to Rob then?" He raised his eyebrows, clearly expecting a 'yes', before Rose informed him of the opposite,

"You won't be able to. Rob's in London. Ring him, he's got his mobile. Sorry, I've really got to go or I'll be late," she turned her back on him, signalling the conversation was over. He stood there, watching her, thinking how attractive she looked.

She got in her car to leave. He gestured for her to open the window,
"Is everything all right? I mean, with Rob, him being away and all that?" He kicked himself the minute he said this. It felt over familiar as the words came out, and he remembered their failed kiss. Momentarily, Rose stopped looking at him, fiddled with the car heater, then looked him straight in the eye,
"Of course, why wouldn't everything be all right?" before she drove away.

"I'd like this area behind me, just this wall, in the pink I showed you, and the rest is fine in cream. Also, the flooring needs to go down before the units in the kitchen but I think we've already discussed that and, er... one more thing, yes... that's it, please would you make sure no one switches on the new fridge, once it's delivered. I'll sort it out. I want to make sure it settles properly as I really don't need any unnecessary expenses cropping up because things haven't been treated properly," Rose smiled expectantly. Mick looked a bit put out by this comment,
"We would never switch on an appliance without reading the instructions first, wouldn't dream of it."
"Good, I think you're doing a fantastic job, it's just I have to mention these things for my own peace of mind, if nothing else. Please don't take anything I say personally but you have lots of guys here and it only takes one to make a mistake... think he's helping, you know what I mean."
"Don't worry, we'll be finished soon and out of your hair," he laughed. She smiled back,
"How much longer do you expect it to take?"

"A week to ten days, maybe two weeks, certainly not three."

She did not push it because even three more weeks sounded fine to her except she did not want him to know this for fear that he interpreted it as there being no rush to finish up. It gave her time to sort out the things she needed to do. She felt now was a good time to leave him to get on with it,

"Great, well I'm just going to take some measurements for blinds then I'll be gone. It's certainly taking shape. I'm very pleased with what you've done, so far."

Back home, she scooped the letters up from the floor, as she opened the front door,

"And another one for good, old Nicky Turner! Can't the postman read?" She dropped it on the floor, near the front door, to deal with later. She wedged the remaining letters behind the pepper mill, on the surface, in the kitchen.

She took a cup of tea upstairs and sat on the edge of the bed to remove her shoes. She loved them. They flattered her legs and made her feet look neat. Unfortunately, her feet hated them. They had moulded into the shape of the shoes. Her toes looked like they had been tightly bound into a fat, tube shape. Her feet slowly, and uncomfortably, began forming back into their intended, more-spread-out shape, as if they were being reinflated.

Without warning, she suddenly felt her energy levels plummet. It was like someone had pulled the plug. Rob, Nicky, Will, the coffee shop, the children all charged around her mind until she burst into uncontrollable tears, again. She feared Rob's suspected infidelity might make him believe that they would be better apart.

She was startled from her state by noise from the kitchen. She realised it must be Jan. Rose had not expected her to be here but, of course, Jan still had a job to do. Rose waited until she was sure Jan had returned to the hut before easing herself off the bed. She swallowed another sob. She did not want to cry any more. Her body seemed reluctant to stop. She willed herself to be strong. This would not break her. Nothing got the better of her for long. She would fight for Rob, if necessary, because she loved him, because of their children and because of the life they had together which she cherished.

Comforted by a bath, and more make-up, Rose went out to speak to Jan. Rose could see her busily typing on Rob's computer, through the window. Rose knocked on the door.

"Come in, oh, hi Rose, is Rob OK? It's just that he's not answering his phone. I don't want to keep leaving messages. It's so unlike him. He didn't leave me any instructions as to what to do, like he normally would, if he knew he was going to be away from the office for long."

"Oh, right," said Rose, as she sat down, "have you got enough to be getting on with, for now?"

"Well; yes. It's just Rob is normally very particular. I don't want to miss anything. I'm probably doubting myself unnecessarily. In fact, I'm sure I haven't missed anything."

"I'm sure you haven't either. Rob is helping his brother decorate a flat, emergency, apparently, a leak or something, had to get it ready for a new tenant as the old one bailed, unexpectedly." Rose surprised herself at how easily she told Jan all of this, considering her suspicions as to why Rob had gone away so suddenly, "So, I don't think Rob had time to sort out much, at this end, before he left. I imagine he thought you'd manage. He's always telling me how capable, and competent, you are." Jan beamed,

"Well, I've answered all the emails, opened the post and really got on top of the filing and tidying up."

"Thank you, Jan. I'm sure he'll be happy with that. I must go as I'm going to drop yet another letter round to Nicky before I collect the children. Do lock up when you leave, please."

"I will, thanks, Rose. Just one thing, are your eyes OK? They look sore."

"My eyes?" Rose thought she had done a sterling job with her make-up but women always seemed to notice things amiss on other women. *Damn*, she thought, *if you're too nice to me, I'll cry again*. "Oh, it might be my new eye liner. How annoying. I seem to react to so many things. It wasn't a cheap one, either," she lied.

"You want to try 'Lusheye' drops. They're brilliant. The chemist in town stocks them."

"I might get some. Thanks again, see you tomorrow, Jan."

Rose drove straight round to Nicky and Ed's. Instead of just popping the envelope in their letter box, she decided to ring the doorbell. She refused to be afraid to face Nicky. Rose wanted to give her the message that she was very much present in their lives with no plans to shrink and disappear.

Rose thought she saw a fleeting look of fear, or was it guilt, she could not tell, in Nicky's eyes, as she opened the door,

"Hi Rose!" Rose regarded the woman in front of her, for a moment, the harlot. Rose resisted the urge to grab her by the hair and force the truth out of her,

"Hi Nicky, How are you?" *Like I care*. Rose sniffed the air, "Nice perfume, Nicky." Rose held up the letter. Nicky looked more relaxed once she saw it and nodded before taking it from Rose and thanking her, adding,
"The perfume was a present from a friend of mine." Rose ignored this,
"Perhaps you should phone the post office and find out why we keep getting your post. It's happening far too often now and you wouldn't want to miss something important, if we were away, would you?" Rose was being purposely curt and wanted to add something along the lines of, *Don't you thing you're getting a bit old for mini-skirts and such bright lipstick?* but thought better of it. Nicky must have sensed Rose's thoughts because she looked nervous again,
"I appreciate you bringing the letters round, thank you. You're very kind." Rose resisted the urge to say, *So kind I even let you use my husband.* Rose could feel anger rising inside her so fast she felt giddy. Before she could stop herself, she blurted out,
"Funny, your perfume is exactly the smell I got off the collar of my husband's shirt. I noticed it when I was loading the washing machine but then there is probably a very good explanation for it. It is, after all, a very common scent, every other woman wears it."

Nicky looked shocked and stepped back. She was momentarily speechless before looking triumphant,
"Your husband, lovely Rob, is much kinder than you may think, actually. I gave him a friendly hug the other day as he's offered to pay off my credit card for me. He's so generous. I happened to mention it to him when he stopped by for coffee, after dropping off some post, actually. He offered to help me. Why would I refuse?" She smiled like the joker in the batman films. It took all Rose's self-control not to shove her,

"We'll see," was all Rose managed to say before turning on her heel leaving a superior-looking Nicky in the doorway.

Rose's debilitating sadness had been sidelined by anger, the fighting-back sort. How Rob would even want to be near a woman so scheming she did not know. Rose was his wife, the one he had chosen to be with. She had built up history with him. She was the mother of his children. She was not going to give up on him, regardless of what he had done. Nicky was just some woman that had got in the way. She came much lower down, in the pecking order, as far as Rose was concerned. Sex was sex. It was not love, compassion, understanding or companionship; some of the things Rob and Rose's life together was built around.

Sitting in the school car park, Rose had five minutes to spare. She sent Rob a text. Nicky would not get a penny out of him, if she had anything to do with it,
"Hi Rob, Hope you're enjoying your time with Andrew? I just wanted you to know I love you very much. Whatever your reasons, I do NOT agree with you giving Nicky Turner a penny of our money. I do not trust her, or even like her. What's mine is yours and you are not to give her anything, regardless of what she says. Talk tomorrow. Busy now. Love Rose xx"

Rob tried to ring her, almost immediately. He tried three times. Rose purposely did not answer, leaving him to sweat. Eventually, a text message came through,
"OK, not sure what you mean?! I love you too. Rob xx"

Of course you know what I mean. For now, she would not grant him the luxury of explaining anything. A just punishment, and a lesson learned, in case temptation ever came his way again.

She was in no mood for school-gate chat. She reached the playground just as Anna and Thomas were let out. They came running over towards her, smiling with their arms wide open to hug her, their backpacks like big shells.

"Hello you two! Good day?"
"Yes!" The duo replied.
"We've got to get Evie from Granny's."
"Yes," they said, again in tandem, as they skipped off towards the car park.

"Come in, cherubs, good to see you all." Cathy turned to Rose, "You've time for a coffee haven't you?"
"Yes, please," Rose hung up all the coats on the pegs inside the front door, before joining her mother in the kitchen,
"Rose, you look exhausted and your eyes look sore. I hope you're not over doing it. I bet you didn't take even a minute off today." Rose smiled,
"My new eye liner has made my eyes sore and yes, I'm too keyed up to relax, Mum. I'm full of ideas. You know what I'm like. I'm making changes and I can't stop for anything," she joked, easing her way past her mother, to grab a warm place near the Aga. She knew the children would have already made themselves comfortable, on the bean bags, in front of the television, in the sitting room, probably with a Kit Kat in each hand.

Rose sat down with a cup of tea. Cathy offered her a biscuit.

"No biscuits, please, Mum. I put on a pound every time I touch one. I don't need fattening up!"

"OK, only offering! I'm sorry to keep saying it but you do look tired. Please don't take on too much. You are a mother of three and one of them doesn't even go to school yet. Get Rob to put the children to bed tonight, and give you a break. Get a takeaway, have a night off."

At the mention of Rob, Rose could no longer maintain her composure. Tears stung her eyes as they forcefully formed. Her throat felt dry, like sore lips about to crack. She managed, stifled by sobs, to say Rob was with Andrew before she completely broke down. Cathy, remaining calm, put her arm around Rose's shoulders, "Oh love, what is it?

"I think he may have cheated on me, Mum." She sobbed into her mother's chest, like a child who had been left out of a party she wanted to go to.

After telling her mother everything, she calmed down,
"I'm such a mess or rather it's, this, is such a mess. What am I going to do? I probably shouldn't have told you any of this as now you'll hate Rob and I want you to like him because I still love him."

"Hang on, love, who said I would judge? Yes, I'm cross, very cross, with him, for upsetting you so much, but it sounds like you've been having problems for a while. It's not the end of the world and chances are Rob feels rotten too." Cathy was desperate to make things right for her daughter, "Everyone's allowed one mistake, a once-in-a-lifetime holiday, if you like, and, sadly, a lot of people, men especially, take it, if it's offered on a plate. No excuse, I know. It should be treated with the flippancy it deserves. It's more than likely over now. I've seen the way he looks at you, Rose. He loves you.

I bet he's full of remorse, really suffering, I have to add; with any luck."

"Shouldn't I say something to him, Mum? I don't want him to think he's got away with it and I want him to know that if he were to do it again that would be it."

"It's probably killing him the fact he doesn't know whether you know or not and that might just be good enough for him, you know, to bear the guilt, alone, because to be able to come clean might make him feel better. This is about you, not him.

"What about Will?"

"As for him, I would say nothing, to anyone, and stay well away. He sounds used to seducing women and you were caught off guard, a bit slow, if you don't mind me saying. One could even say he took advantage of you, but no need to go there. Some things are best left where they are, love. All this should evaporate, naturally. Nothing is worth making yourself ill over.

"You know, I love spending time with the children. I will always babysit for you, if I can. Perhaps, once Rob is back, you should try to go out together more, on dates, just the two of you, rekindle the reason you two decided to build a life together, in the first place."

"I know, Mum. Everything you've said makes sense, but, what if Rob doesn't want me any more?"

"Want you?" She laughed, "He adores you. I've never doubted his love for you. He's made a mistake. Aim to move on."

"I hear what you're saying, Mum," Rose cut in, "but, if he's cheating on me, and giving her money, then surely I need to confront him?"

"But, Rose, you have no solid proof, apart from what this manipulative-sounding Nicky has said. What good would it do? He has made the mistake so he can live with it. No one's marriage is perfect and you still have a chance to grow old together."

"Oh God, Mum, you're such a pacifist."

"Yes, Rose, and there's no harm in that. If you still love him then fight for him. Have you thought about marriage counselling?"

"What, so some bearded hippy can tell us how to have sex?" Rose laughed, cracking the stickiness on her face. Cathy looked serious,

"Come on, love, it's only a suggestion. It might help."

'I know, Mum, thanks. I really appreciate you listening to me and thank you for not slagging Rob off as a lot of mothers-in-law would do, I'm sure, given the opportunity."

David brought Evie into the room, holding her at arms length, "I'm afraid she needs a nappy change." He handed her to Rose before quickly retreating. Cathy raised her eyebrows at Rose before Rose found herself laughing,

"Oh Mum, I'm going mad. My emotions are all over the place!"

As Rose was leaving, Cathy stuffed some notes into her hand,

"Get your hair done, your nails, a massage, a new top, whatever you want; my treat. Look after yourself, Rose." Cathy kissed her daughter on the cheek. Rose felt overwhelmed again,

"Oh, Mum, no, I can't take this. You already do so much for me. You're always helping with the children."

"I want you to have it." Cathy put her arms behind her back and smiled. Rose kissed her mother on the cheek,

"Oh, Mum, thank you ...for everything, for being objective, and, especially, for your discretion."

TWENTY-SIX

Only when their father had died, had Andrew ever witnessed Rob sobbing, uncontrollably, like this. Andrew was not aware of anything that could have upset Rob this much. Andrew put his hand on Rob's heaving shoulder and waited for him to calm down. Eventually, Rob managed to tell him, between laboured breaths, to just go. Andrew agreed, saying he would be back, shortly, with some food. Then, they would talk.

Andrew returned, twenty minutes later, with sandwiches from the local delicatessen. Two cups of tea and a new box of tissues complemented the offering. Rob was sitting on the edge of the bed, with the duvet pulled around him, like an inflatable, protective pad. Lint, from the toilet paper he had used to stem his tears, was stuck in his stubble. His face was swollen. He had a thumping headache. Before Andrew sat in the armchair, next to the bed, Rob asked if he could have some headache tablets and a glass of water adding,
"I would get them myself, mate, but I am literally spent." Andrew dutifully rushed off to get them while

Rob took a sip of tea. It was soothing, much appreciated. Andrew returned with a packet of painkillers and released two into Rob's upturned hand. Silence fell between the men until they had finished their sandwiches. Andrew was first to break the silence,

"Are you going to tell me what's going on? I'm not aware of anyone dying," he winked.

"Andrew, mate, I wish I could laugh but I've really messed up..."

"What do you mean? Rose and the kids are OK, aren't they? And, your work's going well, you told me that yourself. I know Mum's OK so, what is it?"

"I cheated on Rose." Andrew stared at him with a mixture of disbelief, confusion and pity. "Yep, you heard right, I cheated on my lovely wife." Just saying it made Rob stifle another sob but this time he clenched both fists as if he was willing the pain to leave, literally trying to get a grip on his emotions. "I had sex with our neighbour, the one at the bottom of the garden. I don't know why, or what made me do it, but I did and now I have to live with being cheating scum, just like all the other cheating scum out there." Rob ran both hands through his hair, which looked greasy, "How I wish I could go back and not do it but I can't." Andrew looked concerned. He straightened the watch on his wrist, which did not need straightening. Clearly feeling like they needed more than just tea, Andrew went to the kitchen and returned with two small glasses of whisky. He handed one to Rob, who took a mouthful. Andrew took a sip of his and put the rest down on the windowsill,

"Does Rose know?"

"I don't know," Rob grimaced. He looked like he was in pain.

"You absolute, bloody plonker," was Andrew's unhelpful response, "What the hell were you thinking?

You struck gold with Rose. When did things get so bad that you had to go looking for favours from your neighbour? I mean, honestly, Rob, you've got it all."

Rob said nothing, for a while, as he believed he deserved to hear this. He felt even more desperate now the reality of what he had done continued to embed itself deep within him,
"Things have been different, lately," said Rob, "You know, we moved out of London so we could have a slower, less frantic, pace of life, a garden, more room for the kids. Rose was so keen for another baby and to be a full-time mum this time round. It was all going so well, according to plan if you like, but, lately, Rose has become distant, you know, not as interested in this life, what we both planned. She's rented a coffee shop at the top of town. All of a sudden, she doesn't want to be at home any more, she wants to be bloody working again. It's like, where do I fit in to all this? We have more kids, are busier, decide to renovate our house and she decides to start a business. I repeat, that's not what we agreed!" Andrew shook his head,
"What? For God's sake, Rob? Isn't she entitled to change her mind? She's an intelligent, educated woman. Surely you didn't think she'd want to spend the rest of her life chained to the kitchen sink? How ridiculous of you! It sounds like just because she wasn't giving you enough attention and things weren't quite panning out as you wanted, you thought you'd go and get some attention from your neighbour. Honestly, Rob, get over yourself!"

Rob looked horrified,
"Don't hold back, mate, beat me more and take Rose's side. It wasn't so long ago you cheated on your wife..."

Andrew seethed, at this comment. He leant right into Rob's face and cut in almost hissing the words,
"Except, Lucy had gone off me, and our life together, long before I cheated on her. As you know, she'd had two affairs herself in our five years together and never wanted sex, not with me anyway, always had a headache or a period, any excuse she could think of, so it was a bit different.

"Don't punch low again, Rob, because you've messed up and you know it. Oh my God, I know you don't want to hear this, mate, but this is Rose we're talking about. Could you not have worked something out before you... before you... honestly, Rob..., have you told her? Will the neighbour tell her? Does anyone else know?"
"I don't know. Of course, I haven't told her and I don't think Nicky, that's her name, will tell anyone. She wants me to pay her off though."
"What? Pay her off? What do you mean? What are you talking about? Are you mad?" Andrew looked utterly horrified, "How much?"
"Only two"
"Two hundred?" Rob looked sheepish,
"No, grand."

Andrew took a big gulp of whisky prompting Rob to take another mouthful of his. Andrew gasped after his gulp then exclaimed,
"Two grand! So, next time it might be three? You're being blackmailed, mate, she'll do it again. She won't stop."
"I don't think she will ask again if I pay her this time," said Rob quietly, "I just don't think she has a lot of money and thought she'd grab her chance to get her credit card paid off."

"She sounds so nice, husband-stealer and blackmailer," said Andrew, sarcastically. Rob looked sombre,

"Somehow, Rose knows about the money."

"But not the affair?"

"I just don't know. Nicky must have said something about me helping her with her bill because Rose sent me a text saying I wasn't to give her a penny. But, I don't know what's been said, whether Nicky has told her or not."

"Rob, she may well have guessed. Women have a sixth-sense for this kind of thing." Rob sighed loudly, a defeated sigh,

"Look, Andrew, I made a mistake, a massive mistake, OK? It was only once and can't you see I'm broken from it? I don't need you telling me what a fool I am because I'm quite capable of telling myself that. Andrew, I love Rose so much and want our marriage to work for the rest of our lives. I don't want to cheat on her ever again but she's been so distant lately. You have no idea. I know that doesn't make what I've done all right but I'm trying to explain."

"Do you still like her?"

"What, Rose?"

"Well, I think that one's obvious, no, I meant Nicky."

"Not in the way you're thinking. I don't think she's very happily married."

"So, you thought you'd step in and make her happy?" Rob shot Andrew a withering glance and Andrew apologised for what he had said straight away. Rob continued,

"Like I said, it wasn't like that. It just happened. I didn't plan it."

"Spontaneous?"

"Well, yes." Andrew raised his eyebrows,

"Christ, Rob, you've put your marriage on the line because of a spontaneous moment." Andrew rubbed his face in disbelief while Rob finished his whisky,
"Yes, when you put it like that. It was just sex, a one-off. I love Rose so much. This is cutting me up." Rob stifled another sob. Andrew felt sorry for his brother,
"I know, I'm sorry, mate. I can see you're a mess. It's just Rose is a cracking girl." Rob managed a smile. He looked like he might break down again. Andrew noticed this and moved to sit next to him. He put his arm round him, "You'll just have to fight for her, Rob. You know, I'm here on my own in a flat while the ex enjoys the house. Hands up, I screwed up but you, Rob, you have it all. Fight to keep it that way. I think that I fell out of love with Lucy and vice versa long before we had affairs. They were just the final straw. Your situation is different. Even so, I wouldn't advise confessing to Rose because you'll just be unloading your guilt. That never works. You're just going to have to live with what you've done."

Rob knew his brother was right,
"Really, Andrew, I'm surprised you're single. You seem in touch with how women think." Rob seemed to be regaining his sense of humour. Andrew laughed,
"Lots of practice and lots of thinking. One more thing, don't give that woman a penny."
"Seriously, you really wouldn't pay?"
"Nope...be strong about that. I guarantee she's trying it on and it's none of my business, I know, but may I suggest that, perhaps, you and Rose ought to consider a few sessions of marriage counselling?"
"What? Are you serious? So some floating woman in a kaftan can interfere in our sex life? God, no thanks!" Rob acted out a mock shudder. Andrew smiled,

"I think you ought to go home tomorrow morning, mate, and stop hiding. See your wife and start to put things right."

Rob arrived home, the next day, just as Rose, with Evie, returned from the morning school run. Rose was relieved to see him back home. She had woken, during the night, gasping for breath. This level of anxiety she had not experienced since her early days at university, caused by the shock of leaving home, her sudden placement in the adult world.

Rob got straight out of the car and ran across to Rose. He planted a quick kiss on Evie's cheek. She seemed unmoved by his return and wriggled off Rose's hip, towards the front door. He briefly embraced and kissed Rose. He looked drawn. Stress was etched on his face.

They went inside. He kissed Rose tenderly on the top of her head.
"I'm sorry," he said, sincerely. He noticed a distance about her, which indicated that it would be wrong to grab her and hug, much as he wanted to. He reminded himself that he had left abruptly,
"I missed you," he offered and kissed her cheek again before throwing his arms around her anyway. To his relief, Rose did not push him away,
"It's OK. We must move forward."
"Yes," Rob gently agreed.
"How was Andrew's?" Rose enquired. He noted how strong and stoic she seemed. Wariness would be inevitable. A lot had, and would, remain unsaid between them.
"Andrew's was great, thanks. He sends his love."

"Did you do much?"

"Well, a little," he smiled, "some painting." She smiled back. She did not imagine Rob had done much decorating at all. Rob asked,

"Has everything been OK here, while I've been away?"

"Yes, the children are fine. Mum's helped me out so I'm not too exhausted."

"Good; Look, Rose, I'm sorry I just took off like that. I had to get away. I really do love you so much. I missed you an awful lot."

"I know. I feel the same," she smiled, "I'm sorry for being distant, not taking enough notice of you, especially lately." She stayed silent, for a while, before he spoke,

"What I'm trying to say is that I haven't exactly tried very hard to touch base, shall we say, with you, lately, either. Rose, I really want to make it up to you."

"Well then, let's move forward and forget the past. Before we try though, I meant it when I said you're not to give Nicky a penny. I don't care what her reasons are for wanting it. The bigger the distance we put between them and us the better. That's all I want to say on the matter." Rob looked worried,

"Has she said something?"

"Not really, why, has she something to say?" Rob looked uncomfortable and exhausted,

"Um... no, no..." he tailed off.

"Rob, I know you don't like the idea of me working but I'm going to have a good go at this business. It's not that I don't want you or to be a mum. I just want to work. I need to."

"I know you do. I'm sorry if I haven't been supportive enough."

"That's OK. You've done your best or what you thought was best."

"I think we need to focus a bit more on us though, you know, as a couple."

"Yes, maybe we do." Rose paused before looking Rob straight in the eye, "Do you think marriage counselling might help?" Rob looked surprised then Rose could have sworn she saw a flicker of amusement in his eyes before he answered,

"Maybe, if you think it would help."

"It might do. Plenty of people go. We could try it," she said, brightly.

"Ok, Rose, we'll go." She felt surprised, and relieved.

Before they could say any more, they heard a crash, coming from the sitting room, followed by screaming.

"Evie!" Rob and Rose gasped in unison before running to her aid. She was sitting, crying, in a puddle of water, surrounded by broken glass. She had pulled a vase of flowers off the windowsill. Glass, water and bits of flowers were splashed all over the carpet and up the wall. Rose carefully stepped through it and rescued Evie. She was fine.

"Rob, you take Evie upstairs and change her clothes. She seems all right but be careful to check that I haven't missed any glass stuck to her. I'll clear this up."

"Bloody hell, Rose, we need some help with the kids. They're taking over."

"Well, I'll look for a nanny as well as a counsellor," she said, half-joking. As Rob took Evie upstairs, Rose could not hide her smile. *I'll show you, Nicky Turner, that our marriage, and the life we have together, matters. There is nothing you can do to finish us, or get a penny out of us.*

TWENTY-SEVEN

Nicky had done three pregnancy tests over the course of two weeks. The first had been negative, the second one ambiguous, with one strong line, the parallel one faintly noticeable, but the third test had been unmistakably positive, with two equal lines. She could not believe it. A quick moment, in a hot tub, barely counted, surely?

Rob had barred her number so she hovered around the boundary for days, hoping to catch him. He never came. She certainly was not going to go round to the house, for fear of bumping into Rose. Maybe this had been a blessing because, in the meantime, Nicky had decided there was no actual need to tell Rob about the baby at all. After all, she had choices. She could pass it off as Ed's, even though they had not had any intimate physical contact for a while. It would not be too difficult to fudge the dates and indulge in some urgent cover-up work. As all this ran around her mind, she reminded herself that she could emigrate and have this child on her own. Australia needed nurses. Of course, she could just quietly get rid of it and forget any of this had ever happened. She was not sure about that option. This could be her last chance to become a mother.

In the end, fate decided for her. After around two weeks of knowing she was pregnant, she woke, in the middle of the night, with strong stomach ache. It was like severe period pain accompanied by giddiness and nausea. In fact, she was quite unsteady on her feet. She knew straight away that this baby was not viable, just like the other babies she had lost. She was filled with a fresh sense of loss. What broke her heart was that she could no longer blame Ed for her not having any children. She had always liked to think that he might be the reason she was childless, that there was something wrong with him. All hope evaporated. The evidence was there. She also knew, deep down, that staying with Ed was never going to make her happy. They had drifted too far apart.

Despite initially joking about it, Rose had decided to get some help. She had set up interviews with three nannies that had responded, on the same day, to her advertisement. Rose had also set up an initial meeting with a marriage counsellor, Francine Parish, in the next town. She did not want anyone, who knew her or Rob, to know that they had got so far out of their depth that they needed outside help to stand up again.

Rose felt guilty looking for a nanny but comforted herself in the fact that it would only be part-time and would provide her with the help she needed. A worn-down mother was never any fun. She was taking a step out of, what she saw as, the dependent haze she had become unintentionally embroiled in. A fresh face would be good for the children.

As Rose had stuck her advertisement for a nanny in the newsagents' window, of all the people to pass by, it had been Nicky. She, Rose discovered, had changed. The friendly, 'happy go lucky' person she had been was gone. She looked markedly older as she came straight into the shop and up to Rose,
"Ooh, a nanny, what will you do with yourself, Lady of Leisure? I'd be so bored if I stayed at home all day doing nothing."
"Me too!" Rose smiled, not rising to the bait. She turned and walked away, leaving Nicky looking surprised and, she hoped, feeling a bit silly.

Rose no longer cared what her husband and Nicky had or had not done together. The fact he was willing to try counselling showed his commitment to her and his family. They would get through this. Had Nicky not been snide towards Rose, in the shop, Rose would not have done what she did next but she felt the need to retaliate.

She penned a note, carefully disguising her handwriting. She remembered that she had written the Christmas cards. She did a good job, unlike Ed who was, frankly, a bit of a fool, for the effort he had made with his note, she thought. She remembered the prize for calligraphy that she had won at school, at eleven, so she did not find it difficult writing in a very different way to usual. She dug out her old pen, which still worked surprisingly well. She used some paper at the bottom of a drawer, in the sitting room. She wrote the following,

'Dear Ed,

You ought to know that your wife, Nicky, is having an affair.'

271

This would deliver a swift blow. Rose carefully wrote Ed's name and address on the envelope and placed the note inside.

Ideally, she would have liked a different postmark to their local one but did not want to go to the inconvenience of driving to the next county, or the awkwardness of asking someone else to post it for her. She wanted to remain anonymous so, obviously, no one else could be involved. This minimised her chances of being found out. Ed might work out who it was from anyway. She and Rob had not taken long to work out who the spiteful note to Rob had come from. This note was not a personal, childish attack on someone she had decided she did not like. It was factual, responsible even, giving someone the right to information affecting them.

On her way to collect the children, Rose pulled into a lay-by and posted the note. She got back into the car in a haze of adrenaline. It felt good, for a moment, before she began to feel spiteful. After all, did she not always pride herself on not getting involved in other people's affairs? It was too late. It was done now and part of her did want revenge on Nicky. She had now taken to openly insulting Rose and whatever happened in the future served Nicky right.

That evening, once the children were in bed, Rose had a bath. She added some of the fizzing bath bomb her friend had given her for Christmas. She had just got off the phone from another prospective nanny and had arranged an interview for the following Monday, after the initial two.

Rob appeared in the doorway with two upturned, wine glasses in one hand and a bottle of red wine in the other,

"Fancy a glass? I've checked the children and they're all asleep... amazing! I can't remember the last time this happened. There's a whole evening ahead of us."

"That would be lovely, thank you." She noted how attractive he looked, clean-shaven with a strong, defined jaw. It was a while since Rose had admired him like this. He raised his glass as he handed Rose hers,

"I want to toast your new venture. I'm very proud of you. Cheers!" They both took a sip of wine. She was pleased he was coming round to the idea of her business,

"I'm very excited and, thank you, Rob, that means a lot. In fact, I just had a phone call from another prospective nanny, Katrina Wells. I'm interviewing them all on Monday, if you want to be in on it?"

"Sure, I can be there. I'll be able to tell a lot by the way they interact with the children. I once read somewhere that the children should always be present."

"Yes, you're right, I heard that too. I plan to have them there from the start, you know, see how each nanny copes, especially when Evie interrupts." There was a short silence where Rob and Rose savoured the taste of their wine. He was first to break it,

"Did you make the, you know, counselling appointment?"

"Yes, Wednesday morning at ten, in two weeks time, Francine Parish, a thirty minute drive from here. I don't want anyone knowing our business."

"Ok... and, you still think we need to go?" Rob raised his eyebrows questioningly.

"Yes, it can only help, I think. Why, don't you?"

"I suppose so," Rob said noncommittally, "It's just I don't know if I can take some floating, hippy woman telling me I'm another useless man, from the army of

them, and where I've gone wrong and how I should put
it all right." Rose gasped,

"Rob, they're meant to be fair and non-judgemental and
listen to both sides and she sounds fine to me.   It's
booked now so, at least, let's go once, and see if it helps.
If it doesn't, we won't go back."

"I know. It's just, well, I'm sorry, but once you have to
get a third party involved in your marriage, I think
you're on rocky terrain, don't you? A different road, if
you like. God, I can't stop using clichés. It's like a
different tongue. You know what I mean. I'm just
worried, Rose, that she'll turn you against me because I
really love you and I want us to get back to how we used
to be. I suppose how we were before we had Evie, and
you gave up work, and everything changed, and we
moved here, and, before you say anything, I'd have Evie
a hundred times over, again, so it's not anything to do
with her." Rose looked concerned,

"But, Rob, we can't go backwards, only forwards, and it
has been rubbish, lately. We've been so busy. I have
felt like my identity has burned away. I've always
worked, ever since getting my first Saturday job, at
fifteen. I simply can't get my head round not working
any longer, outside the home. It's just not me. I think
all this has unnerved you. We need some help." Rob
looked sympathetic,

"Rose, I just want you to be happy but I also want to see
more of you, so if this Francine can help, we'll go." She
smiled, and nodded, before changing the subject,

"I wanted to ask you, how's Will finding the building
project, that is, our home?"

"Well, lots of materials arrived today, as you probably
noticed, in the drive, and round the side of the garden.
He seems to be getting on with it although he was really
off with me, on the phone, earlier today, for some
reason. I didn't have him down as moody but hopefully

it's a one-off, as that will start to bug me, if it carries on. Fancy watching a film, tonight, after dinner?"

"Sure, thriller or comedy?"

"I'm in the mood for a thriller and I've got a good one on a DVD Andrew leant me. We never got round to watching it together. He said he's too busy at the moment so I took it. Shall we watch it downstairs or in bed?"

"Downstairs, I don't like drinking in bed and might have a bit more wine later."

Will, in contrast, was having a different sort of evening. He was sitting at his desk mulling over what he had inadvertently witnessed in the hot tub. He knew it was none of his business and had managed, mostly, to put it to the back of his mind. However, the injustice of it all continued to niggle him. He felt that no man should have to go through what he did with Stella, especially not the secret deceit. Ed had a right to know what was going on. Will felt, under the circumstances, an anonymous note should do the trick. While he did not intend to break up a couple, or, indeed, a family, he felt it was somehow, justifiably, his duty to speak up.

He put the note into an envelope, marked it Ed Turner, then hid it inside the back cover of a tap brochure, to allow him time to decide how he would deliver it, anonymously. Feeling satisfied he was doing the right thing, he sat there, for a while, thinking about his own life. He was not getting any younger and he was becoming tired of his single lifestyle. The 'no strings attached' relationships, which he had to admit had been rather sparse, recently, had lost their appeal. They offered nothing concrete, nothing he could build on. He felt glum. Luisa entered his mind. *Shame she is so independent and opposed to settling down because she could be a perfect match for me.*

TWENTY-EIGHT

Nicky had started work at seven, in the morning. Her boss had phoned her, only the evening before, to ask if she was able to cover the early, nine hour shift, possibly twelve, if they could not find anyone else to take over from her. She had jumped at the chance. She needed to keep busy and out of Ed's way, so, the more she could work the better. During her break, Nicky spotted an advertisement, on a noticeboard, for trained nurses, like her, to work in Australia. They offered temporary long, and short-term, contracts, as part of a job-swap scheme. She noted the number. *Good to know it could be possible*, she thought.

Having been disturbed by Nicky's ablutions very early that morning, the shuddering shower pipes being the main culprits, Ed had decided to get up early too. He planned to spend the day pottering around the garden, uninterrupted. The weather forecast was good and he rather liked the thought of having the place to himself. He found Nicky a bit too fizzy sometimes and, although he loved her, over time, their relationship had become more like that of a brother and sister than lovers and, definitely, he thought, more a relationship of convenience than passion. Still, it was better than being lonely, he reckoned. He did wonder, though, if anyone would really miss him much if he disappeared. After all, Graham, his brother, only tolerated him because he was useful, good at decorating and trustworthy. Graham, without worrying, could give him the keys to various flats. Nicky stayed because she liked the house. With no mortgage, the money she earned was pretty much all hers, to keep or spend, as she wished.

Ed watered the new bushes he had planted in the autumn. He planned to cut them into animal shapes, once they were established. He enjoyed, and was good at, gardening. It always filled him with hope, as he watched things change and grow. He thought about how perhaps Nicky and he could rekindle their relationship. While the hose was unravelled, Ed decided to water the plants at the front of the house as well. It had been pretty dry, for the time of year. Later, he would weed the beds. The postman waved and smiled towards him, as he drove away from the house. Ed made a mental note to check the post later.

Background machinery sounds reminded Ed that Rob and Rose's building had started. He was not looking forward to his peace being disturbed by heavy drilling and loud, gruff banter he knew would come on the finer days. *Typical*, thought Ed, nastily, *his lordship has started excavating, typical London-types, always up for changing everything, especially if it costs lots of money. No making do for him, the arrogant toff, over there, born with the silver spoon. God, he's annoying.* Ed knew he did not have a good reason to have any gripe with Rob. Ed was just hideously jealous of him. Ed could not get over this and that was why he had sent Rob that note, to bring him down a peg or two. *Bet that rocked his boat,* Ed smiled to himself, *Rob has no idea I sent it, which is great.* Ed took a drag from his freshly lit cigarette. He paused to bask in the thought of Rob reading the note. *What? Someone actually doesn't like me? Whyever not?* Ed chuckled, to himself.

He was walking round the side of his house, on his way back from the garden shed, at the back of the house, with some compost to top up the pots, at the front, when he caught sight of something slipping into the wheelie bin. The last bag had not been compressed down enough, creating a gap, preventing the bin from fully closing. *What was that? Was it what I think it was?* He lifted the lid. A rat poured slowly out of the bin, leaving a greasy mark behind it. In no apparent hurry, it sloped off into the bushes, towards the back garden. A narrow stream ran through the garden, normally only a trickle, except after heavy rainfall, when it filled up, to stop the garden from flooding. He knew that where there was water, rats would not be far away. Even so, they were disgusting, dirty creatures. He went to get a spade to compress the rubbish so he could close the lid. He was pretty sure rats were unable to lift these lids, once they were properly shut. He would still buy some poison.

To be able to compress the rubbish, in the bin, Ed lifted out two large bags, full of decaying rubbish, and placed them on the ground next to him. After much jabbing, with the spade, he realised it would be easier to climb into the bin and stamp on the rubbish. Having created enough space, he placed one of the sacks back in the bin but as he lifted the second one, the bag spilt, spilling some of the contents onto the ground. *For pity's sake, this is typical.* Grabbing a new black sack, he started clearing it up. This was when he came across the used, pregnancy test. Using the guide, on the side of the box, he realised that it was positive. He knew, instinctively, it was Nicky's. Who else would it belong to? He also knew that it was not his baby. He steadied himself against the bin. He felt sick. He had expected something like this might happen. A vivacious girl, like Nicky, needed more than he could offer but it was still a shock to be faced with the reality of this. His heart wrenched as he realised he still loved her and wondered how things had gone too far, too wrong to save them. He would not know where to start to improve, or reconcile the situation that had become their relationship.

It was as if time stood still. The air was motionless. Ed could not hear a sound. Even the birds had stopped singing. With the shock, his brain had slowed everything down, like a slow-motion film. He willed himself to be steady and managed to go inside for a cup of tea. He wanted to carry on with the day he had planned but it increasingly seemed pointless to him, especially if he had nothing to look forward to. The solace he usually found in completing garden jobs was no longer there. He had to sort out the rats, though. That was a priority today.

At the hardware shop, Ed bought rat poison and rope. He had been meaning to replace the rope on the bucket of the ornamental well, for ages. Today seemed like a good day to do that. He even joked with the shop assistant about just pleasing the missus and how she had requested he buy enough rope to hang himself. The uninterested shop assistant was only half listening and laughed back, taking the cue from Ed.

Back home, he opened his post. He read the anonymous letter from Rose. It was the final straw. As he read it, he lowered himself onto the bottom step of the staircase, in the hall, feeling spent, the last bit of hope that, by some miracle, maybe the baby was his and Nicky had only just realised she was pregnant. She could be a couple of months gone, or more, but wouldn't she have told him? Somehow, he sensed Nicky would leave, soon.

He looked up at the beam above him, initially for some kind of inspiration. He noticed an abundance of cobwebs. He wondered how neither he, nor Nicky, had noticed them before. The doorbell intruded, crudely, into his thoughts. It was Will,

"Hi Ed! Sorry to disturb you but I'm just on my way over to Rob and Rose's to keep an eye on things now the building has started. I wanted to call here just to confirm that. Any problems, give me a call. Here's my card in case you can't find my details. I'm not sure I've given you one before." Ed said nothing but took the card and looked at it before placing it on the table by the front door. Will noticed the rope under the table and gestured towards it,

"Making a swing?" He quipped. Ed looked uncomfortable which, later, when Will relived their conversation, made him wish he had not been so flippant and familiar, and, perhaps, a bit nosier. Ed informed him,

"I'm fixing the well bucket round the back, outside, where the rope has been worn down by the weather," he paused, "Or hanging myself, I haven't decided which, yet." Ed had laughed loudly, but not warmly. Will had laughed back,

"Surely things can't be that bad? Enjoy the rest of your day." Will had waved, got in his car and driven off to the Clarkes'.

He had rung the doorbell and explained to Rose that the brochure he was lending her included all the best kitchen taps, with all the specifications. Prices were included, plus VAT, at the back of the catalogue. She had smiled as she accepted the catalogue, before he had checked with her that the building was starting all right,

"Everything OK in the garden?"

"So far, yes," smiled Rose, "but it's early days. I hope we never get to the 'tearing our hair out' stage but we'll see. We'll take it a day at a time!"

"Well, there's no hurry, with the taps, but, obviously, the sooner we order the sooner we get another thing ticked off the list."

"Yes," said Rose, "I'll have a look, with Rob, this evening and see what we settle on. I'll ring you first thing."

"No problem, we'll talk tomorrow." As Will left, Rose was glad that any unease there might have been between them seemed to have evaporated.

Ed had shut the front door after Will left and returned to the anonymous note before setting light to the corner of it and putting it in the fire grate. He would not want to leave Nicky with the guilt of him knowing what she had done. He entirely blamed himself for driving her away. He knew he had been emotionally unavailable, depressed even, for a long time. She never criticised him or berated him for it, or patronised him into cheering up. She remained the same, stoic companion as he slowly withdrew. Now, he had really lost her. There was no fight left to try to win her back. It was time to let her go. He felt inadequate and demeaned. He could not even get a job, except for the scraps his brother gave him. He only had this house because of his mother. He could not give Nicky the children she wanted. Someone else had seen to that, instead. No wonder Nicky had gone elsewhere.

He wrote her a note saying he was sorry, that the house was hers and everything else he owned. He hoped it would compensate her for him being an inadequate spouse. He promised no one would contest this as his brother was not interested in anything of his or hers, and had made his own money, anyway.

Ed left the note on the kitchen table with the name and address of his solicitor, his wallet and the pin number for his bank card, before calmly getting the stepladder from the shed and the rope from under the hall table. After a couple of attempts, he managed to throw the rope round one of the beams, in the hall, make a strong loop, place it round his neck and kick the stepladder away.

TWENTY-NINE

The screaming could be heard, possibly for miles. The noise came from a desperate female in unimaginable distress. The builders heard it first, above the noise of their digger. They turned the engines off to listen carefully, to identify the direction from which it was coming.

"Oh my God, help me, please," was followed by another agonising scream of shock, "Please! Somebody! He's stuck! Oh my God, oh God, oh God, oh God!"

The builders ran towards the bottom of the garden and squeezed through the gap. They found Nicky, collapsed on her knees, in the hall, the front door still open. Ed dangled, eerily motionless, from the beam, the stepladder, on its side, beneath him. The sheer horror of it all rendered the builders speechless as Nicky, in her navy uniform and flat, black shoes, continued to groan.

The malignant spectacle was surreal. Stunned, no one seemed to know what to do. Ed had gone, all colour had drained from his face. It was grey, swollen and cold looking. Eventually, the tallest of the three builders reached into his pocket before muttering,

"Damn, I've left my mobile on the site. Is there a phone around here? I'll make the call."

"I have one, mate," said the one still wearing his hard-hat. He dialled the emergency services, "Um...I'm not sure. I think we might need all of you as this bloke's just gone and hanged himself." Pete, the shortest and burliest of the trio, put his arm around a whimpering Nicky and tried to encourage her to get up. She did not appear to notice and carried on lamenting, no longer on her knees, but, leaning to the side, her black tights laddered, from rubbing on the floor.

Rose had heard the screaming that had now stopped, thankfully. She was sure to find out later what it was all about. Hopefully, it would be nothing too serious. It was time to collect Anna and Thomas from their after-school-tennis lesson. Rob was on a client visit so she would try to remember to ask the builders, next time she spoke to them.

Rob returned home to an empty house and to an unexpected, odd silence, in the garden. *Surely the builders had not knocked off already?* Rob walked round the back to see what they had done. He ascertained that they must be coming back as the keys were still in the digger's ignition and there was a mobile phone, which had been left on a pile of bricks. Probably a break, he guessed, as he walked towards the hut to deposit some paperwork. This was when he met the builders on their way back from Nicky's. Before they could say anything, Rob jumped in,

"That Ed hasn't been giving you grief about anything has he?" They looked really uncomfortable. Initially, they all looked at each other then the ground before the tall one decided to fill Rob in,

"Don't think he could. He's gone mate, just hanged himself."

"What?" Rob gasped, then, unexpectedly, to his own surprise, laughed, "you're joking, right?"

"Wish I was, mate, he was hanging from the beams in his hall."

"No way..."

"Yep, and his missus has just been taken off in a separate ambulance, in total shock. She's the one who found him, after a long shift, apparently, barely able to stand up. Police are examining the premises but don't think anything suspicious is likely, looks like a definite suicide." Rob just stood there. He could not think of anything to say but thought of Rose,

"Does Rose, my wife, know?"

"She wasn't around so don't think so."

"Right," said Rob tensely, "I'll go and tell her now. She should be back from the school run."

The tallest builder, looking forlorn said,

"Well, we're off for the rest of the day now, after all that. It's turned our stomachs, hasn't it, lads? We'll be back early in the morning." All three nodded, flatly.

"Of course, of course I understand, thanks for what you've done today and err... yes, see you all tomorrow." Rob walked back towards the house looking down, at the lawn, in disbelief.

Rose was surprised, on returning, at how quiet it was in the garden too. She had expected the clunking of tools and loud banter from the builders as they prepared to go home, but it was as if they had deserted the project, already. Thomas and Anna chimed how hungry they were and asked what was for their snack.

Rose eyed the tap brochure. She knew what she wanted, a tap that resembled a graceful swan. She would look for one, later. She just hoped it would not be prohibitively expensive. She had a tendency to choose the most expensive items, every time she leafed through a catalogue. She would then have to look again, a bit dispiritedly, for something similar, within her budget. Rob came in, through the back door, looking very glum, just as Rose sat the children down, at the table, to have their drinks and snacks,

"Rose," he said, woodenly, before considering she had just got home and was busy with the children,

"Yes?" Rose stopped what she was doing and looked concernedly at him. He looked stressed. "What is it?" she felt worried. He gestured to the children as he boiled the kettle, "See to them first, Rose, and I'll tell you. Don't look so worried, I'm OK ...I'll make some tea." Anna and Thomas were soon settled in front of the television. Evie had gone on an adventure with her teddy, tucked into her toy pram.

Rob placed two mugs of tea on the kitchen table,

"Sit down, Rose, yours is the floral mug. I've got some sad news, I'm afraid. It appears Ed committed suicide this afternoon."

"What? Ed? Are you sure?" Rose frowned. Rob looked solemn,

"Well, yes, that's what the builders told me. They heard screaming, went to see what was going on and found Nicky, distraught, having just opened the front door. Apparently, Ed was hanging from the beams."

"Oh my goodness," Rose put her hand to her mouth in shock, "That's awful, how sad. I heard screaming but had no idea. You see, I didn't want to be late for the children and thought it could even be someone playing a game. That's really awful. Poor Nicky, I suppose I'd better go and see her. Maybe, we should both go." This was the last thing Rob wanted to do and, luckily for him, he remembered what the builders had told him,

"Well the builders said she's gone to hospital, total shock apparently, said she was hardly able to stand."

"Oh, how awful." There was a silence that seemed to last for ever, apart from the orchestra, in the background, on the television, playing along to the cartoon about Mr Bear's first day at school.

"Drink your tea," said Rob as he took a gulp of his. Rose drank the soothing liquid. Suddenly, she remembered the note she had anonymously posted to Ed. She felt giddy. What if she had triggered his suicide? What had she done? "Are you all right, Rose?" Rob asked.

"No, not really," she wiped away a couple of tears, "It's just so horrible to think someone so near to us was that desperate that they took their own life. What a mess. Did they say why he did it?"

"No, they didn't but you and I both know he wasn't right, Rose." She agreed,

"I know. Ed was always hostile, always moaning about something, sent you that nasty note... oh, I suppose none of that matters now he's dead. It's just, I suppose, no one saw it coming. It's a shock, that's all." After a few minutes, which felt much longer, Rose got up from the table, "I'd better start the dinner." She smiled as Rob got up too,

"I'll be in the hut finishing some work. How long have I got?"

"About forty minutes," she smiled as he pecked her on the cheek.

"Try not to be too upset. Ed was mad. Hopefully he'll be happier, now, wherever he's gone," said Rob.

As the spaghetti was boiling, Rose tried not to think about Ed and started to flick through the tap brochure. She found the one she liked on page five and the price was surprisingly within budget. *That was easy*, she thought, satisfied with her quick choice. She held the catalogue in her left hand as she leant over to grab a pen and piece of paper to note down the code number and price. As she leant over, the catalogue nearly fell from her hand but she had a firm grip on the spine. An envelope fell from it and landed gently on the floor. She picked it up. She recognised the writing as being Will's. It was addressed to Ed. *There is not much point posting that now*, she thought, before wondering what Will had put. The fact that it was hand written indicated that it might not have been penned for professional reasons. She turned it over. It was sealed. She slid it back into the brochure before putting it near the front door so she would remember to give it back to Will as soon as she saw him.

The mood at dinner that evening was pretty sombre. The children were tired and Rob and Rose sat mainly in silence. They both had plenty on their minds, unaware they were both thinking about similar things. Rob kept wondering whether or not Ed knew Nicky had had an affair with him. Rob hoped Ed had not known, as Rob did not like to think he might have been the catalyst for a suicide. Rose wished she had not sent the note to Ed.

THIRTY

Nicky returned home, numb, in the back of a taxi. The doctor had prescribed something to calm her down. She had refused to take it. She did not want to be tranquillized. She wanted this nightmare, and the finality of it all, to go away except it would not, could not. As she opened the front door to her home, poignantly alone, everything seemed haunted. Ed's body had been removed, along with the rope, but the stepladder, that horrid, metal stepladder, had been folded and left against the wall, seemingly innocently, ready to be used again, a wretched reminder for Nicky in case she should forget what had happened only the day before. She immediately took it outside and propped it up against the black bin. She would never, ever wish to use that again.

She spotted the new, plastic, shoe-box-sized container, with the round hole at the end, placed behind the bin. She knew it was a rodent trap and knew Ed would have put it there. *Why*, she thought, *would a man who took such a pride in his home, and garden, suddenly commit suicide?* She wished she had taken more notice of him. Then, she might have noticed his fragile mental state. He might still be here. She reached into her pocket for a tissue, to wipe away more tears. She opened the bin to dispose of the tissue. It was staring right at her, the positive pregnancy test. She quickly dropped the lid down, with a bang, and ran into the house. She collapsed onto the bottom stair, mumbling to herself, "Oh God, what have I done? He knew, he knew. I killed him." She heaved sobs into her knees, as she hugged them, rocking back and forth. She managed to climb the stairs and flop into bed. She feared she would crack. Eventually, she was roused from her mournful stupor by the doorbell. She ignored it, at first, hoping whoever it was would go away, but they rang twice more. She felt compelled to answer it then, in case it was important, so she smoothed her hair down and wiped her face on the sheet before hurrying downstairs. She had been in the dark, as the curtains were drawn in her bedroom, so her eyes had yet to adjust to the daylight. She opened the door to an uncomfortable looking Rob and Rose. Nicky looked at them, said nothing.

Trying to cover up her surprise, at seeing such a dishevelled Nicky, Rose broke the silence, "Hi Nicky, I know this is an absolutely dreadful time for you but we just wanted you to know how sorry we are for your loss." Rob chipped in, "Yes, err, we are very sorry about Ed and if there's anything we can do to help, let us know." "What do you mean?" Nicky's eyes shone with fresh tears, "You both hated Ed and didn't think much of me either. I know that." Nicky looked straight at Rob as she spoke. He looked down at his feet before reiterating,

"I know this is the most awful time for you, Nicky, but, like I said, if you need anything..." Nicky managed a small, weak smile at them before replying,
"I don't need anything, from either of you, thank you." She closed the door.

"That went well," said Rose, sarcastically, as they walked away from the house. Rob raised his eyebrows before sighing and putting his arm around Rose.

Will had left a cheerful message on their landline,
"Hi Rose and Rob, it's Will here! Hope you're all well. It's a long shot but was just wondering if you had noticed a letter, addressed to Ed, in the tap brochure," (pronounced 'broshore'), "only," he laughed faintly, "not much point posting it now so," he paused, "if you do come across it, just hang on to it for me. It's not important but I seem to have mislaid it. I'll call by tomorrow morning, first thing, to collect the brochure if you've decided what you want. Bye for now." The answer machine beeped the end of the message before announcing robotically,
"Thirty minutes recording time left."

Rose was now intrigued. If the letter was not important then why did Will feel compelled to ask if they had it, and, why was he having to point out it was nothing important? It clearly was and Rose immediately retrieved the envelope from the catalogue. Without hesitation, she managed, with the help of the kettle steam, to ease it open. The note inside informed Ed that his wife was having an affair. Will was letting him know so he could not be made a fool of. It was signed "from a well wisher".

Rose sat down, slowly, at the kitchen table. She reread the note three times before carefully placing it back in the envelope, resealing it and wedging it back into the brochure. The note had not said whom the affair was with but she already knew, even without concrete evidence, that it was Rob. How did Will know? It pained her to think that maybe everyone knew, that she had become one of those clueless women she had heard about. She imagined that people would nudge each other, when they saw her, whispering how unfortunate it must be to be married to such an untrustworthy person. Perhaps Nicky had told everyone herself and perhaps that was why Ed had committed suicide. Rose remembered an article she had read saying that it was normally a long list of things that built up to a suicide. Rarely, someone committed it on a whim. There was often a final catalyst. She had no proof that it was the note she had sent him.

Will had lain awake all night, worrying that Rose might have read the note. It could have awful consequences if someone got hold of it. After all, as far as he was aware, Rose knew nothing about Rob and Nicky. It should really stay that way. Enough damage had been done already without Rose finding out or Nicky knowing someone else knew and jumping to the conclusion that everyone else did too. Rose did not need the heartache of it either.

Frankly, Will was sick of it all. He should never have written that note and should never have even thought to interfere. Indeed, it was none of his business. What could he do to change things? Better to stay out of it, just as everyone had, including his mother, who had felt every bit of his pain, back when Stella had misled, and then abandoned, him. What he had seen, that day, in the hot tub, had nothing to do with him at all. If any good would come of it, it would be that the whole thing had made him re-evaluate his priorities. He had realised that he could only control himself and his own actions, never those of anyone around him. He felt a new urge to settle down. Where did he want to be in ten years' time? He needed to be able to trust women again and be worthy of their trust. He was, otherwise, in danger of missing out on companionship and a family of his own. Nicky was now free, he thought, but she really was not his type. His type, if he was really honest, did not entirely exist but Luisa came pretty close. If only she would make some kind of commitment.

Will visited Nicky. It felt like the proper thing to do, under the circumstances. She answered the door looking exhausted yet younger, almost girl-like. She wore no make-up. "Hi Nicky, I just came to say how sorry I am to hear about Ed. I suppose life goes on." He regretted that the minute he had said it, before concluding that anything could be taken the wrong way right now. "If you need anything, you know where I am. Here's my business card." Will held it up. She did not take it,
"Did you tell him?" She looked angry,
"Tell who what?" Will was clearly taken aback by this comment.
"Cut the crap, Will," she was furious, "I saw you, out of the corner of my eye, that day, when I was in the hot tub with Rob. I know you saw us and I know you pretended you hadn't but I saw you and I know for sure it was you because that was the day you put something in my letterbox, wasn't it?" Anger flared in her eyes, "So, I want to know, did you tell Ed?"
"No,"
"Really? Are you sure?"

"Yes, absolutely, I did not tell Ed a thing. I was going to because I was taken for a mug once by a woman, my ex-wife, a long time ago. It nearly finished me off. I wouldn't wish what I went through on any man but I promise you I've told nobody. You've got to live with what you did and it's none of my business."

"I know, thank you," she whispered, "You know, Ed was very hard to live with, a lot of the time, you have no idea. I had thought of leaving him but we were companions and I liked my life here and I liked living in this house so I never got round to it. Ed has left it all to me." She smiled weakly, "He was always very generous to me. Anyway, what you saw, it was a one-off, really it was. There's nothing keeping me here now so I'm moving on. I'm going to sell this place and I'm going to Australia. I saw an advert at work for job swaps for nurses and medical people so I'll work there and see how it goes."

"Well, I wish you the best."

"Same to you, thank you...you know, for not saying anything. You're right, I've got to live with all this and it's very hard."

As Will got back in his car, he felt sorry for Nicky. She should have finished with Ed before she engaged with Rob but he reminded himself not to be so judgemental. Life was rarely that simple. He cringed anew at the number of women he had blatantly been with, not caring whether or not they were in relationships with anyone else. Will just, metaphorically, stamped all over them. He thought about Rob, *He's got to live with it too. Weird he did it at all because Rob really does seem to love Rose.*

Over the next few days, Will become consumed with guilt, the intensity of which he had not faced before. It became bound around him, like a snake. He needed to face up to his past encounters with women, cleanse himself of any wrongdoing. He endured many nights of poor sleep. Also, he punished himself for not realising, at the crucial time, what the rope in Ed's hall had truly signified. Will did manage to comfort himself with the fact that he had had no reason to suspect anything harmful.

What was happening to him? He had felt mostly happy, and carefree, until now. He wanted to talk to someone about it, but who? He had never burdened his mother with any problem whatsoever since Stella. He felt that no mother should have to do that more than once for any adult child. He would have to deal with this alone.

He decided to check his email and put off any work he did not have to do today. Perhaps, he could visit the driving range, get rid of some adrenaline, even guilt, if he was lucky. There might be a few friendly, fellow golfers at the nineteenth hole. He could make an evening of it.

An email from Luisa was waiting in his in-box. Before he clicked on it, his mother knocked and poked her head round the door,
"I don't like to disturb you but have you got five minutes, Will?"
"Sure, Mum,"
"Would you like a coffee, first?" She smiled, "I'll make it." Sensing he was not keen to be held up for long she added, "That is if you've got time?"
"Of course I've always got time for you. I'd love a coffee, please," he laughed although he had to admit to himself that this was not the best time. Even so, Joan very rarely interrupted him during work hours and,

hardly ever, in the evenings. They both acknowledged a need for boundaries, while living in such close proximity to one another. She returned with two coffees,

"That one is yours," she smiled as she put it on the coaster on Will's desk before taking a seat on the firm sofa, adjacent to his desk. "Everything's all right is it, Will?" She enquired.

"Yes, mother," he raised his eyebrows, "any reason why it shouldn't be?"

"Of course not, Will, only I was at the post office this morning and Mrs Teeter informed me that the man, can't remember his name, with the property that backs on to your new clients, committed suicide a few days ago. You must know that and didn't even tell me. I just thought it odd but then you've probably been busy or didn't think it was news I'd be interested in." Will was about to say something but his mother raised her hand in a 'let me finish' gesture before continuing, "It's just, I've noticed you've been very quiet over these last few days and, well, I'm your mother and I care. What really got me thinking was that rumour has it that this man's wife, Nicky, was having an affair. How true or not that is I have no idea but I know what you went through with Stella and sometimes you can think you're over something and it comes back to haunt you," she cleared her throat, "I mean much later on, something like this can trigger painful memories so what I'm trying to say, in a bit of a clumsy way, I know, is that I'm here if you need to talk."

Will stared into his half-full coffee mug and managed a weak,

"I'm fine," before becoming mortifyingly aware that he was about to burst into tears. Why did mothers always know what you were thinking? It was almost like the feelings went telepathically through the air. Generally, Will felt he was a master at hiding his true feelings. It was how he had managed to be so carefree in Dubai. He turned to his screen hoping to find some reason to dismiss his mother. Nothing jumped up to help. He was trapped. He heard his mother ask coyly,

"You aren't the one who was having the affair with her, are you?" His mother's hand, on his shoulder, was the trigger. Once he started crying, it all came out like a tidal wave. His mother held him at first and then, after handing him a packet of tissues, from her pocket, sat and listened to him as he poured out his feelings around his anxiety at being left alone all his life. What would he do then, when she, his mother, had gone? Joan laughed kindly,

"Let's not be dramatic, Will, and get carried away here. I do wish you wouldn't bottle things up so tightly. This isn't the last-ever, desperate situation known to man or indeed the first and it really isn't the worst thing you've ever faced because you are more in control than you were with Stella. You're still young; you have time. Perhaps Nicky's the one?" His mother looked him straight in the eye before Will started crying again but this time with a mixture of laughter,

"Gosh, Mum, you really do think I play way harder than I actually do. I have not had an affair, or anything remotely like one, with Nicky Turner. I can assure you of that. Like I said, I just feel guilty for not realising what Ed had planned to do with the rope that day. That's all I'm upset about, as far as they are concerned." There was a calmer, lighter atmosphere in the office now. Will and his mother sat quietly before he broke the silence,

"I'm sorry, Mum. I don't know what came over me. I don't like to burden you with my woes."

"Why?" She was taken aback, "I'm your mother."

"I'm supposed to be a proper grown-up now and not need to cry on your shoulder over what are basically my bad life choices." She laughed,

"Oh! Hilarious!" She threw her hands up in the air,

"You're no burden. I love you. You're my son. I have a sixth sense for knowing when something is bothering you. And as for being alone, what happened to Luisa? I like her. She's fun. And.... you always look very happy when you're with her." His mother paused and smiled expectantly before Will cut in,

"Luisa would never make any kind of commitment to me or anyone else for that matter. She values her freedom too much. She's told me that."

"Like you?" His mother smiled knowingly.

"She's different, Mum, amazing really, so independent."

"But everyone needs a companion and everyone needs to grow up at some point. People change their priorities just like you have." Will thought about this for a moment before stating,

"You don't have a partner and you're happy."

"My needs are different to yours, Will. I have amazing friends who are like family to me. I have my sister and I have you, my grown-up child. It's enough for me." There was silence between them before his mother got up and collected the coffee mugs, "Well, I've got to get on with my day. None of my business but why don't you give Luisa a call?"

Ten minutes later, Will was sitting at his desk, leaning back in his chair, recovering from a new shock. He was literally open-mouthed at the email he had just read from Luisa. He had read it three times. Each time it had said the same thing,

'Hi Will,

Hope you're well? Remember all that fun we had after Christmas? Well, I'm pregnant and it's definitely yours. Ring me, when you can, as we need to talk. Love Luisa xx'

Despite the surprise, he felt excited. He called Luisa, straight away.

"Hello, Ronson Estates, Luisa speaking,"

"Hi Luisa!"

"Hi Will, I knew it was you really, just playing," she laughed. In fact, she sounded happier than ever before, "You read the email then."

"Yes... and..."

"It's definitely yours and if you don't want to be a daddy that's fine but I'm keeping it. I know I said I never wanted kids but I've changed my mind, Will, or rather this has changed it for me. I know in my heart, this is what I really want. You have a right to know, whatever you think."

"Well, Luisa, I have news for you because I'm absolutely thrilled and I'm not going anywhere. I am so very ready to be the best daddy ever. In fact, I'm over the moon, couldn't be happier! A child... wow! It's the best news I've ever had. When can I see you? I need to see you!"

"Well, as it happens, I'm coming over to see my sister next week so..."

"Next week it is then! Please come and stay! I think we'll have plenty to talk about!"

"OK, details later. I've got a client meeting in five. Ring me this evening, not too late though. We're four hours ahead and I need my sleep more than ever now."

Will ran round to the annexe, hoping to catch his mother. She was there.

"Mum! Mum!"

"Are you all right?" She looked concerned.

"Yes, yes, I'm fine," Will said, breathlessly, "It's Luisa! She's pregnant." His mother raised her eyebrows waiting for more information as he continued, "Well, it's mine of course! The baby's mine!"

"Wow! Congratulations!" She smiled, "And you're..." Will cut in before she could finish,

"Sure it's mine? Yes, definitely!"

"Well, at last you two are seeing sense. Clearly, Luisa has realised that she might not want to be wafting around Dubai now she is getting older, 'botoxed' up to the eyeballs and alone. Even the most keen of partygoers tire of it in the end. I can imagine that sort of lifestyle could become very superficial. Perhaps she's waiting for you to take the lead now, show some backbone and offer to look after her and the baby, not that it's any of my business," she paused as she reached for her coat before hugging Will and kissing his cheek, "It's good to see you cheerful. I have to leave now, as I want to be on time for Liz. I'm meeting her in town in half an hour."

"Oh, of course, Mum, you must go. I don't want to hold you up. I just had to tell you."

"You will ask Luisa to marry you, of course?"

THIRTY-ONE

Rob was half-listening to Rose philosophising,
"Funny how a shock in one's community can shake up
absolutely everyone, and make people step outside
themselves, in the immediate aftermath, and re-evaluate
their goals, and count their blessings. I think it serves as
a reminder to us all just how fragile life is, and, indeed,
gives people a sense of their own mortality."
"Yes, Rose," Rob paused. He was sitting on the bed,
putting on his socks, "You're thinking deep there, or, did
you swallow a self-help book?"
"Oh, stop poking fun at me. It's true, isn't it? There's a
lighter atmosphere around here, at the moment. People
seem friendlier, in the village anyway, you know... since
Ed died."
"If you say so, Rose," he got up and kissed her head,
"Coffee?"
"Yes please," she turned back to the mirror. Having just
showered and dressed, she was about to do her make-up
and hair, something she did every morning, without
thinking about it, yet, something felt different. She
looked good again. Evie was better settled, Rose's

business was proving popular and their home was forming into the one they wanted. Generally, everything was better. Rose felt like she was where she should be.

Rob returned and placed coffee in front of Rose, "You look nice."

"Thank you," she smiled.

"You look different, new make-up?"

"I haven't put any on yet. You've just said more than the right thing," she beamed, "must be all that undisturbed sleep I'm now getting."

"You certainly seem happier."

"So do you."

"I love you, Rose."

"I love you too." Now was a good time to remind him, "Remember, we've got the counselling session at lunch time. You're not off the hook just because you love me." He groaned,

"But we're much happier now..."

'Still, won't do any harm to go a few more times, will it?"

"Suppose not," he mumbled and went downstairs.

Evie was stacking bricks next to the bed. She kept adding more until it toppled over. She realised she was being watched and smiled as she patiently began building again. Rose wondered at what point people started putting pressure on themselves to succeed, seeing lack of success, like the bricks falling, as failure, even if what they were trying to achieve was out of their reach, perhaps through no fault of their own. At what point had Ed decided it was better to leave? It was hard to comprehend. Rose took Evie downstairs.

"You're not going into the shop today are you?" Rob asked Rose.

"No, I'm going to spend some time with Evie, then there's our 'sesh'," she made an inverted-comma sign with her hands. Mum will look after Evie for us. Georgie will keep things going at the shop. She's proving to be fantastic with the customers and good with the business side of things."

"Jan says word on the street is that your coffee and cakes are the best around. The lessons have had a good press too. She says she's heard loads of people are planning to try them. I'm proud of you, Rose."

"Why, thank you, darling."

"I must get on, a few things to get out of the way before lunchtime. Come and get me later when we need to go."

Rob insisted on driving to the session, this time. He drove too fast. Rose put it down to silliness because he was nervous. She was grateful that he could be bothered to come. She had read that when the man, especially, stopped trying, in a relationship, there really was a problem.

"What do you think she'll be like today?" Rob asked, eyes firmly on the road ahead.

"Francine?" she enquired.

"Well, I'm not talking about anyone else," he said, tetchily.

"Watch out for the cyclist," she exclaimed.

"I've seen him! I can drive, you know." She decided to try a different approach,

"What are you hoping to get out of today?"

"Oh God, you sound like her now. You've got to admit that she's a bit flaky. Today, it'll probably be all, 'and where do you think you've gone wrong because it's obviously your fault, Rob?' and, 'how about lighting candles, around your house, and floating through, like you're high, then having sex in each room?'" This was all said in a mocking, childish voice. He was now on a roll, "Oh, except didn't you say you've got three kids and a secretary that pops in when she feels like it? Oh, Rose, that must be so hard for you, my love. In fact between you and me, I hate men, useless creatures, only good for one thing...'"

"Stop it, Rob," shouted Rose, "Get over yourself and stop behaving like an idiot! Can't you just go with an open mind? She was lovely to you last time. She's unlikely to be completely different, this time. She won't be wafting around in an oversized kaftan, with candles lit everywhere, because she had ordinary clothes on last time and I doubt she hates men, otherwise, she wouldn't be able to remain impartial and counsel couples, would she? She hasn't given any indication that she doesn't like you." Rose spat the last few words. Her throat was dry.

The car ground to an abrupt halt. He wrenched the handbrake up,
"Well, we're here now," he snarled. Rose was more than glad to get out of the car,
"Let's go in then, shall we? And, please, try to remain civil," she looked pleadingly at him.
"Unbelievable," he muttered, under his breath, as he strutted up to the door and forcefully rang the bell.

Francine answered the door. She wore a navy jumper dress and trendy ankle boots with buckles on the sides. *Definitely nothing to waft*, thought Rose. Francine's neat bob, with a grey streak, at the front like a skunk, suited her. It made her look funky and distinguished. A large cocktail ring, on her left hand looked chic. *All in the accessories*, thought Rose as she wondered if Francine was married or divorced, or either. Francine warmly invited them in,

"Please, follow me," she indicated a door at the end of a long corridor. She followed them towards it. They both looked at her. The door was shut.

"Please," she indicated with her hand, "Do go in and take a seat." They sat in separate seats facing her, in her single chair. Rob and Rose felt a little more at ease. The first session had been the hardest. Francine had introduced herself before asking them a few questions like their doctor's details at which Rob had jumped in,

"But this is meant to be confidential, isn't it?"

"Yes, of course, and it is but I have to take these details in case you both collapse or I deem either of you to be in danger," she had smiled. Rose and Rob had looked at each other uneasily before supplying the information.

The session today progressed well. Rob and Rose felt closer, towards the end of it. Francine asked how they met and all about their wedding day. This made them reflect on why they had got together, in the first place. Francine pointed out that a common problem with busy couples, especially with children, was that they ended up putting their relationship last.

Back in the car, Rose was first to break the silence,

"I'm not so sure we need to come here any more. Would you go again?"

"Maybe..."

"Well I'm not sure. Anyway, what does maybe mean? I thought it was great. It's just I don't think we have a massive problem. We seem to be sorting things out ourselves. Are you gaining anything from it?" Rob sensed an aggressive edge to her voice. He sighed. He was driving a lot less erratically,

"Rose, I really love you. I'm sorry I've upset you, lately. I will go again, if you want me to, because it's made me really think about why you're so important to me and has served as a reminder as to why I want to spend the rest of my life with you. I lost my way a bit and Francine has helped me realise that. She's actually really good and she doesn't seem to hate men... not yet, anyway," he laughed and Rose smiled,

"Of course she doesn't, thanks."

"Thanks?"

"Yeah, thanks for putting in the effort. It means a lot to me. I think we'll be OK, don't you?"

"I would say so," he smiled.

Back home, Nicky was on their doorstep, talking to Cathy. Nicky turned around, when she heard the car. She looked guilty when she saw it was Rob and Rose.

"What does she want?" Rob said quietly, and tersely, under his breath.

"I don't know but she is our neighbour who has just lost her husband so try to be nice."

"You're too nice, Rose."

"Maybe...." Rose got out of the car and walked towards the house. Nicky seemed cheerful,

"Hi Rose, and Rob, I was just telling your mum that I'm selling up, moving to Australia!" Rose smiled, but said nothing, thinking what fantastic news that was. She did not want Nicky to know that, though. Nicky continued,

"In a month's time! Anyway, I was just wondering if you would keep an eye on the house while I'm away, keep the keys for a few days. I'm going to Devon, to stay with a friend, clear my head a bit, have a short break. The house is actually up for sale now but the agent said no one will look round, for the next few days, while I'm away. There's photos to do and I suppose the details to type up."

"OK, we'll do that, won't we, Rob?" said Rose. Nicky looked straight at her,

"Thank you and I'm sorry I haven't been a fantastic neighbour but... well... Ed and I were unhappy for a while and it probably showed, in its own way. Maybe I should have left him. I don't know. It doesn't matter now. Here are the keys." She dumped them in Rose's hand, as she turned to leave, "Nothing to do, just keep an eye out."

Rose shot her mother a glance as if to say, 'can you believe that?' as Nicky sauntered off. Rob had not said a word or even, it appeared, looked at Nicky. He was, or rather was pretending, to be engrossed in something on his phone. This was typical of him, thought Rose, to hide from anything he found too much but then, if her senses were correct, Rose translated this, also, as a sign that he was definitely not interested in Nicky any more.

Once inside, and with Rob dispensed in the hut, Rose turned to her mother and announced,
"Good riddance, Nicky can't go soon enough, in my opinion. Had she been talking to you for long, Mum?"
Cathy said she had not. Rose was still ranting, "Did you notice that Rob didn't have a word to say?"
"What did you expect him to say, love? I can tell he's not interested in her. She's all tits and bum anyway. She's no match for you and she knows it."
"Oh Mum, you're always so kind to me!"
"Rose, some things are best left unsaid, to avoid possible, and often unnecessary, upset. Maybe, Rob understands this and, maybe, you need to too. As I always advise, leave what you cannot solve, or understand, and move on. It takes a strong person to do that. You and Rob have a great life here. No one can take that from you, unless you allow it. Rob loves you. I can see that. This counselling you're going to, it's none of my business, but, sometimes it's best not to

probe into everything, just to leave things be. I know I suggested it, in the first place, and it has helped, I'm sure, but I don't think there's anything to uncover that you don't already know. It mustn't become an exercise in trying to back Rob into a corner, into confessing, or anything."

"I understand. I think I know what you're trying to say, Mum. I don't think we'll see the counsellor much more. She got us to think about our wedding day today. It really was lovely. We've just let life get in the way a bit, really, you know, we've neglected each other."

Cathy felt a change of subject was in order,
"You have Nicky's keys! Well, Rose, the agents may not be showing anyone round, for a few days, but I'm going for a good nose around, in a minute, because, if it's on the market, I may be interested."

"Mum... why? You've lived in your place forever."

"Because I might want to move. I might buy Nicky's place because I'm ready for a change."

"Really? Well, that's wonderful news!"

"That is, of course, if you and Rob don't mind me being that close. I figured the gardens are big enough to separate us. We can't see each other's houses, anyway, so we'd still have our privacy. I would change its name, though, to something like 'Treetops', for no reason other than I could. And, the best bit would be that my lovely grandchildren could visit any time they wanted to."

"Hang on a minute, Ed killed himself in there." Rose looked upset, "I mean... suicide, Mum." Cathy prepared for this comment,
"Nothing the vicar can't sort out, dear. Once he's blessed it, I'll be safe. God will watch over me. Hopefully, Ed was sorry and won't haunt me," she laughed, "You know, people live near graveyards, and buy second-hand-engagement rings, all the time, without

worrying or being superstitious. You make places your own. Houses are houses but a home is different. I would fill it with love and positive energy. I'm so excited! You know me. I relish a challenge. I would manage to confine the sad story, in that house, to the dusty history books, where it belongs."

THIRTY-TWO

"You've never brought me here before, I can't believe it. It's like a secret place, so beautiful," said Rob.
"That's because I didn't think you liked woods. I often walk Bobble here. It's always peaceful. If I'm lucky, I see deer."

Rob had refused to visit Francine again and Rose had taken her mother's advice, to leave the past alone. Even so, Rose did not want to make it too easy for him, even if she was, secretly, relieved. She said that she would not push him to go, any more, on condition that they spent an hour, maybe two, together, on their own, once a week. This time, she had suggested the woods. Rob had to leave his phone behind and they could not mention work, the house or the children. Inevitably, they did,
"I saw Nicky leave, this morning, on my way to the post office," said Rose, "She got the taxi driver to stop, when she saw me. She gave me her new address but I don't think I'll keep in touch. Well, I might send her a Christmas card. It can't be the same, you know, Christmas on the beach."

"I'm glad she's gone. They were rubbish neighbours. We can all move on, properly, to the next phase now. I'm glad your Mum will be moving in soon."

"Really? A lot of men might not like their mother-in-law so close."

"I'm pleased. We all get on well. There's enough physical space between us and your mum's always been really good at not interfering. I think it will work well." Rob really did not mind. He felt himself to be very lucky that Nicky was off to the other side of the world, for good, he hoped. He really could not believe how fate had taken care of that nicely. He was hoping Cathy would remove the hot tub as it would be a bit disconcerting, an unwelcome reminder, to be invited into it, with his mother-in-law. He visibly shuddered at the thought.

"Are you cold?" Rose enquired.

"Someone walked over my grave, that's all.

"I had a word with your mum about a few nights away together, just you and me."

"Sounds lovely but..."

"What is it?" Rob looked concerned. Rose sensed this,

"Nothing is wrong, I want to go, just sometimes I worry I'm putting upon Mum too much. She has her own life too."

"They are her grandkids and she loves them. Let go for a change, Rose. Let everyone manage without you. Step back and watch it work. Cathy's happy to take Thomas and Anna to school and of course we have Katrina, the nanny, starting next week so your Mum won't be doing absolutely everything. David will help her, too.

"Katrina said she's willing to do everyday, while we are away, and be on call, in the evenings, if your mother needs any extra help. Jan said she'd help in the shop, with your Mum, if she is needed and you have Georgie, of course. I may even have another architect by then as I'm interviewing two tomorrow, so, I probably wouldn't need to bring any work with me. Come on, what do you think? Rose, we deserve a break together, and, I promise to allow you an afternoon of shopping, on your own, without me hovering around."

"You'd allow me? Listen to yourself," Rose laughed, "OK, you win, the shopping has swung it for me. Seriously, though, I want to make sure Katrina is settled first as I mean it, I want to be fair to my mother. I don't want to start taking liberties, assuming she's just there, at the bottom of the garden, waiting for me to use her."

Rob pulled Rose close, "thank you." As they cuddled, she breathed him in as she glimpsed some deer trotting stealthily along the hedgerow beyond the lake, their ears pricked up. She noticed Rob, and herself, clearly reflected in the water. It all made sense.

ABOUT THE AUTHOR

Louise Allison lives in East Sussex with her husband and 3 children. The Strength of a Woman is her first novel.

Visit her website at www.louiseallison.com

www.ingramcontent.com/pod-product-compliance
Lightning Source LLC
Chambersburg PA
CBHW030546200626
46812CB00022BA/2086